THRIVE

SHAIN ROSE

Thrive

Copyright © 2020 by Greene Ink Publishing, LLC

All rights reserved.

No part of this book may be reproduced in any form or by any electronic or mechanical means, including information storage and retrieval systems, without written permission from the author, except for the use of brief quotations in a book review.

This is a work of fiction and any resemblance to persons, names, characters, places, brands, media, and incidents are either the product of the author's imagination or coincidental.

Editing: thewordfaery.com, Jolene Parker
Cover Design: Bookcover Kingdom
Formatting: Stephanie Anderson, Alt 19 Creative

Subscribe to Shain Rose's newsletter here so you can be the first to see teasers, be a part of giveaways, and get updates: https://shainrose.com/newsletter

Join Shain Rose's Lovers of Love Facebook Group to keep in touch and get sneak peeks: https://facebook.com/groups/shainroseslovers

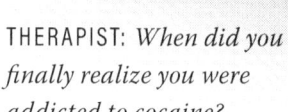

THERAPIST: *When **did** you finally realize you were addicted to cocaine?*

JAY: *I'm addicted to partying. Not any drug in particular.*

THERAPIST: *Okay. Tell me about the time when you figured that out.*

JAY: *Maybe I always knew. Being the life of the party comes with a cost. For me, it was a big one.*

CHAPTER ONE

JAY

THE METAL SCRAPED against the glass table as I shoved the powder into one last white line. I'd snorted only two. This last one wasn't going to push me over the edge into addiction. Tomorrow would be better.

Tomorrow, I'd stop the partying.

I sniffed it up off the table and tilted my head back to the ceiling as I brushed the excess from my nose.

"Feeling it now, Jay?" A redhead with lips that shined like a wet lollipop whispered in my ear as she dragged her hand over my jean zipper.

The rush kicked in and had I been standing, it would have knocked me on my ass. Stars burst behind my eyelids as I closed them, the woman's hands suddenly felt like velvet, and the beat of the music swayed me like the waves of the ocean.

I wondered why I wasn't hard as a rock under her hand. I grabbed her by the hips and moved her to straddle me. "I'm feeling you, sweet thing."

She giggled and shoved her tits in my face. They were fake, but they were round, big enough to be a handful, and accessible.

Just as I was about to lick her cleavage, the voice of reason and everything I didn't need in that moment blurted out, "Jaydon Stonewood. You were supposed to meet me an hour ago to go over your script."

Mikka Chang. My miniscule, overly organized assistant stood in the middle of the club, arms crossed, tapping the front of one of her pink stilettos on the floor, staring me down. As always, those shoes had extra high heels and were like an extension of her. She walked with precision in them when most would have fumbled just like how she walked through life. Of course, she was wearing a pink sweater that matched her footwear perfectly. My eyes trailed over the rest of her. Her skintight jeans covered her curves like latex and I nearly growled when my dick decided that was the moment it should jump to attention.

The redhead continued grinding on me and started kissing my neck like she'd finally succeeded in her efforts to turn me on. She didn't pay any attention to the little wrecking ball in front of us.

Mikka was a tiny little thing. And yet, when she stared us down, she didn't avert her gaze, not even for an instant. I knew my night was taking a turn. When that woman doubled down on a mission, nothing could shake her from it.

She proceeded to remove her worn leather book bag, the one she always carried with her, from her shoulder and take out a copy of the movie script we'd been working on.

"Are you kidding, Mikka?" I groaned.

"No. I'm not." The papers thwacked onto the table near our drinks. She dug in her bag for more files and threw them on the table too. "I could have stayed in tonight if you'd told me this was your plan. Instead, you scheduled me in for the evening a week ago."

"Can't we reschedule?" I motioned toward the woman on top of me who I had to give props to—she hadn't come up for air.

Mikka glared at her for two seconds. Then, she snapped her fingers in the woman's face. "Hey. Take a breath. Go get some fresh air. Think about if you really want to sleep with a man who just made you sign an NDA, which you did make her sign, right, Jay?"

I winced as my lollipop-lipped girl scoffed and climbed off me. "Find me later when your drama leaves."

As she walked off, my security nodded to her. They'd been the ones to make her sign an NDA, not me. "Meek, what the hell?"

She cleared her throat. "Keep to your schedule, Jaydon, and quit taking advantage of me. I'm your only real friend in this town, not your doormat. This is the third time this month you've blown me off and honestly, I'm starting to worry."

My mind skittered around trying to nail down what she was talking about. Days had blurred with the partying and my nights had gotten jumbled. I didn't want to admit that to her.

She was about the only person I didn't want to admit that to.

"That can't be right," I mumbled and reached for her hand. "I wouldn't do that to you. You know..."

She stared at our hands entangled, her dark eyes starting to glisten. "Can you please take a breather from the partying? We have a lot on our plate. I'm hard on you now because I know you can do better."

And there went the wrecking ball. She could demolish me with just a plea. Mikka and I had met at about the same time in our careers. We were both new to the LA film industry. She wanted to get into scriptwriting, and I wanted to act in movies. Being a Stonewood with a father who ran half of a large city could have gotten me a higher profile personal assistant, but I saw the same hunger I had in Mikka's eyes.

We took a chance on each other.

And it worked out. She was the Bonnie to my Clyde, the Sundance Kid to my Butch Cassidy, the Beyonce to my Jay-Z. And she was the one thing I worried about hurting in this city.

In four years, we'd completed six rom-coms and hundreds of interviews and built a persona for me that every male and female in their teens to their sixties enjoyed. Mikka worked for a large agency now that represented me and handled most of my business.

We were brilliant together. But she was still ruthless, still had that hunger in her eyes. And the fact that I saw pain and vulnerability there because of me made me wonder what the hell I was doing.

"You're frustrated." I tried to deescalate or, rather, I tried to nail down what the fuck was happening. The night was flying, spinning, messing with my emotions. The last thing I needed was her mad at me. She never pushed this hard because she knew it wasn't the right angle to take with me.

Mikka was my rock, a steady little pebble that was solid as hell. "But, you're also off. What's wrong, Little Pebble?" I looked her up and down trying to find her injury or ailment.

Had I been sober, I could have pinpointed what was askew, and I immediately regretted indulging for that specific reason.

"Don't call me that."

She hated that I hadn't dropped the nickname, but I'd met her lying on a sandy California beach sunbathing. She was always tiny, but her personality was hard to crack. I'd called her a little pebble that day when I'd picked one up by her side and told her she could fit right in my pocket.

"Nothing's wrong except that I had to google locate you after being stood up. I'm your PA. Not your babysitter." She cleared her throat and glanced away from me. She fisted her hand, and I knew she was holding back. The club wasn't a place to cause a scene and we both knew it. She sighed loudly as she eyed the crowd that was moving to the beat.

The music blared so loud; it practically pumped my blood. The lights flickered brighter than the sun and I probably could attribute that somewhat to the cocaine I'd ingested. Even so, I couldn't shake her tension, the way she stood like someone had rattled off the location of a timebomb to her.

"You're lying, Meek."

She placed a maroon-colored nail to her temple. "Can we please leave?"

"Can you please tell me what the hell is wrong?"

"This isn't the place to tell you anything."

"But something *is* wrong?" I didn't let it go. She needed to unload whatever it was she was holding on to. We stared at one another, her dark eyes holding something, an emotion I couldn't put my finger on.

"Yes."

If I couldn't get it out of her, I'd find a way to make it better. There was something painful there, and my friends didn't have to deal with that if I was around. "Do you want to forget about it?"

"That's not possible."

"Of course it is." If there was one thing I knew how to do, it was how to forget about problems and enjoy the moment. I pulled her toward me and slid the bag from her shoulders. "Follow me."

"Jay," She sighed. "I don't want to party."

Mikka was following me though. Once in a damn solar eclipse, I would get the girl to stay late and enjoy a few drinks. She rarely ever stepped into the clubs. She'd had this longtime boyfriend ever since the day I met her. I know because I asked. And I was positive he didn't let her stray far from his side. When I first met her, I imagined her in every damn sex fantasy I'd ever had. She looked like a Megan Fox with plump lips, dark hair and curves. Then, you mixed in her mother's Taiwanese roots. Mikka had inherited her long, bone-straight hair with the almond eyes.

I asked about her boyfriend the day I met her because, had she been single, I would have found a way to bed that woman.

Now, we were so far friend-zoned, I knew damn well I shouldn't have been looking at her even when every man was eyeing her up.

"You're here. Just have a drink. Take a load off." I pulled her farther into the VIP section where the music quieted. We found a little high table to park ourselves at. The stools had my legs bumping into her jean-covered ones.

A waitress that hovered in the area buzzed over as I lifted my chin at her. "Can you get my very sober friend the drink of her choice?"

"Water," Mikka ground out.

"She'll have a vodka soda with lime, and I'll do a vodka red bull. Heavy on the vodka. Bring us lemon drop shots too." I winked at Mikka.

She brushed her hair out of her face and stared me down with her black-as-midnight eyes. "Did you forget about our meeting or did you just blow me off?"

She wasn't letting my lack of scheduling go. I should have remembered; I shouldn't have been out partying. Except, that's what you did here in LA. I had an itch and I had the money to scratch it, so I did.

"I was out late last night, Mikka. It just slipped my mind, okay?"

"Not really. I schedule your calendar. You get notifications on your phone."

"Would it make you feel better if I admitted to turning them off?" She was neurotic and as my PA, I appreciated that. The company we worked with appreciated it too. "You had time scheduled in for when I could take a five-minute break some days, woman. I think I recall one of them recommending that I take a piss."

She narrowed her eyes and cocked her head to give me a patronizing look. "Don't be ridiculous. I wrote 'go to the bathroom if you want.' I wouldn't have put 'piss.'"

"You realize—"

"I realize that I'm being anal about your schedule." She held up both hands. "In my defense, though, you made it known you needed that. I was being a good friend and a damn good employee. If you had any other PA on your payroll…"

She stopped herself from carrying on. I would have let her, too, because Mikka on a tirade was a sight to see. She didn't get flustered easily and she let a lot of shit roll off her back. But when something wiggled its way under her armor, she was like a bull that had seen red. She targeted and plowed through the problem effectively and efficiently.

"I'm not going to go on and on. You know I kick ass." Her ego was justified, and she damn well knew it. "I'm irritated that you held up my evening for nothing, okay? If I was just your PA, fine, but that's not what you do to your friend."

I rubbed my forehead and tried to burn off some anxiety by letting my leg jump up and down under the table. Mikka didn't usually confront me about my actions, so her doing it now meant it was serious. Either she felt—or someone had talked about—my neglect of my schedule and job.

She cleared her throat and it was like she was clearing away the fear of blurting out what she asked next. "How high are you, Jaydon?"

I reared back. Mikka was my girl, the one who stood by me, the one who would never accuse me even when the industry had. She'd worked to spin story after story. She knew better than anyone that my drug habit was recreational, a fun twist on a night. Nothing more.

"Are you serious?"

She grabbed my wrist and turned it upward where she dug a finger in to feel my pulse. "You're sweating and it's cold in here. Your heart's going a mile a minute. And the dead giveaway—you have powder on your nose."

I yanked my wrist away to wipe my hand across it. "You let me sit this whole time with powder on my nose?"

"No. There's nothing there, but that's a great indicator."

If it had been anyone else, I would have got up and left. The girl was one of my only true friends in the large city though. I knew I owed her an explanation or an attempt at one.

"I'm sorry I missed our meeting, okay?" I winced when I looked at her and saw real frustration in her dark cat-like eyes. Mikka barreled through some of the most irritating situations and she didn't complain, didn't appear flustered, and didn't show discomfort.

"I need you to commit, Jay. If you can't, then let me know and let me find someone who will. I've made a name for myself. It means a lot to me." Her words came out barely above a whisper. As our waitress dropped our drinks off, I suddenly felt wrong downing mine.

Commitment wasn't something I did well. It wasn't something I contemplated. I was committed to my lifestyle and that was to not commit, to have fun, to live fast.

I downed the drink we were both staring at and then I eyed hers. "Bottom's up, babe. I'll talk business with you in a day or two."

Her fingers went to the glass. She held them there so long without moving them that little drops of condensation collected at her fingertips. "That'll be a hell of a day, Jay."

I leaned in close to her and smiled, "Then, let's make tonight a hell of one too."

She tipped the drink back and stared at me as she took the whole thing down.

I whooped at her sudden resolve to finish it. "Time to have fun." I signaled for another round of drinks and added shots to it.

She downed those along with me too.

By that time, we'd gained a bit of a crowd with my liveliness. I stood on the table reciting some of my lines from a movie that had just been released. Mikka stared up at me, giggling along with the others. Then tension in her shoulders had subsided and I knew she'd let go of our little tiff.

Laughter was the best form of medicine and the idea was to forget the troubles throughout the day, to get lost in the fun, to move away from the problems that crept into our minds so easily. Up on that table, acting out lines, I saw bright white smiles on everyone's faces. I saw fun rolling through everyone, and I felt alive.

Mikka rocked to the music in the bubblegum pink sweater that matched her glossy lips. Her hips rotated to the beat and her dark hair swayed in the flashing lights. As she let go of her worries, she became the most intoxicating woman in the city. I swear at least ten guys flocked to her and I had to warn off each of them by explaining over and over she had a boyfriend.

"She's got a man at home. Back off." I stood in the way of another's path of pursuing her.

"You cockblocking me for another dude?" The guy played with his gold chain and curled his lip at me in confusion.

"Yup. Dougie would do the same for me." I scratched the scruff on my jaw and then cracked my neck. I was lying. Dougie wouldn't do shit for me or anyone else for that matter. Her boyfriend was a selfish prick.

"My man. You're a good dude. I'd have hit that the second she came out without her man." He shrugged and backed away.

I bit the inside of my cheek and turned to take another shot at the bar. I didn't warn off the redhead who ambled back over soon after. I needed someone to distract me.

We all danced, we all partied, and we hit the alcohol hard.

Mikka was solid like that. When she committed, you knew she wasn't going to let you down. She would exceed expectations every single time. Even if it was with spending a night out.

A song came on and she squealed before rolling her hips to the beat. I found myself behind her as another guy tried to swoop in. I rolled my hips with hers, held her closer than I normally would have. And she didn't move away. She dropped low in those high heels and brought herself back up as she giggled at her antics.

We ended up in the corner of VIP, laughing uncontrollably at the fact that I was trying to shake the redhead that had been following me around all night. I'd thought she'd be able to distract me from Mikka, but no one could hold a candle to her flame.

"You're supposed to help me get rid of the groupies, Mikka." I chuckled and leaned against the wall as she collapsed into another fit of giggles right next to me.

"Oh, please. Half the time you want me to be your wingwoman. And, honestly, I can't." She sucked in a breath, laughed again, and then tried to get control of herself. "She's on you like white on rice. I promise I know what that looks like."

She cracked up again and I tipped her chin up to get a look at the girl that never let loose with me. "You're special. Not because you can make a joke about who you are but because you know who you are. This place is filled with so many who don't. God, why don't we do this more?" I sighed.

"Because we can't party every day, Jay. It's unhealthy."

She said it like she wanted to get a point across, but my body wanted to get a point across to her too. Before I could stop myself, I caged her into the corner. "Do I look unhealthy to you?"

The question was bait. I didn't expect that she would take it though. Dougie, our friendship, and our jobs had always stopped her.

She looked up at me, something new in her eyes as she let them roam down my body and back up again.

For the first time, I saw what I'd had for her since the moment I'd laid eyes on her.

Hunger.

Need.

"Little one, you aren't answering." I let the words roll out even though I shouldn't have. Standing over her, though, I could smell her sweet lip gloss and see down her shirt. I could imagine what she'd feel like under me and, with her looking up at me, I got a vision of one sexual fantasy I'd had.

She shut her eyes before she answered. "I'm assessing our situation."

"Did you come up with a good assessment?"

"Well, you look drunk and high. I'm definitely drunk and we have business to talk in the morning. So, is that good or bad?"

"The blush on your cheeks and right here"—I brushed the top of her cleavage—"tells me your assessment went a different direction."

"Jay, we're good friends."

"Is that all that's stopping you? Because if that's it, I'll remedy that right now." I growled in her ear.

She wanted more; I could practically feel her vibrating under me for more. When she whispered, "How?" I almost took what I wanted right then.

"Want me to show or want me to tell?"

"Oh, God. It doesn't matter." She practically moaned. "There's Dougie."

I hung my head and took a deep breath. I pulled back. I might hate him, but Dougie was right for her. Dougie made her happy and she deserved it.

"Not that Dougie seems to care what I'm doing." She sighed and then looked up as if she was holding back tears from spilling over.

"What's that mean? Is that what's been wrong with you?"

"Other than you standing me up?"

"Fuck me, woman. I'm sorry, okay?" I sighed and dropped my hands from the wall, giving her some space. "You told me something was wrong. Tell me what it is."

"It's nothing. We'll get through it. I'll make sure we do. We aren't clicking like we're supposed to." She combed her fingers through her dark hair, and I tried not to imagine how soft it would feel gripping it. "He thinks I work too much; I think he doesn't work enough. He wanted me to stay home tonight and I was going to."

I nodded, not giving a shit. I hated her boyfriend like most everyone who knew him. He was riding her coattails and they were getting tired. I just couldn't tell her that. "You'll figure it out."

"Will we?" She questioned and then lowered her voice. "I even dressed in lingerie for him earlier today, Jay."

I tilted my head. Mikka and I didn't ever discuss that much of her life, probably because I avoided it like the damn plague. I didn't need to think about her like that. I didn't want to. Not anymore. Not after she put me in the strict friend zone.

She rubbed a palm over her face. "I know, TMI. TMI. TMI. But I'm just drunk enough to admit how embarrassing it is to dress up for your boyfriend only for him to laugh at your attempt. He laughed and said I better just get the work clothes back on and go. He was already playing videogames."

"He passed on you in lingerie?"

She shrugged like it was nothing, but I wanted to immediately punch her boyfriend in the face. "Are you still wearing the lingerie under that sweater?"

"Are you kidding me?" She rolled her eyes at me, but the smirk made it worth it.

"Meek, sending you on your way with a guilt trip instead of sleeping with you is pretty messed up."

"Right?" She practically screamed and waved her hand in front of me. "I can't believe I always fall for it too. Every single time. And as I'm walking out the door, he grumbles for me to have fun at my joke of a job. Although, in his defense, this is a joke of a job right now. I'm sitting here drinking my body weight..."

"Oh, cut the shit." I ground out. "He's being a dick. The guilt trip only goes so far. He could have fucked you sideways and had a good night. He wanted to have a bad one instead and we both know it."

She smiled and rubbed my shoulder. "Thank you for that."

"For what?"

"For being a good friend even while high and drunk and after ditching me earlier."

The problem with Mikka and me, I wasn't just her friend. She didn't get that. I was her actor, I was her sounding board, I was her go to.

And she was mine. She was the tool I used for everything in LA. She got me movie deals, she got me out of sticky situations, she had even helped me bed one or two girls on the rare occasion that I needed her to talk me up.

She did everything for me.

She was my path, my avenue, my road to hell and back.

And in that moment as I listened to her bitch about her boyfriend and as I looked at everything I wanted in front of me that I couldn't have, I felt the wrecking ball of pain and jealousy crash right into me.

So, I used her as my go to again. This time though it was to deliver my own self destruction.

I took what I'd wanted for a long time.

I grabbed her small waist, pulled her up against my chest, my abs, my dick. I plastered her to me.

And then I kissed her.

I tasted every inch of her mouth, sucked on her bottom lip, and took my time brushing my tongue over hers. It was intentional the way I ran my fingers over her hips like I was memorizing her. I knew this would be the first and last time she'd let me take what wasn't mine.

She gasped and then she melted into me like we fit together, like she was made for me and I was made for her.

The world spun faster, the music beat even louder, but the light faded. Everything went black and I knew that wasn't the cocaine or the alcohol. That was my pebble: solid, bold, and soul-crushing, pushing away everything else in my life and making it crystal clear who was the only one worthy of standing before me.

Then she shoved me away. "What in the ever-living fuck are you doing, Jaydon?" She yelled at me, fear in her eyes. Fear of having felt what I just did or fear of having to deal with my shit in the morning?

"I'm tasting you. I should have done it a long time ago."

"You're high. You're so freaking high, a dog could be kissing you and you wouldn't know the difference. Me, I'll remember it all in the morning and have to clean up the damn mess." She shoved me back farther, harder with fury in her eyes.

"This isn't a mess; this is what it's supposed to be. Me and you, Little Pebble."

A look of confusion and then devastation marred her features. "I'm with Dougie, Jay. And you're high." She sighed and scanned the area to find her book bag. She checked the zippers and then hugged it to her as if it was a good barrier between us. "I love you and that's why I'm going to tell you this. Don't throw your career away. You keep doing this, you will. You'll end up doing something really stupid and ruin your reputation. You think the executives aren't keeping tabs on you? You think your audience will take you seriously if you don't show anyone how deep you are beyond this lifestyle?"

Her words pelted into me like bullets. "What the hell are you saying?"

"You need to change something. This partying has to stop. I'll help you. I'll do whatever you need."

Her hand went to my arm and then she snapped it back because I'm sure she felt the electricity between us like I did. "But you need to stop. Stop the *cocaine*." She blurted out the word like it was acid in her mouth.

She ducked under my arm and stalked away from me, heels clicking as they always did. I started to follow her and then turned back, shaking my head, trying to shake the fog of the drugs from my mind. "Fuck!" I screamed and pulled at my hair. The woman had to be messing with me, but she never messed around with words like that.

Something formed deep in the pit of my stomach; it was heavy and solid, like a boulder crushing my life underneath it. I'd pushed her and she'd responded.

Maybe I wanted it, maybe it was my cry for help. Surrounded by everyone that admired me but no one that loved me, I hammered the last nail into my coffin. I let the night spiral, I let the drain I'd been circling swallow me up.

I could blame it on the events but that wasn't it.

Drugs, my habit and my friend, the real thing I'd been close to for the last year were to blame. I wouldn't know until a few weeks later that my friend, the white, white powder was really the enemy. And addiction was the fear of the unknown without it.

I remember getting into the bathroom with the redhead. I remember snorting two more lines off her chest. I remember more shots.

I don't remember much after that.

LESSON OF THE DAY:
People only see a tiny window into someone's life. Make sure you show them exactly what you want them to see.

CHAPTER TWO

MIKKA

ONE KISS.
One mistake.
One little misstep.

It knocked our friendship so far off course, I wasn't sure we'd ever get back to where we were.

I was his pebble, and he was my rock. This solid, charming, larger-than-life rock that made everything in my life a little brighter.

We didn't talk the next morning. I wasn't even sure he remembered what happened. I thought about it day and night. I tossed and turned next to my boyfriend and felt the guilt of that kiss. I turned to Dougie in bed, ready to tell him. And then I turned away, cowering from the idea. Dougie and my relationship had been rough lately. He had been closed off and distancing us from one another for months.

Adding to the turmoil of my current relationship, I still felt the lust, the desire, and the pull toward Jay instead of my boyfriend.

So, I held onto the secret. I let it fester until I knew what to do with it.

I flew out to the film set in the warm San Francisco air days later. The heat and humidity hugged me as I watched Jay finish another scene with his costar. They stood under the dome of the Palace of Fine Arts where the large white pillars encircled them as they kissed over and over again. The small lagoon lapped nearby as the sunlight poured in on them while filming.

The location was romantic, held the hearts of so many Californians and was meant to spark hope in culture and in art. It was a great fit for the movie.

And I told myself it was all for the movie. Even if Jay stared into her eyes and grabbed her like he had me, it was a job. They were executing the perfect amount of emotion and the cameras were rolling to capture their orchestrated tension.

Still, kiss after kiss felt like punches to the gut. I wondered if he tasted like he had that night, if he kissed her like he had me. Did feelings barrel through her too? Did he think more about me than he did when he leaned in each time to taste her lips like I'd thought about him when I'd kissed my boyfriend?

It didn't matter.

Had he meant any of it all?

It didn't matter.

I repeated it to myself.

It couldn't matter.

I was there to provide assistance, talk him through lines and his schedule. He needed me to make sure his affairs were in order, that he'd make the right flights, that his interviews would be attended on time. He even needed me to make sure they'd filled his trailer with his favorite lollipops.

He didn't need me there to discuss a kiss. One that meant nothing at all.

What mattered was that Jay was finally filming *the* movie,

the one that would shoot him into Oscar-worthy territory. Mr. Guillermo, the director, yelled for them to cut the scene. He nodded and walked away. He never said much, but you knew he was happy if he walked away.

Jay bee-lined for a red lollipop from the bowl near his makeup station. I heard his makeup team tell him to stand still as they studied under his eyes. The circles there were darker, and I knew it meant he'd been partying again. His body was starting to tire of his lifestyle, and I didn't know how to approach it, didn't know if it was my place to say any more than I already had.

He strode over as he unwrapped the sucker and popped it in his mouth. My nipples tightened as I watched his lips fold around it. "That's the scene that'll make the world fall in love with us, right?"

He vibrated with excitement; his smile so wide around the lollipop that I knew he loved his job as much as people loved seeing him do it. They'd parted his hair, dressed him in jeans and a collared shirt. He'd always made my mouth water, but the good boy look had my thighs quivering.

Or maybe it was his proximity.

Or the fact that I knew what his mouth tasted like.

I squeezed his arm and focused my attention on what mattered. "It's a great scene."

He nodded. Then he whispered, "You okay, Meek?"

I didn't want to dwell on that night. I hoped he didn't remember and was just asking how I was. I skirted around his question by shrugging and then adding, "You know, the lighting could be a tad darker for the camera."

He narrowed his eyes and scanned the area, instantly focused on work again. "Right. Let me get Guillermo over here to discuss it with you."

I stepped back. "Absolutely not. Don't tell him I said that."

Jay smirked. "Little Pebble, you need to take credit at some point."

I shook my head and waved it off. "I'm going to go get some coffee for you. I have to meet my mother after we wrap for the day. I'll fly back then."

"I can come hang with you guys," Jay offered.

I narrowed my eyes at him, not sure why he would want to. "No. She's going to give me enough grief when I get there. I don't need you both trying to irritate me—"

"I'm coming."

"No." I shook my head and hiked my book bag up my shoulder trying to stand my ground. "You're not."

"Want to bet?"

I poked my tongue into my cheek, trying to not give in. But I remembered the last time we'd played this game. He'd won and I was a sore loser, or rather I always felt the need to prove myself.

"I'm going to win," I blurted out.

I didn't.

I freaking lost.

And now we were standing in front of my mother's business.

The coffee slipped from his fingertips, crashing and spilling all over the cement. He didn't even glance down to see the damage. He had spotted my mom's shop and couldn't look away.

"So, before you say anything, I don't want anyone at work knowing about this." I grumbled, taking a step toward King Chang.

"You told me she owned a restaurant, Mikka Chang."

"No." I shook my head and dusted some imaginary fuzz off my blazer. Everyone assumed my mother owned a restaurant when I rattled off the canned line that her business did very well in San Francisco's Chinatown. "I never said that. I just said she runs a business."

He choked back that guttural laugh the whole world loved and attempted to reply. His mouth opened and closed repeatedly without finding any words.

I curled my lip and scrunched one eye to look at the shop, trying to see what he saw. "Sort of a shock?"

He laughed and I stared at him in all his hysterical glory. Jay Stonewood with a full-blown smile on his face in faded denim and a collared shirt caught more than a few women's eyes as they passed by.

I shook my head at him. He thought he knew everything about me.

I'd globbed onto him like glue when we'd met a few years back and he'd let me become his PA.

I considered us close friends.

Great colleagues.

But nothing more.

Except for that kiss.

And except in these instances when I could observe him without him knowing, when he got lost in a moment of pure joy. And Jay lost himself all the time in every one of his emotions. It was what made him brilliant in front of the camera and pretty irresistible to the opposite sex.

"Get a grip," I mumbled but couldn't help being infected by his laughter.

"Oh, I'm sure I'll be gripping tons when I get in there," he managed. "Meek, how could you not have told me?"

"I don't know what there is to tell." I wanted to stomp my foot. "Your ass isn't even supposed to be here."

"I know, little one, but you lost the bet."

I winced at the name and at him pointing out what I was trying to forget. My competitiveness had gotten the best of me again. "Everyone on set cheated."

And they had. I swear his makeup artist was in on it. She'd gone and counted those damn cupcakes for him and when he'd bet me he could get closer to the right number, I stupidly thought he'd play fair.

Jay charmed every woman he met—including the lead actress he'd had to make out with twenty times that day for the film set under the Palace of the Arts—and used them to swindle his way into everything he wanted. Including winning the bet he'd made with me.

"Stop being a sore loser," he chided, his thick, dark eyebrows waggling at me.

"I'll stop being a sore loser when you stop cheating. Did you sleep with Betsy just to get the exact count?"

"Does it matter?" He wrapped his arm around me and pulled me in for a bear hug. He swallowed me up into his expansive chest as he grumbled, "The crew had a meeting and I wasn't staying for that."

"Wait, what?" My hand flew to my book bag to find my planner for Jay. "I didn't have that scheduled."

"Because it wasn't. I'm not sitting around to listen to them complaining about irrelevant issues—"

I wanted to scream at him. "Jay, this is the role of a lifetime. If they want you to make small talk, you do. If they want you to sing, you do. If they say jump, you're supposed to say how high."

"It'll be fine. They'll get over it," He said it so nonchalantly that I almost believed him. "I honestly didn't want to sit there with Betsy and Lela. I've tasted every part of Lela's mouth and I'm about done there. Plus, you needed company. You always bitch and moan when you have to go visit your mother. Now, I guess I understand why there's moaning."

I slapped him hard in the stomach, trying my best to feel irritation at his lewd jokes, but instead my body took note of how rock-hard his abs were beneath my hand. I cleared my throat and tried to get out from under his arm. "Let's get this over with."

"Okay. Fill me in."

"On what?" I tried not to roll my eyes and readjusted the leather bag on my shoulder. It always held my scheduler—my lifeline, the hardcopy of everything I needed to remember.

He started toward the front doors. "Well, for instance, when you told me you were lucky enough to have a mother who created a successful business and you were able to learn so much from her, I would have definitely liked to know that business was in porn."

"Oh, here we go." I grabbed the metal handles that connected to clean steel doors. "This is the reason I don't share this with people."

My mother was meticulous in her design of the shop. She wanted straight lines, bright neutral tones, and white lighting. The furniture placed throughout had tufted cushions and carved wood frames all stained white. She claimed her store was a boutique of sex and fantasies, and most of her customers did too.

"Does Dougie know?" Jay asked about my boyfriend.

I waved off his question. "Why wouldn't he know?"

Before I swung open the door, Jay's hand was on it, holding it closed, and he was up against my back. I smelled his pine aftershave and a hint of the sweet lollipop he'd eaten earlier.

"Meek." The gravel in his voice when he said my name low like that sent shivers down my spine. It shouldn't have affected me like that. "It sucks that you told him and not me."

I tried to laugh off his comparison and how close he was to me. "I've been with Dougie for years, Jay. He's my boyfriend." Jay would look twice at any woman and so the reminder was always a good one for him. Normally, I didn't need that reminder. My friend was a natural charmer, a man who couldn't be tied down. I had someone much better than that at home and I knew it.

Except right now. Except when Jay was in front of me and Dougie was brushing off another night with me.

"And we've been friends for approximately four years now," said Jay. "Every time I flew into LA, I called you. When I moved here, you were there. You were the only one I kept in touch with when I flew back and forth. I tell you everything, my whole life." He whispered it into my neck, like he was working the words into it, massaging them in until they found a home.

I closed my eyes and reminded myself that Jay charmed everyone, that we were just friends, that I had a boyfriend who wanted to stay with me, to commit. "You tell me your secrets because I'm your PA. I know all about your family because they're American Royalty. You share everything with everyone."

"Not true." He smiled that winning smile, where one side lifted just a bit more than the other, showing off perfectly straight, white teeth. "You know my friends, my family, my darkest secrets. I want to know yours. If I'm still this close to you after tasting your mouth the other night, it means I want to know everything about you, Little Pebble."

"Jay," I whispered, not sure what to say. Not sure where we went from here. The uncharted waters looked dangerous, risky, and too deep to wade into. "You remember?"

"Couldn't forget if I tried." He licked his lips.

Words. I should have been saying them, telling him we had to forget it ever happened, that I was going to tell Dougie, that our friendship would never go further. I stood there speechless instead.

"I'm sharing. I expect you to, Meek." He didn't stand there any longer. He pulled open the door for me and ruffled my hair with his other hand. "You're my favorite LA girl by far and you know it. I'd share the world with you if I could."

I combed my fingers through my dark hair, hiked up my book bag, and scanned the place to see if my mother was up front. I couldn't focus on what had just happened, couldn't even consider that Jay was my best friend and also the man I was lusting over.

I had a boyfriend. And, sure, Dougie wasn't talking to me and was acting like I didn't exist half the time, but he was still the man for me.

"So, my mom is going to try to make us stay the whole night. We have to get back to the airport on time."

He nodded, eyebrows raised with a little smirk that said to me he wasn't listening to a damn thing I was saying.

"I'm serious, Jay. I don't want to restock and organize all day."

"And normally I'd agree with you, Mikka. I would. Today, though, is the opportunity of a lifetime. Whoever gets to say they restocked a porn store?" He practically shook with excitement.

"Are you twelve?" It was a remark I pulled out for most people when they learned my mother owned a porn shop.

"I honestly think in my heart of hearts, I am."

I tried so hard to continue to glare at him but looking back over the years, I knew his statement was true. If there was an opportunity to be a kid or immature, Jay was the first to take it. He shoved our boss into the pool at a formal event just because he thought the man was being too stuffy.

Anyone else would have been fired. Jay jumped in after him and claimed he was saving him. Bob laughed and laughed.

I was no different because I cracked under his charm. My mouth lifted of its own accord and I spun away from him.

"I saw that, Meek. You know as well as I do there's no reason to be a damn stiff. I'm fucking pumped!" He whooped at the end of his proclamation and the laugh I had been holding in burst out of me.

"You're so ridiculous."

He nudged me as we walked down an aisle looking for my mother. "It's the best way to be, woman. You and I both know it."

"I beg to differ, but it works for you. And for me, I guess." I shrugged. Jay's success meant my success, quite frankly. I'd moved to LA with dreams of screenwriting but got to the top with my over-organized nature and handling everything for Jay. I got to see the movie made, I got to read the scripts and Jay always asked me for input. Jay Stonewood was my biggest client, my best friend, and the whole female population's eye candy.

Jay moved much slower than me as we searched the store. He stumbled upon a box and picked it up. "What the hell is this for?" he asked, eyes wide.

"Can we not do this?" I crossed my arms over my chest.

"I'm serious. Do you know?" He glanced at me and then back at the box in his hand. "You don't know. Your mom probably never let you in here."

He was baiting me. I knew he was. But the need to prove myself and be the best pushed me to answer. "It's a new type of vibrator, waterproof and dual action. The motor is mediocre. I'd recommend the more expensive version. If you can't orgasm with that one in five minutes"—I dropped my voice and slid my hand over the box seductively—"you probably need to see a doctor."

His mouth dropped, and I snatched the box out of his hand. "That was hot, Meek. Tell me more. Where has this side of you been hiding since I've known you?"

I blew a raspberry. "Want me to continue your fantasy and say it's locked away until I get home or be honest and say, newsflash, not even Dougie gets that side of me because it is fake."

He crowded me into the shelving and lifted my chin with the knuckle of his finger. "I don't believe you. Maybe you haven't met someone to unlock that side of you. But it's there."

We were both looking at each other's lips. I licked mine and he licked his. I remembered how he tasted, how soft his lips felt, and how he'd demanded everything from me as he controlled the kiss. The world was fading around us and all I could see was him, all I could focus on was that we had fit together that night, that I'd felt more alive in that moment than I ever did anymore.

I took a deep breath and closed my eyes. "It's for the sale, not reality. I know how to sell product. My mom made me work on commission and I didn't want any loans in college. I worked hard and it paid off. Dougie was happy to know I didn't have loans going into our relationship."

He grumbled something about Dougie that I didn't ask him to repeat. I knew he wasn't a fan of my boyfriend and didn't need the reminder. I shoved the product back on the shelf just as my mother appeared from the back room.

"Mikka, face the picture forward." My mother's voice berated me from across our store. How she could see that I was restocking wrong, I didn't know. She was a ferocious mother, driven by her need to succeed in the porn store business.

I turned it the right way. "Mom, it doesn't matter, every side has the same picture." I whined like a petulant child. Still, I knew my mother would correct it like she did everything. It was a pastime of ours to argue the semantics of product display. I'd known when I'd come that's what we would be doing. We wouldn't discuss much else.

"They all need to be presented uniformly. You know this. Can you get one of the boxes in back?"

"I came to have lunch, not work, Mom."

My mom shook her head like she didn't understand. She wouldn't because she never left the store. It was her baby, her home, her first real child. My father passed away from a heart attack not long after she became pregnant with me. This store they'd built together, it was the last thing, other than me, that tied her to the love of her life.

I was the little minion that came after their firstborn and I gave her all the hell a second child normally did, or so she told me.

Hell was getting one A minus my senior year and partying in college, which most kids did.

"We are eating." My mother carried out to go boxes from the back and placed them on the glass display counter where her sculpture of Yue Lao sat. She rearranged him pointedly in front of us.

Jay jumped at the bait. "What's the story behind that guy there, Mrs. Chang?"

I rolled my eyes and groaned but my mother was already revving up. "Oh! How nice of you to ask. No one asks about this man here."

Everyone asked about him.

"This is Yue Lao. He is an old man on the moon that knows who will marry who. He'll tie a red string to you and your partner's ankle connecting you forever. That will be your soulmate, the one you will always find your way back to."

"Oh." Jay smoothed a finger over the top of the sculpture's head. "That's an intriguing story, Meek. So, you and Dougie are tied together?"

I swear he was baiting me, but my mom jumped in. "Of course they aren't. Dougie's tangled up her string. I'm very frustrated with it all."

So she'd told Dougie specifically the last time he visited.

"Wow, Meek. Should we discuss this?"

I grabbed the food. "I'm not engaging with either of you. What do we have to eat?"

The gold nipple rings and expensive BDSM jewelry shined brightly in the window case below our food as my mom said, "Well, you will be happy to know, I ordered from the good restaurant. Wren made special take-out for you."

My mom liked to claim Wren made special things for me. He didn't. Wren was also Taiwanese and owned a business. My mother therefore saw him as the perfect suitor for me.

I saw him as a slimy creep who came on to me every time I was within ten feet of him.

"Did Wren make special takeout for Jay, too? This is my friend, Jay. I work for him in LA. He wanted to tag along today."

My mother squinted as if debating her options. After a couple seconds, she cocked her head, "Will you be helping restock?"

I rolled my eyes. "No, Mom, we won't be here that long."

My mother scoffed and curled her lip at him, completely unaffected by his smile the way most women were. "Then, no. There isn't any extra food for Jay."

A laugh burst from him. "Don't let your daughter speak for me. I'm happy to help restock. I told her I would spend the rest of the day here if you needed help."

Her beady brown eyes lit up, all of a sudden utterly taken with him. I wanted to kick him or punch him in the arm. Instead, I grabbed my takeout and stalked to the back of the store. "This is rude. I didn't come here to work. I came to visit."

My mother's voice carried over the vibrator aisle. "You should come to work. I need help."

I heard Jay mumbling that he would be happy to help any time and my mother giggled, a sound I'd never heard out of her.

I grumbled to myself and texted Dougie that I might get back to LA later than expected. He'd be thrilled I was spending extra time here with her. It meant he wouldn't have to visit her with me any time soon. They had a mutual dislike for one another. My mother thought his lack of a job was stunting her daughter's potential. My boyfriend thought my mom was way too uptight for a Taiwanese woman who owned a porn shop in the middle of San Francisco.

They were both right in their own ways.

"Jay!" I peered around the aisle to see my mother happily chatting with him over the nipple rings and Yue Lao, munching on Chinese food. Weirdly, the picture of them calmed me. Two of my favorite people getting along had me sighing and succumbing to what I knew would be a day of dick jokes from Jay and commands from my mother. "If we're staying, we have to talk over the movie script."

His blue eyes sparkled and crinkled around the edges. A tiny dimple appeared next to the others over his cheeks. It was how I knew his smile was genuine. "I'll do anything to stay here forever, Meek."

"Oh, shut up." I walked back over and opened my Styrofoam box. "At least Wren makes good egg rolls."

"Nah." Jay shook his head. "The food's good but nothing compared to what you make."

My mom nodded and stood a bit taller than her full five foot three inches. "I taught her to cook good Taiwanese food. No shortcuts. Wren takes some in his business."

Jay nodded and then I saw the mischief forming as he tilted his head. "She doesn't make the food much, though. I can't remember the last time you had me over for dinner, Mikka."

He sounded affronted and when I turned to my mother she looked as offended as he did. "Mikka, why haven't you cooked Taiwanese for Jay lately?"

"Mom." I didn't know where to even start. "Of course I cook Taiwanese. I just make it for Dougie and me."

"Dougie doesn't deserve a meal." She mumbled as she picked up her food and turned to sort through some receipts. "Did he find a job yet?"

I tried not to slam my fist onto the glass counter especially when I glared at Jay and he followed up by fluttering his obnoxiously long eyelashes at me. "Yes, Mikka. Answer the question. Does Dougie have a job yet?"

"You're technically jobless half the time, Jay," I retorted and shoved some rice in my mouth.

He pointed his fork at me with narrowed eyes. "You know as well as I do my career hiatuses are not the same as being jobless."

My mother was sorting things and didn't look up to agree with him. "I saw Jay's name in the magazine over there." She pointed toward a little lounge area where she did set up consultations for new customers wanting to explore their fantasies. "The magazine says he makes millions. You should find a man like Jay, cook for him."

She nodded like that was the best idea ever and Jay nodded along with her, completely proud of himself.

I snapped the Styrofoam box shut and pushed away from the counter. Time to change the subject and start the wheels in motion to leave as soon as possible. The two of them would kill me if I didn't get out of there soon. "What can I help you with, Mom? We can only be here a few hours."

"Look around." She made an all-encompassing circle above her head, still not glancing up from her work. "The store is a mess."

It was immaculate. Jay side-eyed me. "So, um, Meek, why don't you show me what I can do?"

We spent the rest of the afternoon working. Jay was enamored with my mother's take-no-shit attitude and helped change lights that weren't even dimming but only he could reach. He cleaned imaginary cobwebs from the corners and carried heavy boxes to the front of the store for us to unpack.

At one point, he wiped the imaginary sweat from his brow and unbuttoned his collared shirt. "What are you doing?" I hissed.

"It's hot, little one." He winked at me.

"Get real," I said, but it sounded breathless as I glanced down at his abs. I'd seen them before, but the eight pack looked more accessible, and somehow more defined than ever before. I licked my lips because my mouth was suddenly very dry.

Jay grabbed my hand and brought it to his stomach. "All yours, Meek. Whenever you want it."

I yanked it back. "Are you always this idiotic? How are we friends?"

"You're friends because he's a good worker, Mikka." My mother rounded the corner into our aisle. She enunciated the word "worker" and I almost screamed at Jay for being such a good sport through the day.

"Yup. He's a great *friend*, Mom." I enunciated the word in rebuttal.

"I'm happy to be more any day, though, Ms. Chang." Jay leaned against the shelving as he re-buttoned the shirt, completely relaxed and enjoying our not-so-subtle banter.

"He's lying. Jay can't commit to what he wants to eat for lunch, let alone a woman."

"Anyone would commit to you, Mikka. You're the best. You're worth it to anyone." My mother was hard on me, but she was fiercely proud of me too.

I blinked a few times before I pulled her in for a hug. I hated coming and working through every visit I had with her, but I also loved the hell out of it. I missed her when I was in LA, especially because she'd been my only friend back in San Francisco for so long. "We've got to go but I'll text you when I get home tonight."

She nodded and turned to Jay. "Take care of my daughter in that godforsaken city. No one there takes care of her."

And we were back to me hating the visit. I started to protest and remind her of Dougie, but Jay cut me off. "Of course. I don't know if you saw my last few movies, but I'm always happy to help a damsel in distress."

"Oh my God, are you kidding?" I shoved him as he went to give my mom a hug. "She doesn't watch rom-coms where the guy never puts his shirt on."

"Right, well, you need to find me better movies to star in then, right?"

"Yes, she does. Mikka, Jay has more talent than that. He told me when we were putting in the lights. Also, I do like his movies. They are funny."

"See, she likes me and my abs."

"I do. You will need to pose for a poster here one day." My mom always brought the conversation back to her store.

"Mom, you can't just ask for free advertising!" I took a deep breath and looked at Jay who was holding said abs as he laughed. "This is so embarrassing," I mumbled.

"This store is a part of the family, Mikka. You should be excited to get advertising for it, not embarrassed."

"Excited isn't the word I would use. None of this, not even the vibrators, excite me anymore."

"Well, they paid for your college education; that's pretty exciting to me." My mother stood there proudly with her arms crossed. Her coarse grey hair wove between her black locks, but other than that, she looked just a tad older than me. Her slanted eyes, her thin, small frame, and her still-smooth skin had me hoping I would age as well as her. Even having lived the hard life she had, she'd amounted to a person that didn't look worn, didn't act worn, and approached life without fear of defeat.

Jay appeared shocked that this porn store was that lucrative. My mother and I smiled like we had a secret. We did. We laughed all the way to the bank as people frowned upon what we called a healthy lifestyle with a balance of adventurous sex.

"I'll text soon, Mom."

On our way to the airport, Jay pried further. "So, all your life, this is the store she owned?"

"Yup." I shrugged and checked my phone to make sure our driver was making all the right turns. We needed to make our flight, but we'd left little time to get to the gates before they closed. "I learned early on to take the snarky or dirty comments in stride. I have a thick skin and a big bank account because of that store. It taught me a lot over the years."

"Then you should have told me about it." Jay yanked on the neckline of his shirt.

"Are you scolding me?" I teased him.

He lowered his head seriously. "Yeah, actually, I am. We're supposed to be friends, Meek. I need to know about the things in your life that make you the way you are."

Jay knew more about me than any other friend I'd ever had. He knew my family, my job, what made me tick.

And what my kiss tasted like.

That night my phone rang as I got out of the Uber at my apartment.

"Mikka, he's got to shape up," my boss complained. He was frustrated to hear Jay hadn't stayed for the meeting. That damn meeting that would have definitely happened had Jay shared it with me and I'd be able to put it on my calendar.

"I know. The meeting wasn't scheduled. If I had known, I would have made sure he was there."

There was a long pause. "He's one of our best, but we can't afford not working with this director again because of Jay's lack of commitment to this role. He needs to show it's important to him, stop putting other things first, and prove that this is the role for him, and only him."

I nodded. I agreed. It was his role; he nailed each line. But acting was only half the job. He needed to showcase a different persona off-screen too.

"I'll talk to him. I swear I will."

I added it to my calendar. I was going to do it first thing in the morning.

I didn't get the chance.

LESSON OF THE DAY:
*Life is never what
you think it is.*

CHAPTER THREE

MIKKA

JAY HAD NUCLEAR-BOMBED his career. I got the call at six in the morning that he'd partied even harder than we had two weeks ago.

"I'll text you updates, Mikka. But this is bad," Bob grumbled into the phone. Bob had been Jay's advocate for so long, an older jolly boss who absolutely loved Jay like his own son. "We can't keep him tied to the company if this movie deal falls through."

"I'm sorry, what?" I shot out of bed to walk to the other room, scrambling to put together what he was saying.

"It's just guilt by association, Meck. You understand. We either get this done or we have to let him go. Guillermo specifically wants him in rehab or he loses the movie too. You need to get that done, get him there, or his career is over and we reassess the clients you work with."

After we hung up, my phone buzzed with another text from my boss: screenshots of a headline. Someone had caught Jay with lines of coke in the club bathroom. Another paparazzo caught him in the parking lot with a hand up some blonde's skirt. Picture upon picture upon picture.

Bile rose in my throat at the thought of going to see him, knowing that Jay had partied this hard after hanging out with me and my mother. After he'd injected the idea of him and I together in my head. I couldn't forget how he'd gripped my hips, run his thumbs along my skin and kissed me like he was desperate with hunger for me.

I guess he'd caught amnesia though. Or he just didn't care; charming women was what he did.

Our agency wanted me to go retrieve him, to get him in order. But my life was spiraling out into a disorganized mess too. I still hadn't told Dougie, who was asleep in the next room, what had happened.

How could I? Our relationship had been rough the past few months as it was. My boyfriend through college, through my coming of age, through everything, was on the brink of being my ex.

And that wasn't an option.

I needed him and he needed me. We'd grown together, found jobs together, lived together. We could beat our little bump in the road together too.

The bump that likely could turn into a mountain if I didn't come clean about it immediately.

I didn't dwell because I couldn't. I needed to wake Dougie up, tell him what had happened, and then go retrieve Jay.

I grabbed my book bag from the table and made a list. If anyone could do this, it was me. I just needed to execute each thing one by one. First on that list was "tell Dougie."

I looked at him lying on the bed, his light brown hair mussed and his mouth slightly open. He inhaled, and the pale blue sheets over him rose and fell with the motion. We'd picked out those sheets together, the first Egyptian Cotton set we could afford.

Jay had landed a rom-com deal because I had pitched him the idea. He asked me if I thought it was a good move. I remember just how he looked at me, like he really wanted my honesty and I gave it to him. I told him the movie was shit but the payday would be lucrative. He nodded and said that we could both use a payday.

He hadn't needed one, but I had.

Those sheets marked my first taste of luxury with Dougie but also the point of trust Jay and I had with one another. Since that day, I was honest, and he was Jay, this larger than life fun-loving persona that everyone admired and enjoyed.

Yet, no one saw the toll it took on him to drive that happiness every day.

"Dougie." I shook his shoulder to wake him.

He grumbled and then cracked an eye open at me. "What time is it?"

"Too early." I sat down at the edge of the bed. "We need to talk."

He squinted at me, rubbed his eyes. "What's going on?"

"It's my day off, but I have to go handle some things for a client."

"Do I want to know?" He sat up and stretched one arm over his head while he yawned.

"I don't have to remind you that we all signed NDAs." I stopped and took a calming breath when he rolled his eyes. "I'm just reminding you. Jay's in some trouble. I have to pick him up from a hotel and deliver some news."

"You don't have to remind me about the NDA every time. We've been together since you took on this godforsaken job."

"Why do you say it like that?" I saw the swell of anger and resentment gaining momentum, but I didn't know how to stop it or know if I really wanted to.

"Because that job causes all our problems."

"That job pays all of our bills." I threw back at him.

"So, you're mad all over again about me not working. I thought you said you wanted me to find my passion like you found yours."

I combed my hand through my hair. "I do want that. You know I want that."

"Well, then, you should let me find it."

Fighting him and pushing him wasn't the answer. I held back the need to drive him, to nudge him in the right direction. It wasn't my place, I was supposed to be his partner, not his accountability coach.

I sighed. "We need to discuss something before I leave." I pushed the words out just as I knew I would have to push my confession out.

He cracked his neck. "It's the ass crack of dawn, Mikka. Jesus."

"Still, I have to be honest with you." I wrung my hands together and swallowed down the new fear that was bubbling up. The words stuck to my mouth, not at all near ready to come out.

I folded my hands in my lap to stop fidgeting and told myself that doing what was right sometimes meant doing what felt like was wrong for you. Living a lie could have appeared beneficial, but the truth always came out. No one deserved to be in the dark.

I took a deep breath.

One in and out.

One in and out.

"Jay and I kissed two weeks ago."

It seemed both of us held our breath as his hazel eyes widened. The blotches of red filled his skin as his face crumbled like my words were finally registering. "What?" he whispered. Then, he yelled, "What?"

He jumped off the bed and paced up and down the room.

"Dougie, like I said, things got out of hand. Jay got carried away with partying and... It isn't his fault. I got carried away. I drank too much and let it happen."

He slammed his hand into the wall hard. Harder than he should have. When he turned back to me, his eyes looked wild. "You let it happen?"

I lowered my head into my hands, and my hair fell around my face. "It's not an excuse. I'm so sorry." I shook my head and pushed the palms of my hands into my eyes. "I'm so..."

Before I fully registered his hand in my hair, I'd been yanked up from the bed by it. "You cheated on me with him? After all the denials and the bullshit you spewed about him being a friend?"

As he said the words, his hand squeezed tighter and the base of my neck and scalp throbbed with the pain. The shock started to wear off and fear started to ebb its way in.

Dougie had only ever gotten physical with me a few times before. There were other factors to blame then too. He'd drank too much one night, we'd been provoking each other another night. It'd been so long ago though.

I trusted him again. I trusted that he was the guy that could make me feel safe even if he was a whole head taller than me. I was always the small girl who put on shoes to gain height and when I curled up next to Dougie, his size dwarfed me even more.

His size had always made me feel safe.

Safe until the moment I knew I wasn't.

I'd reasoned that he'd never hurt me again. He'd apologized for days, begged for forgiveness, got me present after present. This was the man that when I'd first started dating him, he'd seen me jump at violence in a movie and he'd changed the channel. He had even shielded my eyes if I cut my hand while chopping vegetables one night.

"Dougie, you're hurting me." I whispered the words like a plea, like a reminder, like I knew this wasn't him.

"I'm hurting you?" he asked, his voice full of condescension. He jerked his hand away and my head fell forward at the abrupt release. "Do you know how bad it hurts to know you did this to me?"

"Dougie, I…"

The first punch to my ribs knocked the air clean out of my lungs. I remembered flailing backward but he followed with a motive to inflict more pain. The next punch was measured and accurately placed in the same exact location. I wheezed out another plea.

He backed away from me, eyes still full of chaos and violence, rabid with the pain I'd caused. "Now you know how much it hurts."

I scrambled farther back on the bed but winced the whole way. The pain shot through my side as I moved. "I'm sorry," I whispered because I couldn't manage to say more, couldn't muster up the courage to say anything else. "I'm sorry, Dougie."

"Stop saying that," he bellowed, spit flying from his mouth.

I recoiled like a beaten animal at the volume. The jumpiness was an instinct I'd thought had been long forgotten. It'd been almost a year since he'd acted out, a year of us rebuilding from the last incident. But muscle memory always took over when adrenaline and fear kicked in. My body instantly didn't trust him, instantly categorized him as a threat. The trust we'd once had with one another was snapped that quickly. Shattered to pieces all over the beautiful tiling of the floor we'd picked out together.

I opened my mouth but found myself silent, keeping stock still. Even as my side throbbed and I wondered how quickly I could escape if I had to, I was frozen. Normally, I acted. I figured out my odds, I worked hard to get out ahead, and I drove forward. Here, in my own bedroom, arm around my ribs, I suddenly felt small, helpless.

Destroyed.

"What do you want me to do?" The words trembled out of me, and I hated that I was folding under his attack, giving him what he wanted.

He cracked his knuckles and closed his eyes like the mere sight of me was pissing him off. "Damn it, Mikka. I shouldn't have done that." His voice rumbled out full of gravel and pain. "You're just everything, you know? We're in this together. Me and you."

He came to me and I let him. His face crumpled like the idea of what he'd done was breaking him and maybe it was breaking me too. His words meant something to me; we'd been in it together for so long. I'd invested my past, my present, and my future in him.

He sat down on the bed and scooted over to me. "Mikka," he whispered and his finger lifted my chin toward him so gently, I felt the man I first fell in love with beside me. "I'm sorry. I can't lose you and I thought I might. It makes me crazy that he did that. And you know I've never, ever hurt you or anyone before. Shit, baby. I love you, okay?"

The words broke down the wall of shock, broke down the fear, and flooded me with emotion. My eyes started to fill with tears and he instantly was there at the corners of them, kissing away the wetness. "Forgive me. God, forgive me. Say that we'll be okay."

I nodded and let him rub my back as he tried to soothe away the events of the morning. "We'll be okay. We'll be okay." I almost chanted the words, like something I needed to remember, like something I needed burned into my mind because I wanted so badly to believe them.

Yet, how could we be fine after this? How could we move forward?

I rubbed my side one last time. "Do I need to quit my job? Maybe I can call to have someone else pick Jay up."

Suddenly, he had the reins and complete control of our relationship. I wanted his opinion on my life and I didn't know why. I didn't see that I'd just handed him the first page to the book of controlling me.

He took it with a smile and a peck on my cheek. "No, honey. No. I overreacted. Let's just start with making sure you know how to get him to back off if he tries something. I'll need his number and I want you to call me when you're with him. Let him know you're with me. He needs to know who's in charge."

I nodded like I could accomplish that list but the bile rising in my throat told me I didn't want to.

"I should get going. I'll be home in a couple hours."

I got up to leave and grabbed my leather bag to hike up onto my shoulder. I gripped the strap tight like it was my only safe lifeline. He followed close behind me. When he grabbed my ass and turned me, my heart jumped to my throat again. "Tell me you love me. That I'm the only one you love."

His face had a new look, intoxicated with new power. "Dougie..."

"Tell me, Mikka. And then lay one on me." His grip on my ass tightened to the point of pain.

I leaned in and said the words. Then, I let him kiss me.

On the way out the door, I left my pride and heart behind. As I walked down the hallway, the first tears fell. In the elevator, the sobs wracked my body and I winced at the pain in my side.

On the way to the hotel, I drove in silence, numb to what had just happened.

I gripped my leather bag in the seat beside me. I would check off my list, I would plow ahead, and everything would fall into place.

It would have to, wouldn't it?

LESSON OF THE DAY:
*One foot in front
of the other.*

CHAPTER FOUR

MIKKA

OUR COMPANY INFORMED me that Jay was staying in the penthouse of the largest hotel in town. I focused on that.

Shock, I learned, does that to a person. When the worst happens, adrenaline shines light on whether you barrel forward or shrink back. Neither reaction is wrong because it is merely the body surviving the trauma.

It wasn't until I pulled up to the valet that I realized my hands were shaking on the steering wheel. I held up a finger to the valet and took a minute to fix my makeup. Powdering over the tear tracks and swiping on another coat of lip gloss, I stared into my own eyes.

I'd never failed at anything, I tried to remind myself. This was just another bump in the road Dougie and I had to get over. And getting Jay to agree to rehab was just another test even if I wasn't going to be graded. The score would come from how people looked at me, how quickly Jay agreed to the company's recommendation, and, most importantly, how well I hid the previous hour of my life.

The adrenaline from my altercation with Dougie pinpointed exactly the type of person I was. I barreled forward, not letting anyone see my weakness.

I got out of my car and threw the keys to the valet. "I shouldn't be long."

I didn't wait for a response as I strode up to the counter. I tapped my finger on it when the bell boy didn't immediately give me his attention. Celebrities were well-known here, but holding yourself with importance made a lot of difference in this city.

The trick would be getting into his room without the hotel's aid. Jay topped most celebrity charts with a larger than life persona and a charm that most weren't immune to. So, even if Jay had paid on the company credit card, the hotel would refuse to let me have a key.

"I'm here to get a key to Jay's room. My agency's card was used." I slid it over. "We need access."

"I'm happy to call him from the front desk for you, or you can knock on his door. We can't give you access to the room, Ms…" He waited, one eyebrow cocked and a smarmy smile on his face.

"Ms. Chang. And I'm happy to call my agency to see if we want to demand the right of entry to the room—"

"I'll call him." His eyebrow fell down into a frown, like he knew he couldn't throw around that much weight. The tall, thin man reached over to pick up a black corded phone and dialed. He looked out over the lobby as he waited and I stared straight at him, not bending under the awkwardness of the situation.

He pulled the phone away from his face, "You know, he looked just fine last night."

I narrowed my eyes at him. No one actually thought that Jay looked just fine because I'd seen the pictures.

But that was this city. They protected their golden boys and girls. Privacy was everything for the famous and when it was a charming celebrity like Jay, everyone looked the other way. Drugs were part of the lifestyle and very much a part that the city was happy to keep buried under its beautiful beach sand.

"Oh, hi, Mr. Stonewood." The bellboy raised his eyes at me. "I'm calling because there is a Ms. Chang here who would like a room key. I wasn't sure if…"

He paused and then replied, "It's eight AM, sir. I told her it was very early. She insisted that I call you."

Another pause.

"Um, yes, she looks, um, awake." He nodded, scanning me from head to toe. "And like she's ready for the day."

He started making the room key. I let out the breath I was holding. I was Jay's friend, but I wasn't sure if he would always allow me to be that close. The top was lonely and even if he didn't admit it, I saw the distrust he had in his eyes when he looked at most people.

The bellboy handed over the key card. "He said to come up in about twenty minutes."

Jay would clean up the scene of the crime and make himself presentable in that time.

I snatched the key card and sped over to the elevators, my heels clicking loud against the hotel's marble floors. I swiped my room key, walked in, and then waited as the cart shot up to the highest level money could buy.

It opened to the mess that money bought too.

Excess amounts of wealth allowed for responsibilities to fly out the window. If you had your own hallway to your own grand room, it was fine to start taking your clothes off in it. A women's red lace bra was in the middle of the hall. I stepped over it and waved my key in front of the door to his room.

You could pay for someone to clean up the bottles all over the floor and pay them to keep quiet about the lines of cocaine on the tables. A woman ambled in, half naked but not at all surprised at being caught that way by me. "You must be the reason I was told to find my clothes."

I didn't respond. It wasn't my job to make her feel comfortable. "Jaydon and I have some business to work on this morning."

Her amber eyes scanned me as if I was her opponent. I didn't wiggle in my blouse and skinny jeans.

"I believe you said Jay told you to find your clothes." I kept my voice monotone and slid my leather bag from my shoulders to pull out a stack of papers. "Do you need help with that? And also, did you happen to sign an NDA?"

The leggy woman put a hand on her bony hip, still standing there in lingerie. "I told Jay he didn't need that with me."

"Nevertheless, I'd appreciate you—"

"He still had security make me sign one. Now I see why, if you always hound him like this." She sneered as she bent at her waist. "But guess what? I don't want anything more from him. You know why?"

I packed up my bag, trying not to engage. The zipper that usually slid closed so quickly snagged on a paper. I pulled it back but didn't get any traction.

"Honey, him in a bed is good enough. Him between my legs..."

Jay ambled out of the bathroom with just sweatpants on, drying his dark mussed hair. Water droplets beaded on his chest.

"Mikka." His voice cracked like the guilt was breaking it. "I told the bellboy I would be ready in twenty minutes..."

Seeing him and knowing she'd been with him just weeks after he'd had his lips on mine cut as deep as the woman wanted it to. It exposed feelings I wanted to keep covered up and left them raw, broken, and unattended on the hotel floor.

"And I received his message, Jay." I looked down and shoved the zipper harder as I realized my vision was blurring under tears I definitely couldn't shed.

I wasn't Jaydon's type, or anyone's type in LA really. I was naturally thin but my muscles weren't tanned and toned like the woman who stood there in all her half-dressed glory.

LA accepted me anyway. Not based on appearance but based on performance.

My clients trusted me to go above and beyond for them. I did. Every single time.

Specifically for Jay.

Specifically for America's royalty.

The zipper finally gave way, as did my drive to overcome my sudden lapse in judgement for feeling something for my friend. I stepped over a pillow and my ridiculous feelings to attend to what was important.

"So, for a hotel party, this is pretty mild. We should start cleaning though." I glanced around and my stare fell on the woman. "Do you need me to call you a car?"

She reared back, her mouth opening and closing when Jay didn't jump to her defense. She threw up her hands and skittered around grabbing her clothes. "I guess I'll go then."

I folded my hands together and waited. I let the awkward silence stretch as the woman turned to him. Jay nodded and some of his manners kicked in. He led her to the door, whispered something charming no doubt as she giggled and then closed the door behind her. Before he turned to me, he leaned his head on the wall. His shoulders moved with the deep breaths he took.

"I'm not here to patronize you, Jay." Even if I wanted to throw accusations, I couldn't. I had Dougie and the painful physical reminder of him every time I took a breath.

Jay turned and the muscles in his neck coiled, his abs flexed. I saw pain before I saw the shame. "You should be. Look at my room."

We both eyed it, me, probably more trepid than him.

"It's not the best I've seen and definitely not the worst." I measured my words because we were on uneven ground. My words weeks before were directed at him maliciously and I should have chosen them more carefully especially because he was my friend, a friend I didn't want to lose over a kiss that meant nothing.

I zeroed in on the drugs at the table. They were illegal, glaringly accessible, and served as a reminder that he had a problem, one we had to fix. "Do you want me to clean it up?"

He cracked his knuckles and I swear his eye started twitching. "No, I… can you just give me twenty minutes?"

The shame. It was always a big motivator. I remember the first time my mother used it as a weapon against me. I'd fought her so hard on cleaning my bedroom one day. She finally surrendered. Little did I know she went and invited as many parents of my friends over as she could. When they arrived with their children, my mom directed them to my room.

Never again did I have it a mess.

"Twenty minutes for what, Jay?" I went to grab a white towel from the bathroom and ran water over it. Then I re-entered and started wiping up the powder.

He stepped in front of me to block my view. "I'll clean up the room. I don't remember..."

"It's fine." I sighed and stepped around him. "Not anything I haven't seen before, definitely something I'll see again."

The truth was I loathed this part of the job. I wanted to help make movies come alive, be there to adjust the lighting, direct a facial expression, make a viewer get lost in something that had the potential to change their life. Instead, I cleaned up mess after mess in the hopes I would get closer by working with actors.

"Meek, I don't remember half the night in this hotel room."

I snuck a look at him. Even standing there with his shoulders slumped, the body of that man after a drunken night's sleep was still perfection. He scratched the scruff of his five o'clock shadow, and my body reacted like any woman's would. He was what made movies blockbusters—his muscles, his strong jaw, his full lips.

It was a glaring reminder, like a bucket of ice water being thrown on me, that we could never, ever work. A pin up model belonged next to him and even if I was competitive in nature, I was also logical. We weren't compatible.

I grabbed a few pieces of clothing that looked like his and threw them to him. "Do you remember who you were with last night? Any damage control I have to do?" I wondered if he remembered what I saw in the pictures, if he knew he'd been caught doing lines in the bathroom, with his hand up the woman's skirt. I tried not to shudder at the thought.

"I think the biggest damage control is that you saw me with her, Meek. I know you got Dougie but we need to talk."

My heart hammered. I glanced around the room, not wanting to meet his eyes, not wanting to admit to myself that I wanted to hear what he had to say. Dougie and I would work through things and I didn't need Jay swooping in as a distraction.

"Little Pebble, she wasn't you, she wasn't like kissing you..."

I bit my lip.

Damn.

My body wanted to go to him. I wanted to scream at him that he was right, that she wasn't me. And how could he risk it all on another night like this with another woman?

A woman that wasn't me.

I reminded myself it should have never been me though. He was planting this little seed in my heart where he had no business doing so. I didn't want my love for him to flourish beyond a friendship or beyond the mistake we'd already made.

I cleared my throat, ready to dig up the seed and toss it far away where it belonged. I picked up a knocked-over chair to push it back under the table. "Jay, that was weeks ago. It's not something we ever need to bring up again. No need to try to soothe my ego." I reminded myself that's what he was doing anyway. "You get a pass from me, I'm your friend, not a woman you've slept with who's trying to stick around. Honestly, just pass go, collect $200 and forget all about it."

"A pass?" He cocked his head. Then he strode over to me. His chest brushed up against my arm and I gripped the top of the chair, trying to stave off any reaction to his proximity. He ran his finger and thumb over a strand of my hair as if feeling the weight of it. "Little Pebble, you know I'm not going to forget that kiss for the next decade. We don't have to talk about it. We don't have to bring it up. But you need to know: I won't forget it. I'm sorry it happened that way. I've had a few bad nights in the past month and that was one of them. I shouldn't have put you in that position. So, if it's a pass you're handing out, I guess I'll take what I can get."

I held my breath. The pain in my side stopped. It felt like the beating of my heart stopped too. I wanted to believe the words so badly, my body leaned toward him as he said them. It was a toxic, damning situation to be in, though. Jay couldn't commit; he was the farthest thing from commitment I'd ever encountered. "I think it's good to just move on. It was a bump in the road with lots of alcohol involved."

He narrowed his eyes like he was about to disagree but then he said, "Does Dougie know?"

"Does he know what?" I jolted away from him at the mention of my boyfriend's name.

His brow furrowed. "Did you tell him about us?"

"Of course. It's fine." The words tumbled out of me and I tried to wave off the growing ball of anxiety in my stomach. "My clients get out of hand all the time."

"Wait." His shoulders bunched. "Who?"

"You're kidding me, right?"

He had the audacity to tsk at me like he had the right to put himself in a different bucket than all the others. "Has Johnny tried something with you? Did someone step over the line?"

I wanted to scream at him. "Isn't that the pot calling the kettle black? Can you please just get ready so that we can go?"

He held his ground, tried to wither down my resolve with his stare, but I didn't fold under it anymore. Jaydon Stonewood came from an astute, ruthless family of businessmen. I knew his father had run most of Chicago with investments and then his brother took over. They played their cards right, they handled large deals, and they always, always seemed to win the war of who was a bigger man.

Yet, Jaydon didn't know a man's competition had nothing on the strength of a woman. I'd have stood my ground for days to prove my point. Add on to that, my mother and I had many a standoff. His retreat was inevitable.

He backed away without a word. We straightened the hotel room. I found more than one line on the kitchen counter, two more in the bathroom and remnants on the bedroom nightstand.

As I cleaned the last one up, he mumbled, "It got out of hand last night. I'm... it's not usually this bad."

I nodded. "Okay, Jay." I didn't need to fight him. Kicking a wounded animal when they were down was never productive.

He pulled at the collar of the shirt he'd put on. "Look, I really am sorry. I need you to know that."

His words bottomed out my stomach. "For what?" Did he know my relationship with Dougie had just changed because of him and his actions, that the drugs put him front and center in my life while his front and center was anything but me?

"I'm sorry for this." He spread his arms wide and his voice broke. "For the kiss, for everything."

I closed my eyes to shield myself from the hurt of knowing he regretted our kiss. He should. I should have too. "Nothing should be happening this way; I'm putting you in a tough position."

"Don't be sorry. Be strong." I stared him down, not bending to his apology. "Make me believe you."

He tilted his head. "Okay, and how do you want me to do that?"

"Go to rehab with the intention of never ever ending up there again."

Jay ran a hand through his hair and then pulled it up in what looked like frustration. "Meek, what?" He whispered. Then he rasped out, "What do you mean? I don't have a problem."

"I think you do. The agency thinks you do too."

"How can you say that?" The way he asked me had me wanting to snatch back my words. "You never see me using. The last couple of times... I mean... I said last night was..."

"You're dancing around the truth," I said, crossing my arms and trying to hold firm. "Every single time you missed a meeting with me last month, you were using. Our company sends me updates on you, I read the headlines, and I've caught you more than once taking a bump."

He raised his eyebrows. "How do you know what a bump is?"

"Does it matter?" I shrugged. I'd never ever used anything other than alcohol for fun in my life but he didn't need to know that.

"Yes, it matters. Someone offer you something?"

"Would it be terrible if they did? I'm surrounded by you and your friends all the time. You think they don't offer me anything?" I practically shouted.

"Woman, I want names because I've told them never to approach you with that. It's dangerous for you to—"

"Do not." I stalked toward him and poked him in the shoulder. "Do not give me a lecture on drugs when you're using them. You need help. I talked to Bob this morning and they want you in rehab, Jay."

He glared at me like I was betraying him. His step backward felt like a mile he was putting between us.

"I'm giving you honesty. Don't look at me like that." I crossed my arms, knowing I was staring him down like my mother would me.

He growled and pulled at his shirt as if everything was suffocating him, annoying him, frustrating him. "I'm just mad, Meek."

"Me too. I'm mad at you though." My voice came out pleading and I dug my nails into my arms, trying to stand my ground and not go to him. I wanted to soothe away his hurt but I knew I'd enabled him for too long. "You put us in this damn situation and you know it. You can't stop. So, I don't know if that's negligence or something worse. Do you?"

"Are you asking me if I have a problem?" The question whooshed out of him, like I was letting all the wind out of his sails.

"I'm asking you to take a look at yourself and assess that question, Jay."

He stared at me like he was begging for me to throw him a lifeline, a get out of jail free card, anything. I couldn't, though.

Not this time.

"I'll go to the rehab center if that's what you want," he said, hanging his head.

"I don't want you to do anything for me."

His eyebrows slammed down as he whipped his face back up. Then he paced forward.

I stood my ground, not backing up even one step. "This has to be for you and your future. This isn't my idea. It's our agency's idea along with the movie director."

I stared into his electric blue pools and let my words sink in. His jaw was ticking and the lines on his face had deepened.

I waited a second longer to emphasize the gravity of the situation and then said the words I knew would pull him down into darker, more ominous depths. "He'll recast you, Jay."

Those beautiful blue eyes widened. Then, he stumbled back and hunched over like I'd socked him in the stomach. This role meant everything to him. He'd wanted it for so long, to be taken seriously as an actor, as more of a rom-com star.

"And our agency will drop you. I was informed this morning."

"What do you mean? We've shot everything except the scenes in my hometown." Jay shook his head and combed his fingers through his dark, thick hair.

"I said the same thing." I shrugged, trying to stay professional and calm. "The director doesn't care. He said this movie is too important to be overshadowed by an actor who's too wild to keep some powder off his nose."

Jay's face dropped.

"Those were his words, not mine," I clarified, not giving him the information about me possibly being stripped of clients too. He needed to do this for himself, not anyone else. "So, this is for you. And for your future. Not mine. I'm fine either way."

I was lying through my teeth. My life was unraveling and I was fumbling to grasp the threads to stop it. Dougie and I would never be the same. And I couldn't lose everything I'd built my life on. Without Jay, without my clients, without what I'd worked so hard for, I wasn't sure I'd ever be able to weave together a life I wanted.

His jaw worked and I could swear he ground away most of the enamel in those seconds. "I'll try it in LA. I don't want my family or anyone else but the agency aware. I want the movie and so I'll do the time they think I need."

"Perfect. Let's get you there." I clapped my hands.

He stepped in front of me. "Wait. I'm not going now. I need to go home and get packed."

"They'll have what you need delivered." I reached for my leather book bag but he scooped it up before I got to it. "I can carry that."

"Mmhmm." He hummed as he took one last look at the room with me.

I scanned the white counters, the lush furniture, and the beautiful view. "Nice place to stay."

"It's nice until you lose yourself in it," He said as his electric blue eyes turned toward the door like he wanted nothing to do with the luxurious life he lived.

I wrapped my arm around his waist and we walked out together. I hoped we were leaving the worst of us behind.

The drive to the facility dragged on for ages. The stretches of silence between us weren't normal. I knew I should have eased his mind by making small talk as I drove but my heart was focusing on so many things.

I could lose my relationship with Dougie if I didn't figure out how to work through our last encounter. I could lose my best friend to rehab. And I could even lose the job I loved.

I whispered my fear because I had to tell him, had to let him know someone needed him to come back. "I'll miss you while you're there."

He chuckled. "I'm sure they'll let me call you, babe. It's LA."

"Jay." I sighed and turned down another street lined with palm trees. The road turned to bricks and the landscaping on the block became extravagant. "This isn't going to be a walk in the park. You drink every night. I don't know how much you're using, but they aren't going to let you make calls if they think you're dependent on a substance. They don't want you to be at risk of relapsing..."

"Meek, it's fun. F-U-N. Not drugs, not dependency, not an addiction. I promise." His blue eyes shined with promise but his leg jittered with fear.

I shot my hand out to steady his thigh. "I'll be here when you're ready to come home, okay?" As I pulled up to the center, my jaw dropped when the entrance came into view. The brick paved driveway circled a stone fountain. Perennials bloomed in sections around it and the pillars of the entryway were made of the same stone. As I put the car into park, our view was the same as the rehab's: The Pacific Ocean lapping at the coastline.

"Doesn't seem too bad. You and Dougie want to come stay too?" Jay joked. His nature was to lighten the mood, to mask the gravity of the situation. Yet, him bringing up Dougie now didn't lighten anything. I wanted to tell him, to share my burdens with my closest friend.

I grabbed his hand and squeezed instead. Today, I would be selfless. And every other day after that. Because Jay needed a friend in that moment. He needed someone to be there only for him. I wasn't sure he understood his addiction, if he was in denial or trying to cover up how bad it was. Either way, I'd seen the wear on his body, on his soul, and he had to be scared it was about to take a toll on his career too.

He needed me to be there for him, not myself.

An older man with a full head of greying hair and a genuine smile stepped out of the front doors. His maroon shirt was tucked into his khakis, and his expensive loafers said he probably made a decent living. He waved at us, and Jay's jaw ticked. "I guess I'll call you when I get a chance."

I nodded. "I would walk you in, but I don't think I'm supposed to."

He chuckled and patted my leg. "No worries, Meek. I'm thinking I'll be out of here pretty quick. The agency will be happy, the movie will move forward. No biggie." He shrugged but his shoulders were tight.

"You're sure you don't want me to call anyone?"

"I will if I need to," he mumbled and got out of the car. He rounded the car and tapped on my window. I rolled it down.

His aqua blue eyes stared at me and I saw the turmoil in them. "Meek, if they say I'm at my worst, prepare for me at my best." He winked at me. "I promise I'm going to get there."

Before I could say more, he walked away.

Jay at his worst was still the best man I'd ever met.

THERAPIST: *For the first time, you were scared to tell your family something. Would you say that's true?*

JAY: *Sure. I've never been a problem for them. We lived a good life.*

THERAPIST: *That's a pattern of yours. To never be a problem.*

JAY: *And that's a bad thing?*

THERAPIST: *When never having a problem becomes the problem, yes, Jay. It is.*

CHAPTER FIVE

JAY

THE REHAB WAS a joke if you wanted it to be. Other celebrities were there and some were trying, sure. Most were on their phones, snapping selfies, talking to their friends, scrolling their social media accounts. At night, one of the women gave me the details on how to leave without them making a fuss or contacting the people who paid for you to be there.

My agency wouldn't be contacted as long as I slid the night duty staff a couple hundred. Where do you get a couple hundred if you didn't bring cash? They would drive you.

And then there were those that tried. I saw the loss of life in their eyes, like they knew their problem had taken over their life, consumed them, consumed their family, and still they were clawing at the edge of giving in as the addiction dragged them down.

I liked to think my partying with drugs and alcohol was a habit. I didn't do it daily. I indulged and partied hard maybe twice a week. Other days, I took a bump here and there to maintain the personality and the charm.

On Day Four of my stay, my habit became somewhat of a nuisance. Why couldn't I party if I wanted to? To prove a damn point to Mikka and the agency? I wasn't telling my family like the doctor on site suggested because I didn't need to worry anyone outside of the business.

And this was a business. They wanted me to have a clean ass bill of health and reputation before the movie released.

The movie was a step outside of rom-com, the one I'd been waiting for. I was the next Matthew McConaughey, sources were saying, I had the acting power but hadn't been given the script. This was that script. Mikka and I both knew it and my agency did too. They didn't want anything tainting that.

So, I would sit at this nice rehab center and take it as a vacation. They offered massages, had a gym, and were stacked to the nines in amenities.

On Day Five of my stay, my habit-turned-nuisance became a strong desire. The desire became a need—the addiction I'd dreaded. Frustration turned to rage. My obliviousness to my problem became an immediate terrifying reality.

My doctor pushed me to accept it. "You need to call the ones you love, Jay. They need to know what you're going through."

"Why? They don't need to worry. It's under control."

"You screamed out in pain last night and begged for a hit of something. You think that's control?"

"No. I realize there's a problem. But I will overcome it," I replied, full of belief in myself.

"You will." The doctor looked down at his notepad. "I have no doubts you will, but your family will help you. And you need that help if you want to continue to pursue what's important to you."

"There will be other movies." I brushed a non-existent crumb from the table that sat between us.

"Sure. But this is your movie, the one you said"—he rustled through his papers—"you believed in and had views that aligned directly with yours. You said, and I quote, 'I practiced nailing this role because I was born for it. It's the role of a lifetime and it isn't one I will ever encounter again.'"

"So, I know I said that but—"

"Don't downplay how you feel now in order to get what you want. It never works." The doc closed his notepad. "Call your family."

Those calls were the hardest to make. Something about their shock and then their support once I convinced them pushed my guilt to new heights.

My parents were together when I phoned them.

"Jay!" My mom yelled into the phone. "Your father and I are vacationing."

"It's not a vacation," he grumbled.

"It is. I'm calling our home in Florida a vacation every time I'm here now. He keeps telling me it isn't a vacation home but it is. Home is in Greenville."

"We're living here half of winter. That's not a vacation."

"It is. You worked without a vacation for most of Jay's life. You want to talk about that? It's why we're here, vacationing for half the year. I get to call it a vacation if I want."

I heard his sigh but knew he was smiling, that they both were.

I hesitated and considered whether I should even tell them. "Look, I'm calling with some news."

Maybe my voice carried over the seriousness I felt but neither of them said a thing. They waited as if they knew the ball was about to drop.

"I'm in rehab." I winced at my words, knowing that didn't cover what I needed it to. "I'm struggling with some things, and I'll lose the movie role I fought so hard to get if I don't shape up."

I cleared my throat to continue, but my mom drove our family. She'd always stepped up to take the steering wheel when we'd veered off the path and would yank on it to navigate us back onto the right road. "Oh, honey. You worked so hard to get that role. All the auditioning and practice you put in... are you okay?"

She didn't ask why I was in rehab, what addiction had sent me there. She didn't pry or say "I told you so." That her first question was one of concern almost broke me. My chest hurt from the support she always gave rather than searching for a place to put the blame.

"I'll be okay, Ma." I didn't admit that right then I wasn't okay, that I wanted to break down, that it wasn't easy and I was used to the easy road.

"What do you need from us, honey? We'll help you overcome this in any way we can."

Her complete acceptance and willingness to help relieved and frustrated me at the same time. I lashed out at her words. "Have you thought I had a problem this whole time?"

There was silence on the other end. I could picture them sharing a look. Then, she answered, "I'm trusting you if you admit to a problem, Jay. You wouldn't give us this news unless it was serious. So, stop trying to find fault and focus on what you need from us to get better."

She was our beacon of light to follow home, to follow back to the right place. I sighed, knowing my anger toward her, toward everyone and everything in that moment was misplaced. But the ball of frustration kept growing and burning a hole in my heart where my empathy was supposed to be. "I'm not sure. I just need time, I think."

It was a clipped, vague response. She didn't deserve it but she definitely didn't deserve me blaming her for something.

There is something completely shameful about not having a reason for your addiction. When you've had the perfect life, the right friends, the good siblings that only razz you a little here and there; it is difficult to know that you fell a victim to drugs or addiction. The guilt piles on because you should have been able to work through it. I was given all the right tools growing up and still was letting everyone down.

The need to not put the blame on myself clawed its way up my throat. I wanted to scream at her and my father for never giving me bigger obstacles. I wanted to lay blame where it wasn't warranted. But I'd been a man long enough to know better.

Instead, I called my brothers back home. I considered calling my sister in law too. She'd been my best friend in high school but she'd dealt with alcoholism in her father. I couldn't burden her with more. She was someone I realized I had to apologize to as part of my therapy. Doing it over the phone felt much too difficult.

I took the rest of the time at the facility as seriously as I could. The director was able to film most of the scenes I wasn't a part of during that time. They did send over contractual updates though and I was happy to see that they hadn't included Mikka in all the details. They were cutting some of my pay, opting to have me drug tested, and pushing for more therapy. It was a stark reminder that other people had a good enough understanding of how bad my lifestyle had gotten.

So, I surrounded myself with the people that were there by choice, trying to change their lives. Those that were there as a part of their job, that cut corners, that offered me drugs and partying, I stayed away from. I attended meetings with the therapists and doctors.

I committed finally to one thing during my stay. It was getting healthy.

My therapists and doctors felt after sixty days that I was ready for outpatient care but that LA would be a toxic environment.

I called Mikka. I wanted her to pick me up, to see how much I'd changed, to see that I could be better. I wanted my friend to be proud.

When she did, I ended up not caring about any of those things at all.

> **LESSON OF THE DAY:**
> *A true friend listens closely to the things you never say.*

CHAPTER SIX

MIKKA

WENT BACK. I'D told myself I wasn't a victim of abuse, that Dougie just slipped up and we would work it all out. Him and I were so much different than the classic case of domestic violence.

So.

I went back to Dougie.

He'd been the boyfriend I'd had for so long and the man that hadn't ever hurt me before. I had been convinced that this was going to be the man I would be with forever, the one I wanted to marry and share my life with. We'd even discussed marriage in the past.

To start over, to leave all the effort we'd put in behind wasn't fathomable to me. It'd been so long since something like this had happened and it only did because I'd confessed to kissing someone else.

I realized I'd broken him; I'd snapped his control and turned him into someone I didn't recognize. My actions had pushed him over the edge and I wanted to be the person to pull him back. He became the assignment I needed to complete, the test I'd failed but could ace a second time. He was the only wrinkle in my dress. If I could iron this out with him, we wouldn't crash into a mess together. We'd soar high instead.

Yet, he beat me every couple of days while Jay was in rehab. Our relationship became a rollercoaster of his viciousness and then his complete remorse moments after.

I bought a lot of great makeup in those days to cover up the damage. I definitely would have aced cosmetology school.

I didn't visit my mother and I didn't really have any friends but Jay. The other clients that I PA-ed for didn't look twice.

The agency couldn't tell. I did my work flawlessly. With Jay missing from the LA scene, the tabloids speculated enough that I had to work tirelessly to keep rumors of his drug addiction at bay. Everyone complimented me on doing a wonderful job and there was even one time when a secretary mentioned that I looked great with my new eyeshadow and a few less pounds. She wanted to know if I'd been working out.

I'd been working on my relationship. That was about it.

When Jay called, I was like a rabid animal who hadn't been in a warm, safe place in decades. I lunged for my phone. When he said he was ready to come home, to pick him up, I sat in my bathroom and cried.

The agency called soon after. They wanted him to do outpatient therapy in his hometown, Greenville, for another month. It would work perfectly as that's where they wanted to film the last scenes. Bob mentioned I could go if I wanted to also.

It was a blessing and a curse.

You see, Jay had just conquered his addiction. He'd faced it dead on and won. Now, in order for him to do his very best as an actor, I was supposed to confront Dougie with the idea of spending time in another town halfway across the country for my job.

With the one man Dougie would never trust me with.

I pulled on my best dark jeans, a light cream blouse, and swiped some lip gloss on while I took deep breaths and tried to weigh my options. Dougie and I had to get better. We were trying. He was trying and he'd been so nice the past couple of days. He'd cooked dinner, cleaned dishes, and told me I was the best part of his life.

I didn't want to risk telling him that I had to pick up Jay, that I might need to go with him to Greenville. Then again, I prided myself on the job I did. It was the part of the job I loved. I'd get to see the last scenes be filmed and I'd get to help keep Jay on track. He needed that. He needed me.

I didn't know which path to take but I knew I had to keep moving forward. It was the first time I saw failure in my future, one way or the other.

Pulling up to the facility in my white luxury sedan felt different this time. I didn't know how I was going to be able to face Jay and keep everything together. I was different, changed by my own problems. And I needed to be strong for Jay.

Yet, when he emerged from the facility's doors, my beige stilettos stayed glued to the floor mats and my hands shook on the steering wheel. He walked out all clean lines, full of confidence, and completely put together. His bright, focused eyes looked aware and his smile was a mile wide. My core ached for him immediately and my body reacted in a way it never should for a friend that could only be just that. A friend.

Not a lover.

I took deep breaths. Then, I popped the trunk and got out to greet him.

His smile dropped the minute he saw me. "Meek?" he whispered.

The nickname from his lips had tears springing into my eyes. I shook my head and held out a hand when he approached me quickly with his suitcase. "Don't hug me. I'll just end up a blubbering mess. Let's get you loaded up and go. We can talk once we're driving."

He growled and shoved my hand out of the way to take the hug I was trying to deny him. He breathed in like he was breathing in my smell, my spirit, my soul. "I missed you. Damn, I missed you."

I nodded and let one sob escape. "I missed you too."

He smelled like the red lollipops he loved and I imagined he tasted like them too. My body immediately heated and remembered just how much I desired him as I held him close. He felt solid, warm, comfortable, and safe. He felt like a home I'd missed and one I didn't want to leave for a very long time.

I swiped at my face and pulled back, trying to right my emotions and myself at the same time. His arms rested on my shoulders as I looked up at him, and he assessed me. "Something's very wrong."

I cleared my throat. "It was a long two months. Let's talk in the car."

He nodded, threw his suitcase in the back.

"I'm driving," he announced he rounded the trunk of the car. As I looked at him, I saw his confidence, how he was sure of himself again. The grey braided sweater he was wearing filled out across his expansive chest. He looked more solid, like he'd been working out but also like his body was finally getting used to a steadier lifestyle.

"Why can't I drive?" I questioned him.

He scanned my face and his lips turned down. "Because you're a terrible driver. It's probably because you wear those ridiculous heels and you'll be even worse when I make you relive whatever hell you've been in while I was gone."

"I wasn't in hell, I was..."

He cut me off. "Did I ever tell you about my best friend from back home?"

"Aubrey?" I questioned. I knew of her. I knew of her story and the fact that she married his brother. She was a beautiful girl who lost her mother in a house fire her father started. They took her in after her father went to jail and she fell for Jay's brother. Their story made national headlines. "I know some of it from the news. It's my job to pry into your life a bit."

That was the truth, but I tried not to pry more than I needed. The balance we had between friends and coworkers was fragile. Most actors I represented didn't want to feel like I was controlling them based on their history or what I'd found out about them. My friendship with Jay stemmed from an organic trust. I tried to wait for him to tell me some things.

I knew he was close with Aubrey. I also knew he'd adamantly denied having the intimate relationship with her that tabloids wrote about. According to him, she was like a sister and definitely a best friend.

Jay motioned for me to get in, and I glanced back at his rehab center before I did. "This it for you?"

"That's it. I won't be back." His words held so much finality and his vibrant blue eyes held so much determination that I believed him.

"Let's go then." I folded into the leather seat and closed the door. He put the car in drive and peeled out of the circular driveway much faster than I ever would have.

I grabbed the dash and yelped. "What are you doing?"

"I haven't driven in a month." He winked at me with a lopsided smirk on his face. "I need to let loose a little, Meek."

"Oh my God. You know how much the fountain probably costs and the brick paving? Calm down before you crash and cost us a fortune."

He laughed and settled in as we traveled down the drive and wound round the hills back into the city. We enjoyed the silence and the breeze as he rolled down the windows. "I feel free," he mumbled.

"I'm happy you do," I replied and meant it.

"I want you to feel that way too."

"What is that supposed to mean?" I asked as I looked out the window, away from him, away from the truth he was about to put on me.

"You have the same look in your eye as Aubrey did the first time I saw her after her father beat her mother senseless. I didn't know it then but I knew something was wrong. I'll never forget that look, Meek. She looked trapped."

"I don't know what you're talking about."

"Little one, what cage are you locked up in?"

I set my chin in my hand and rested my elbow on the door. I didn't look at him. "It's just been a tough couple of months, Jay. I'll get through it."

"Okay." His hand went to my thigh and squeezed it. "I'll find the key and get you out even if you can't talk about it."

"Jay, I promise it's nothing."

He shook his head. "How's Dougie? He a part of this?" He asked the question not one person had asked me in the past sixty days. No one would have ever guessed Dougie was hurting me. He was too reserved, too docile, too much of a pushover. But I hid our defects well. I hid my failures even better, and my relationship was shaping up to be one of those.

"Of course not, Jay. Are you kidding?" The laugh that came from me sounded mechanical, high, and wrong.

He drove in silence for so long before answering me, I finally glanced at him. He was white-knuckling the wheel, jaw locked in place and brow furrowed.

"I'll ask you one more time, and for the sake of our friendship, Meek, don't lie to me. I'm not in a place where I can take liars. Is it Dougie?"

"A part of it's him and a part of it's me, Jay. Like I said, we've had a tough time."

"Are you coming with me to Greenville?"

I sighed. His question was a bigger one than just a trip. "How do you expect me to explain that to Dougie?"

"It's what you do. You PA for me." Jay said it like there wasn't an argument to be had. Yet, Dougie never would allow me to be gone for a month with Jay, not after what had happened. My mind started to concoct excuses for him, because he was right. I had cheated, I had broken our trust, I had jeopardized our family and the job that put the food on the table every night.

"I want to go, Jay. I do. I want to be there for you and I get this movie is big and that you need a PA there. I'm just trying..." I took a breath and combed my fingers through my hair. "I'm trying to figure out what's best."

He didn't hesitate. "It's best for you to come."

"I know Bob mentioned I could go but a whole month isn't

necessary. Maybe in a week, I could meet you out there to check on you."

"Maybe now, we drive to your house, pack your shit, and you come. Tell Dougie it's for the job."

We got to a red light and Jay glanced at my hands. I was picking at my nails, a habit I had to stop. I folded them together. "It's just that I have a lot of other obligations. You aren't the only actor I represent and PA for, Jay."

My tone was chastising and he let it go, or at least I thought he did until he hit a few buttons on his phone screen. Our secretary's voice came over his cell's speaker. "Empire Talent. How can I help you?"

"It's Jay Stonewood. Is Bob at his desk?"

"Oh, sure. One moment."

I whisper-yelled at him, "What are you doing, Jay?"

He shined his smile on me, the one that melted women's hearts around the world. "Seeing if they can spare my agent for a month."

"Don't you dare, Jay. I am not..."

"Jay!" Bob bellowed into the phone. "How are you? You with Mikka? She pick you up?"

"Yep. We're both here, just driving back and I'm feeling good in the LA air, Bob."

He harrumphed. "You know you got to get back to that hometown of yours for just a month, son. Just give us a clean bill until the film crew gets there in a few weeks. This damn movie is going to be it. I can feel it."

"I feel it too." He nodded like there wasn't a hint of a doubt there. I wanted that for him, wanted him to make the movie only he had the acting ability to accomplish. Jay felt people; he *was* them, their pain, their joy, their love. I was convinced that part of his indulgence in drugs was for that reason, whether he knew it or not. He had this gift of seeing into someone's soul and holding their hand through their turmoil. It made him a brilliant actor, but it was also a large burden to carry.

"So, I need Mikka to come back with me." Jay dove into asking for the impossible. He was my biggest actor but I had others, two of which were handling movie deals right now. There was no way I should leave.

"Yes, I told her she should go." I rolled my eyes because he had said I *could* go which was much different. "We got you there for a month at that bed and breakfast you mentioned. I booked her the only other room there." He grumbled like he was looking it all up.

"Bob, I have numerous movie deals." I protested.

"No worries, Mikka. We'll get those taken care of. Jay needs twenty-four-hour care and attention."

Jay belly-laughed in silence next to me. I smacked his chest. He carried on the ridiculousness with Bob. "Yep. You hear that Meek? Twenty-four hours, seven days a week."

I rolled my eyes. As we neared my apartment, though, his joking felt less and less light, his presence weighed more heavily on my mind, our situation seemed more and more dangerous.

"Right." I cleared my throat. "Bob, I'll have to discuss this with my family and iron out details for our agency before I commit. If you could give me a couple days—"

"We're on the way to her house to get her packed right now, Bob. She can fly out with me?" Jay cut me off.

"Sure thing. We'll get her a plane ticket. Guillermo wants someone keeping tabs on you anyway. I'd rather Mikka be there for all that. You agreed to drug tests and I think that's best. You know, just to make Guillermo happy."

My questioning gaze shot to Jay's. This was the first time I'd heard of drug testing. "I'm sorry, Bob. I didn't agree to—"

"I have another call coming in." Bob's voice bellowed over mine. "I'm looking forward to seeing your progress in the next month, Jay. I'll have other script details sent over."

The phone screen lit up with the "call ended" sign.

Jay turned down another road, and I realized we were only five minutes from my building. I had to shut down this idea and keep my home life separate from him, from everyone.

"I can't go anywhere. I can't just uproot my life for a month. I have priorities."

"We just got rid of those priorities," he said with no emotion in his voice now.

"My mother is in San Francisco; she could need me."

"She doesn't ever need you. She's as fierce as you, woman. And you barely visit her. She's fine. You and I both know it."

"Well, I..." I stuttered. "Dougie needs me too."

"Does he, though, or does he need a punching bag?" His question was without emotion but so cold I felt the degrees within my car lowering.

I reared back and glared at him. "What are you insinuating?"

"Something's wrong, Meek. I don't know what, but I know you don't look like you do without something being very, very wrong."

"Look like what?"

"You're a shell of yourself." He stared ahead as he turned on his signal to veer onto the road of my apartment building.

"I told you it's just been hard. Dougie and I have had some disagreements but nothing of that sort."

"Really?" he ground out.

"Really." I folded my arms over my cream blouse as if to shield his eyes from the bruises I knew were under it.

"That's two times you've lied to me on this drive, woman. I promise you I'll break that new habit as quickly as possible. I'm starting with getting you out of this fucking mess of a relationship." His jaw ticked. "A long time ago, I made the mistake of ignoring the signs with Brey. I won't do that with you."

"Nothing's wrong," I whispered.

"Three lies, Meek!" he yelled and I jerked back. He saw it, my recoil, the one my body automatically made now. I was ashamed when he winced at the movement I couldn't suppress. "Not me, little one. Don't be afraid of me." His voice was pleading, full of the pain I knew he felt more than most. "You're done with him, with this bullshit of being scared. We end this now, even if that means we drag you kicking and screaming to Greenville with me. I got a drug problem and it seems you have a habit you can't quit either. I'm happy to remedy one of those issues now. You coming up to your apartment with me or not?"

His hand was on his door handle, poised and ready. What could I say to make this go away? How could I get the truth I wanted so badly to hide out of his head?

He cocked a brow at me. "Either way, I'm going, Meek."

"Just…" My heart raced, galloping toward an outcome that felt out of control. We were going down the hill toward chaos so fast, I was sure a wheel would fly off and send us careening into destruction. And I couldn't stop it. I'd lost the reins and couldn't scramble fast enough to pick them back up.

I could lie. I could keep trying to get around the truth.

I saw his rage as I sat in silence, though. Jay's was different. He didn't show it on the surface. It didn't fill his face with red blotches and tighten all of his muscles. He didn't look ready to burst and take his anger out on me. Jay held himself steady, quiet, filled with a confidence that he knew he could control the emotion even if he was feeling it more than anyone else. He'd never lashed out, never wavered from his fun-loving personality even in his blackout moments where drugs stole his conscious decision-making skills.

When I looked back at Dougie, I saw the signs. I knew them all perfectly now. I sat there disappointed in myself night after night when I combed through all the clues like Carmen San Diego. I'd had a 98% average in my Psychology class where we discussed signs of abusive tendencies and still, I'd missed every single one.

"I just need a minute." I sighed and closed my eyes, willing my emotions to stay locked up. "I need probably a year but just give me at least a minute."

He put his head to the steering wheel. "Damn, I didn't want to be right but I am, aren't I?"

I didn't answer him.

He knew the answer.

I took a deep breath. "I'm going to go get my stuff. I can do that discreetly. If you come up, it'll be hell."

"I'm not letting you go in there alone."

"I've been alone with him for years, Jay."

"Has he been…" He took a breath. "When did it start?"

"That's not relevant." I didn't want to explain that our kiss was a sort of tipping point. We were both broken, and shattering those pieces further wasn't worth the pain for either of us.

"Fine," he grumbled as we parked on the road under a palm tree right outside my building. "I'm trying hard not to push you."

"Weird. Feels like pushing when I have to join you on a plane in two hours and I'm getting no time on my own."

"Little one, I don't regret this for a second. If you think I feel guilty, I don't. I expect you to push me just as hard on random drug tests and keeping my ass in line. You going up or not?"

I picked at a speck of lint that was on my jeans. "Let me talk, okay? I'll deal with him."

Jay pulled at the door handle and shoved it out harder than necessary without answering me.

"Jay, you have a reputation to uphold, remember that." I scurried out of the vehicle after him. "Jesus. Can we put the brakes on this? You just got out of rehab!"

My hand flew over my mouth and I glanced around before I took in the man in front of me, frozen in place. Then he laughed, laughed at my stupidity, at the fact that I could have potentially delivered a crushing blow to his career.

He crossed a foot over the other before he did a slow spin on the sidewalk. He looked like perfection, plain and simple. His longer dark hair had grown in rehab; the extra wave to it now just added to his appeal. His stark blue eyes sparkled brighter contrasting the dullness of his grey sweater.

"Yup, I'm out and I'm healthier than ever, Meek. Not that I wasn't healthy enough to kick his ass before this."

With that, he turned away from me and stalked toward my building.

THERAPIST: *You've mentioned your friend, Mikka, before. Is she just a friend? Even after what happened that night?*

JAY: *She'll never be just a friend. She's a colleague that I trust with my career and a woman that I respect.*

THERAPIST: *Anything more?*

JAY: *A lot more.*

CHAPTER SEVEN

JAY

REHAB HAD BEEN near the hardest thing I'd ever done in all my life. Every day, every hour, and every minute felt like a weight of anxiety now hung around my neck.

I couldn't let anyone down again. I had to nail this movie role and to do that, I couldn't fall victim to the one thing I thoroughly enjoyed while living in the city.

Partying had been my life for years. Drugs were always a complementary friend that tagged along. Withdrawing from it had pushed my body to limits I wasn't capable of understanding before being an addict.

All of that seemed easy, though, sitting next to a woman I considered so close to me and knowing that she had been sucked dry of her life force.

Mikka was the epitome of perfection. If you thought of her as a bug, she was a butterfly; if a cat, she was a tiger; if a dog, she was a purebred. She walked into a room and instantly you knew she was the most intelligent, put-together person there. Then she opened her mouth and her hunger to be better made you strive toward your best too.

Perfection.

And all of it was gone.

Rehab had been easy.

Seeing my friend broken wasn't.

Her infectious energy to live and fight her way to the top had been extinguished. The moment I saw her, I knew. She'd lost weight, put on more makeup, and approached me like a wounded animal seeing a friendly face. When I'd hugged her, her body froze up like every part of her might be bruised.

She ran ahead of me and shoved me back, desperation in her brown eyes. "Jay! Stop." She whispered the last word, "Please."

Her hands didn't leave my chest as I stood there, a fury I hadn't felt in a long time coursing through my veins. "Mikka, what do you expect me to do? I stood by and let it happen before to Aubrey. You know what that does to a kid? To let his best friend go home to a dad that beat her?"

She winced at my story. "It's not like that."

"What's it like?"

"I go back willingly, Jay. I'm an adult. I... It's not like I have nowhere else to go. When things get out of control, if he hurts me, he doesn't hurt me like that." She tripped over her words, none of them really making sense.

Reining in my anger was like taming a wild beast. "Are you hearing yourself? It doesn't make sense. If he hurts you, he isn't? Meek, if he's hurting you, the rest is black and white."

"No! It's murky, and mixed up and a mess, Jay." She swiped at her cheek furiously as one lone tear escaped from her dark eyes.

"Little Pebble, you could be with someone so much better," I murmured.

"Like who? You?" she shot back.

I wanted to nod but didn't get the chance.

"You can't commit to a meeting with me, let alone a relationship!" she spouted. "Dougie's committed and that says a lot about a man."

"Any man would commit to you." I meant it. "You've got a million things to offer."

"Jay, you kissed me, flirted with me in my mother's porn shop, and then went to party with another woman the next day. You hung out with me and my mom, flaunted your abs in my face and acted the complete gentleman with her, only to turn around and have your hands up another woman's skirt later that night."

"Meek, we weren't… I wouldn't have done that had I thought I stood a chance with you." I ran a thumb across the path of her tear to wipe the remnants away. "What do you expect from me?"

"Just, please, let me handle this! I've handled it this long."

I took her face in both my hands and tilted her head up to look straight into my eyes. "And that's too fucking long."

I started to walk forward but she pushed back on me.

I gripped her wrists as softly as I could. "Little one, I can't let you handle it the way you have been. You get that, right? You get that I can't let him off so easy?"

"I still want this to work, Jay. I stayed. I chose to be a part of this life. Me. That's not anyone's fault but mine. I have to figure out what works for me. That might not work for you, but at the end of the day, it isn't your relationship. It's mine. You and I are friends, not lovers. We're colleagues, not partners."

Her words hit me harder than they should have. "You might not be my girlfriend, woman, but you're definitely my partner. You have been since the day I met you."

I rubbed my thumb up and down, remembering how soft her skin was. She leaned into my touch, and I wondered if I was the last thing holding her up. I wondered if anyone else knew, if anyone else had tried to talk her out of staying. I wondered if she'd lost friends over it and knew I couldn't have her lose me when she needed me most.

She sighed and her long lashes swept down onto her cheeks as she closed her eyes. "You're right, okay? But Dougie and I have been a team too. I have to just... I get that we need a break. I get that things aren't right. I'm accepting that leaving for a month will be good for everyone. I just need to handle it my way."

She could reason her way into anything. But she agreed. She was coming with me.

I would make sure she wasn't coming back too.

"I'll fall back and take your lead. But I'm still coming up with you."

She rolled her eyes. "Fine." She didn't move her hands from my chest or turn around. She stared at me for what felt like a minute or more. As she did, her eyes filled with unshed tears, ones I knew had probably resurfaced again and again in the last two months I'd been away. "Thank you, Jay."

She turned then and walked up the cement steps. After she unlocked the door, we strode in. I was shocked to see that nothing was askew. I expected shattered vases, smashed-in walls, something to showcase that they were living in hell with one another.

Her home looked as it always did, though. The white countertops were clean, the porcelain vase was intact with fresh pink flowers in water. The beige throw was folded neatly on her linen couch. Everything was white, spotless, almost innocent-looking.

At first, I thought we'd missed him but Mikka turned to me and lifted her index finger to me to motion for silence. I glanced around and spotted her bedroom door ajar where he looked like he slept heavily.

I nodded and leaned a hip against the kitchen table as she buzzed into her bedroom where I saw through the doorway that she was collecting items. She moved with quiet precision. As someone whose childhood friend was abused, my eye was trained to see her practiced cautious movements. It wasn't just that she tried to be quiet, it was that she winced a bit when the sound was too loud as she set her suitcase on the hardwood floor. As she unzipped the bag, her fingers shook.

Mikka was afraid, and she'd never been afraid of anything.

She inhaled deeply before she zipped her suitcase. We both held our breaths as she walked through the doorway, but the hinges creaked as she bumped it open a little further.

His body stirred. "Baby, you home for the day?" I heard his groggy voice ask her.

It took a new determination, one I'd found in rehab, to stand back, to not burst in and beat him within an inch of his life.

Her soft response just beyond the wall felt smaller than usual. "No. Jay's in the kitchen if you'd like to say hi, but we have to take a trip. The agency wants us to do a stay in his hometown."

He grunted, still not moving from the bed. "For what? They paying us extra for that?"

She sighed. "Dougie, you know I'm salaried."

When I heard the rustling of the sheets, I tried my best to trust her, tried not to barge in, tried to give their relationship the benefit of the doubt.

"They pay you a salary for when your actors assault you?"

Before I could even contemplate his words, I heard her hiss, "Douglass, I told you that was just as much my fault as it was his."

"Maybe we should ask him, huh?" I saw him finally stand as his words shifted the situation into place. I'd been drunk and high. And dumb. So dumb. I should have known our kiss would send that selfish prick into a violent rage. He'd always had a look in his eye, especially when he drank around us. I knew something was off and it took our kiss to confirm it.

Dougie stormed out with Mikka after him, her suitcase in tow. Her brow was furrowed and it finally looked like she might not be able to stand another moment with him.

"You got some nerve stepping foot in my home after the shit you pulled on my girlfriend," the asshole spit at me.

I wanted to correct him. Mikka paid the rent—I knew that for a fact. I'd been shopping with her for the picture she hung on the wall and picked up the vase for her flowers one day. She's what made the house a home. Her home. Not his.

I didn't move from where I stood. I didn't owe him the effort. I would apologize, though. I would right my wrong because it was part of staying healthy and sober. It was part of moving forward with Mikka too.

I crossed my arms and looked at her, breathing heavily behind him, her eyes wild as she tried to figure out what to do next. "He's right, you know. I shouldn't have pulled that, Meek."

Her shoulders slumped a little and she shook her head slightly like she wanted me to stop.

"I have a lot of people to apologize to. And I'm not sorry that I kissed you, love. I'm just sorry it happened when and how it did."

Her eyes widened and I held her gaze. My world shifted, my heart jumped, we experienced something I couldn't put my finger on.

I'd never wanted more with a woman, not more than what was attainable. I had fun with those that wanted to and I had friendships with others. I lived a carefree, commitment free life. Staring at Mikka, saying the words I said, I wondered for the first time if I wanted something more with one of my friends.

Dougie stepped in front of me, puffing out his chest. "You want to apologize to me too?"

"Nope."

He cocked his arm slow enough that I saw the punch coming from miles away. I leaned at just the last second so that his momentum would carry him right into the chokehold I had ready for him. I grew up scrapping with two brothers, and even though Dougie was big, he wasn't a match for me.

"You going to calm the fuck down?" I asked him as I squeezed his neck while he struggled in the hold.

There's something about the way you feel once you get out of rehab. Everything's a little frayed, lines are a little thinner, easier to cross, the edge of darkness creeps closer, and the rage, the feeling of losing control is always pulsing around you, ready to take over. Even when he stopped struggling, I wanted to squeeze his neck harder.

He deserved it.

Mikka's tiny hand grabbed my arm, though. "Stop." Her eyes were on me and then him. "Both of you."

I shoved him forward out of the chokehold, and he coughed as Mikka said in a defeated voice, "Dougie, you promised last night that after everything we were going to try to get better. You were going to try for me. Is that you trying? You can't hit other people."

"Baby, I said sorry. I... He's provoking me." He pointed at me. "I'm trying, I swear." He reached an arm out slowly to smooth his hand over her face and then let it drop to her ribcage where he rubbed. She winced and his hand flew off. "I'm sorry, baby. So sorry."

The next words she whispered sounded strained, broken. "I think we need a break, time apart."

The man appeared soft around the edges, no muscles too big and no smarmy smile to make you think he'd attack a woman. But I saw the red pop up over his face as she said the words. She did too as she took a few steps back and grabbed her suitcase.

"Does it matter that I don't want time apart?" he growled.

"I just... we aren't getting better together. Look at this." She waved her hand between him and me. "You can't attack somebody else and think it's okay."

"What if I come with?" He was back to trying a different angle.

She shook her head and stood taller. "It's this or nothing."

He rolled his shoulders as if he was weighing his options. I fisted my hands under my crossed arms, hoping it would help me to keep from losing my own control. This man didn't get to manage her life. She did that and still I saw how he'd been steering it for far too long.

"Look, man." He turned to face me. He had the audacity to hold his head up, to stand proudly there as if we were man to man. He dragged a hand over his face, wiping away the discomfort of the situation. "Mikka and I have gone through some shit. I'm not proud of it, and I'm not that kind of man. It's just, she's mine. It's hard to process that you both made a mistake. I've got problems doing that."

He kept talking, but the anger inside me tuned him out. The roaring of it was like a thunder too loud for me to hear his words anymore.

Mikka stepped between us, put her hand on his chest like she had done mine, and whispered "Enough. The agency wants me there to PA for Jay for a month. It will be good time away from each other. You do you. I'll do me. We'll see what happens after, okay?"

He gripped her wrist. "A month? Baby, I don't..."

She eyed where his hand was, and he dropped it immediately like he knew he was too far in the doghouse to try anything. The red mark from it remained though.

"Look, fine. Okay. I'll do whatever you want. I don't want you seeing other people though."

"That's not for you to decide."

His brow furrowed. "But not him! Right?" He pointed at me, his voice heightening in desperation.

She scoffed, not even looking back at me. "Jay has better things and women to do, Dougie! Come on."

My jaw worked at her statement. Did she think any woman was better than her?

Dougie barreled on. "We should still talk. I want to keep in touch. I want to hear your voice. I need that. I need to know where we stand."

She nodded and I saw her love for him still there.

I stumbled back. It was a hard realization, finding that my friend didn't want to be saved. And she wasn't mine to save either.

She kissed him, and that hurt just as bad. My mind was scrambling to catch up with the idea my heart had just figured out. Mikka had been my only friend in LA but she'd also been someone I'd developed more than friendly feelings for.

Her kissing him goodbye was the stab I needed to jolt me back to the friend zone.

She turned to survey her place one last time. "Everything is paid through the month. The plants over there"—she pointed toward her dining table—"need to be watered once a day. I'll remind you when I call."

He slapped her ass and smiled at me over her shoulder. "Take care of my girl, huh, Jay? I'm trusting you, man to man."

Would she talk to me again if I broke his nose? I contemplated it for a second too long as she whispered, "Jay!"

I nodded at him but didn't respond. I was saving my response. I knew sooner or later that I was going to give it. It might not have been that day or the next that I inflicted the pain on him that he had her, but there would be a day.

"Yeah, I'll take care of her."

Better than he ever would.

LESSON OF THE DAY:
*Endings are just
new beginnings.*

CHAPTER EIGHT

MIKKA

OUR PLANE RIDE began with turbulence. The flight attendant assured us all in first class it wouldn't last. The bumpy ride between Jay and I continued though.

Normally we shared an ear bud, played a card game, watched a movie together.

Instead, I found myself nudging him after an hour of silence between us. "You excited about the next few weeks?"

"You mean the random piss tests, the calls with my therapist, and the constant behavioral therapy techniques I'll be practicing with my childhood town watching? Yeah, not really," he grumbled.

I winced because this wasn't a vacation for him, nor was it for me. We could lose everything. We were grasping at the last thread and hoping it didn't slip through our fingers. I needed him to survive outpatient therapy, I needed to see him get this movie. I'd prided myself on his success for this long and seeing him fail would be my failure too.

He sighed. "Sorry, Meek. I'm digesting the past couple hours."

I reached under the seat in front of me to pull out my leather bag. When things got tough, I knew how to smooth everything out. I pulled out my planner.

Jay groaned. "No. No. Nope."

"Jay, it's the perfect time to look over a plan for the next month." I opened to the month.

"It's never a good time to do that."

"Why? We can map out what your month will look like and..."

"What if I just want to spend the month with no plans and just you instead?" he asked with his voice dipping lower.

I blinked at the question. "Are you trying to lighten the mood by insinuating that we'll hook up all month? Please tell me I'm imagining the suggestive hint in your voice."

He chuckled and cracked his knuckles. "Someone has to lighten the mood here."

Was I imagining him glancing at my lips with his cerulean blue eyes?

I looked pointedly away and said, "The fact that you have not a bone in your body that cares about the rules of a relationship and hitting on someone when they are in one just shows why we would never, ever actually be able to do anything more than what already happened between us."

He tilted his head in question. "So, you've considered doing more with me?"

"Oh, my God." I tapped my scheduler to get us back on track. "Let's be professional and responsible for once, huh?"

He sighed and looked out the plane window. "Little Pebble, I'm not mapping out the month. How would that be helpful, anyway?"

"Well..." I cleared my throat. "You're going through a lot. It can be overwhelming to think of planning out your days. But I assure you, it actually helps."

"Meek, not happening."

I crossed off "Fly to Greenville" from my list for the day. Below that, I wrote to pick up baggage, drive to Lorraine's Little Lodge, and more. The list provided me with a distraction from Jay and having him so close after all this time, breathing on my shoulder, watching me like I was a new toy.

I turned to face him after scribbling a little heart around the lesson that I'd written in for the day. "Okay. Fine," I mumbled even though nothing felt fine with his lips this close to me. My cheeks heated at the memory of his taste: alcohol and candy, like loose inhibitions and cravings of the most delectable sort. He'd fit perfectly against me, kissing me like I meant something to him. "That's fine. Everything will be fine."

That mouth kicked up a notch. "You sure it's fine? You're looking at me like something might not be, like I might need to remedy it."

I snapped my gaze to his because he'd caught my lingering stare. I was embarrassed that the heat on my cheeks was giving away my guilt. "I don't know what you're talking about, Jay."

He shifted in his seat. "I'm starting to think this trip is going to be more difficult than I thought for reasons I wasn't expecting."

I knew what he was referring to. I didn't ask what he meant or acknowledge his statement. I figured if we didn't say it out loud, the desire and chemistry between us might disappear.

After my long beat of silence, he relaxed back into his seat. "What's your lesson for the day?"

I rolled my eyes. Whenever he saw me doodling in my planner, he asked. This planner contained inspirational quotes that I tried to live by because they were like little dares to succeed that I couldn't pass up. "Endings are just new beginnings."

For the first time on that flight, the corners of his mouth lifted high enough that his eyes sparkled. "Now, that's the truth."

"Yeah, maybe." I grabbed my phone and pulled up an e-mail. "I got the script for the last takes here in Greenville. The crew will arrive to film in three weeks. We need to practice your scenes with Lela. Are you okay with that?"

"Sure. Want to act out all the scenes?" One of his eyebrows raised like he was taunting me.

Of course those scenes had kissing.

I busied myself with lifting the folding table in front of me and sliding the latch into place. "We'll practice what needs practice. We need to make sure you're ready to film."

He leaned his head back on the seat and closed his eyes. "I'll be fine with filming. I know this part. I just need you there to make sure everything goes off without a hitch."

"I'll be there for what you need, Jay." I didn't promise anything more than I could. I was going to try to stick out the month but I considered leaving him once he was settled.

"Mmhmm. I can practically hear the cogs in your brain turning." He didn't even crack open an eye to check. "You're staying and we're working through our problems together."

"I don't have the types of problems you do," I blurted out.

"Don't you, though? You're in a relationship you think you can change. I thought I could change my drug use at any point. You're hoping things will get better. I promised myself they would too. You keep going back to the one damn thing that's hurting you, and I can only imagine the ways in which he's hurt you, Meek." He didn't lift his head or open his eyes, but he'd folded his hands together. The tips of his fingers were white from trying to keep his emotions bottled up. "I kept going back to the partying and alcohol and cocaine. I'm not even sure I'm done going back."

"Jay, I know it's hard..."

"You do because you're doing the same thing. Unhealthy relationships are forms of addiction. I know it's hard to leave; I know you'll consider going back. I know because I'm doing the same thing. We got through LA together. And we got buried in this toxic hole. I'm digging us out, Meek. You can grab a shovel and help or lay there and watch. Either way, I got you."

I leaned my head on his shoulder, wanting to say something, but the words were caught in my throat.

My body melted as I sat there with him and I became pliant in my soul's desire for him. He'd come back from rehab as strong a friend as he always had been but also more appealing than ever. I couldn't control my pull toward the man that was only supposed to be my friend when my heart warmed in his presence.

We touched down and collected our suitcases. Jay navigated me through the small airport, one he'd visited countless times.

"Do you know the bed and breakfast we're staying at?"

"It's Greenville, Meek. It might be the tiniest town you've ever set foot in." He chuckled. "I know everything about everything there."

I wrinkled my nose. As we stepped outside and handed off our bags to the driver, the brisk air hit me. I smelled small town already and I wasn't sure I liked it. I'd grown up in San Francisco and moved to LA. I didn't understand how the other side lived. I liked the desert sun, people who accepted small diverse women like myself, and the hustle and bustle of a big city. No one paid attention to you in the mass; you had to propel yourself forward on your own steam. If you failed, no one noticed, and if you succeeded, you'd done so in front of millions.

I straightened my blouse and entered the SUV. "Are you alright with the bed and breakfast being familiar? Should we have rented an Airbnb?"

He outright laughed at the notion. "Greenville doesn't do that type of stuff." He shrugged. "I don't mind Lorraine, the owner. It's better than being twenty miles out or staying at my parents' house. They could fly back from their vacation home at any point, and I can't deal with that."

I smiled, "Your parents aren't that bad."

"Just wait. My mom is about to give me hell, and my dad never needs to say he's disappointed—you can just see it. It's the businessman in him."

"He's retired," I reminded him. "Your mom loves you and wants to be supportive."

"My mom's only mission is to make sure I get it together for my future family."

I tilted my head in question.

"She wants me settled like my brothers. And she wants grandkids. Sooner rather than later."

I shuddered at the idea of kids. "Children don't do well in LA."

He glanced at me, and one corner of his mouth kicked up. "You look like you're ready to jump out of your skin, woman. You hate kids or something?"

I never had to talk about kids in LA because we were all trying to make it in the film industry, all trying to look our best, and all competing for the perfect life. Children or lack thereof didn't normally fit into that conversation. "I don't hate them, Jay. They're kids."

He studied me longer than I liked. "They make you uncomfortable?"

"I just don't have any, so I have nothing to say about them."

"Do you want some of your own? What's the name of that guy your mom talked about—Yue Lao? He would probably want you to have children."

Leave it to Jay to ask such a serious question with no remorse, as if our lives were an open book to one another. He felt that way, too. He wanted me to share everything with him, but a woman's choice to have children was sacred and sometimes not even her choice. The idea that I could try to have kids and fail just because my body wouldn't produce terrified me. I was used to making things happen and working toward an end goal. I knew that having children didn't work that way.

"This really isn't an idle drive chat," I mumbled.

He draped an arm over the back seat and settled in. "When did you become shy about sharing?"

"I'm not," I insisted. "It's just I haven't really thought about whether Dougie and I can handle kids."

Jay's smile dropped off his face so fast, it was like a ton of bricks had weighed it down. "I wasn't talking about you having kids with him."

I sighed. "Jay, it isn't all bad."

"When you first started seeing him, did it happen?"

I knew my eyes widened, that a blush crept over my cheeks, but I couldn't school my reaction. I wasn't used to the tough questions and pressure from Jay. He normally led people to an answer they never thought they would give by charming them. "No! Just... why are you asking me something so crazy?"

"I don't have time to sugarcoat things for you anymore, Meek. I'm tired and we're going to spend a month together. Get used to this side of me, the one where I push you and you push me. We're here to make each other better, right?"

I looked him up and down, trying to find a crack in his new persona, one I could chip away at to bring back the old Jay. This new one was blunt, truthful, and maybe a little too intense. "I agree that we're here to make *you* better. I'm just fine."

"You're not." He said those words with a finality that made me want to break down. Then he shook his head. "Answer the question. Did it happen early on?"

I turned from him. The city faded into rolling hills where evergreen and maple trees sprinkled the grass and wider curved roads formed. It was like we'd left all the noise and distraction and been given space to focus on each other.

"Does it matter? I've stayed this long. At first, I thought it had come out of nowhere. Now I can see there were signs from the very beginning. They're bold as hell and clear as the light of day. We've grown together for years. I know in his heart he's a good guy. Something, or me, probably, tweaked him over the years. Our encounter just pushed things over the edge."

He didn't respond. He sat there quiet for so long, I tried to let the conversation fade away like the city lights were. We pulled up to the bed and breakfast. It was small, Victorian, cute, and utterly old. The SUV came to a stop on the gravel driveway, and the driver got out to get our bags.

Jay didn't move. Instead, he asked me, "We're giving your ass of a boyfriend a pass and blaming his actions on what you're calling an 'encounter'?"

I waved him off, trying to get past the small butterflies I felt in my stomach every time I thought about that night. "Our kiss, our slip up, whatever."

"Ha," he huffed out. "Slip up? Little one, that wasn't a slip up."

The leather under me shifted as I rubbed my thighs together, trying to stave off what I was feeling. "I don't know what you mean by that."

"I'm not sure what I mean either. All I know is we're more..."

"More what?"

"More than what you're giving us credit for. Don't call what we did 'a slip up.' Ever."

He had his arms spread behind the headrest now and he looked relaxed, in control, and not at all remorseful.

"As opposed to me saying something different? I try not to say anything at all about it. I try not to think about it. I want to forget that we fucked up. You're one of my best and only friends in LA and that could have ruined us."

"Bullshit." He didn't hesitate to spit out the word. "Nothing can ruin us. We've been through my partying and we're about to get through a month together under the same roof, battling through a lot of crap. You're stuck with me, little one, and nothing changes that."

My heart skipped like it wanted to jump right on over into his arms, but I swung open the door, grabbed my work bag, and got out of the vehicle instead. Jay spoke like he could be the perfect one for me, like he knew what being faithful to someone meant.

Our kiss, that kiss, had wrecked my body. Now, whenever I saw Jay, it reacted like a friend never should. It sped up, danced around, and dipped to the ground for him.

I shook off the feeling and stared at the white-stained wooden sign with the words "Lorraine's Little Lodge" painted on it. The bed and breakfast was no wider than the length of the SUV that was leaving us behind. I almost ran after it, but a woman who I guessed was Ms. Lorraine herself sat in a wicker rocker on the white porch, smiling at the both of us.

Jay walked right up to her and scooped her up from the chair. He lifted her off her feet and spun her around until she cackled and whacked him on the shoulder.

I stood back, one hand gripping my bag like a lifeline, and dug my shoes farther into the gravel drive. When Jay set her down, her chocolate brown eyes glanced my way. She was a small woman, hunched a bit by the years that aged us all. Her gray hair was curled, and the floral dress she wore was bright with reds and yellows.

"So?" She looked at me as if I should say something in reply.

Was I to introduce myself?

Hug her? Oh, God.

I hoped she didn't want me to hug her. I didn't do hugs with strangers and I wasn't sure how to talk to an elderly woman who had lived in that quaint little house all her life. Did I discuss the trees with her? They were big—that was about all I knew. The flowers that hung from intricately curled hooks above her porch? They were bright like her floral dress: reds and pinks and whites to match the home.

I stuck my hand out as she continued to study me. "I'm Mikka Chang. I work with Jay." I glared at him. He stood there silently with his arms crossed, like he enjoyed making me uncomfortable. "We've known each other since he's been in LA."

"Right. You're his gatekeeper for the month, I assume?"

Wow. That was a bold statement for a woman I thought looked cute and sweet. "I'm his PA. I work to make sure he stays on task for the agency so that we can deliver the best entertainment within the film industry as possible." It was a canned line, one I used when I was being assessed, and she was definitely doing just that as she eyed me up and down with a curled lip.

"Didn't do such a great job of that back in LA, did you? The boy flew off the wagon into drugs, sex, and alcohol."

My jaw dropped and I dug my nails into my shoulder strap to stop myself from mouthing off. The audacity and complete lack of respect for Jay's private life left me speechless. And then she'd gone and dragged my job into it, making me out to be incompetent.

Jay chuckled and swung his arm around my shoulders. "Lorraine, go easy on her. She's new to town." He turned to whisper in my ear. "She's the best, isn't she?"

I eyed him like he was deranged, and Lorraine blew a little air out at his comment. She waved us in and I let Jay's arm around my shoulders lead me.

Walking up onto the white wood porch and into her home felt like being in a movie. The woven mat at our feet read "Welcome Home," and as I walked past the screen door—something LA homes didn't have—I was overwhelmed by the smell of fresh flowers. The walls were painted soft pastels and each room had decor to match. In every room of the first floor, she had placed freshly cut flowers, big beautiful ones that I definitely couldn't name, in glass vases atop wood tables.

She pointed up the wooden stairs. "Both of you will stay up there. The first two rooms on the right." She waved us on. "The dining room is this way. I'll make breakfast at 8:00 AM sharp every morning. Do you like coffee, Mikka? Jay drinks tea and I'll brew it just the way Nancy does for him if you want that."

"Huh," I said out loud, a little baffled. "I've never seen you drink tea."

"No one in LA makes chai tea like they do here in Greenville."

Lorraine patted his back like he'd made her day. "That's right. Remember where to get the best of everything, boy. It won't be at some party sniffing God knows what."

Jay's shoulders tensed, and I knew she'd struck a little too close to home.

I stepped in front of him and changed the subject. "I'd love to try the tea tomorrow."

Lorraine glanced between us. She was assessing again. This time, I must have passed her test. She nodded. "Great. I'll order dinner from Bob down the street tonight and leave that out for you both. I'll probably be at Ray's for a drink later. Jay, call them if you need anything."

With that, the tiny woman disappeared down the hall, not at all concerned that she was leaving us to fend for ourselves.

Jay rolled his head around and shrugged off the tension and most likely the comment before he went and grabbed both of our bags to lug them upstairs. "Good to be back," he said as I followed him.

"Is it really?" It seemed like everyone was already in our business and this place was much too small and quaint to hold three of us.

He set my suitcase down in a room full of yellow. The color alone should have made me smile. Yellow was supposed to do that. But the handmade quilt and the fresh sunflowers, no doubt cut from the garden the window overlooked, made me a bit itchy. Everything was too connected, too meaningful, and too real.

I spun to tell Jay this wouldn't do, that I should stay at a hotel, that I was fine driving twenty minutes into town every morning.

He shook his head at me as I opened my mouth. "No, Meek. Remember what your planner said. Some things ended. Now, we start our new beginning."

With that, he disappeared into his room.

I wanted to support him. I wanted to like his childhood town. A friend could do that. I just didn't know if I was that friend.

He had so many others. He was home.

I definitely was not.

THERAPIST: *Is there temptation back home?*

JAY: *There's temptation everywhere.*

THERAPIST: *Do you think partying and drug use will be readily available?*

JAY: *That's not the temptation that I'm worried about.*

CHAPTER NINE

JAY

MIKKA HAD FINALLY met her match. I smiled to myself as I unpacked a few things and thought of her face when Lorraine blasted her about her work and my partying. Her hand tightened on her leather bag so hard, I was sure the leather would be worn in that spot the next day.

Welcome to Greenville, where everyone knows your name, your business, and your dirtiest secrets. She was going to lose it here and I was going to enjoy watching her unravel. The woman needed to let go. She needed a town who knew everything about her so they could help make her whole again.

Greenville was small, but it had a massive heart, one that worked wonders on someone who was broken. It was the perfect place for both of us.

Even if it would be hard as hell to have our problems flying around in the gossipy wind of the place.

At least that wind smelled of pine, autumn, and freshly cut grass. Home.

Lorraine placed peonies on my dresser. The crazy old woman was the sweetest person I'd ever met. She knew we'd grown up with rows of peonies near our windows. She'd helped my mom plant a few.

I sighed at the idea of calling my parents. My mother was going to argue with me about staying at her house again, I just knew it.

She'd offer the space, and probably give me the run of the place if I told her I couldn't relax around family.

She didn't understand that my childhood home would be a crutch. I didn't want that. It may not have been a healthy choice to search out my discomforts, and the therapist said it could even be a potential risk to my sobriety, but it was the only way for me to heal.

I needed to be in a place where people called me on my shit, where I couldn't hide away in my own room. I'd found that out the hard way in rehab. I'd come close to getting comfortable, close to some of the other patients who wanted me to sneak out at night with them. The temptation had almost been too much, but it was just enough for me to realize I needed to surround myself with harsh truths.

Lorraine's place allowed for that. The woman would be truthful even if it killed her.

Mikka's head popped in again. Her dark, straight hair fell like a waterfall toward the waist. "Do you think we're going anywhere tonight? Should I dress for company or for sleep?"

I immediately pictured the woman in next to nothing, ready to climb into bed with me. My mind was mixed up; I hadn't been with a woman since rehab. Mikka had imprinted on me or something. I needed to erase the memory of our kiss; I needed to find a different fixation.

"I probably need to bite the bullet and show my face in town tonight."

"Great, I'll come with." She replied so quickly that I knew she was babysitting, not coming for enjoyment.

"I'm fine going on my own." The words rumbled out of me harsher than they should have.

She rounded the corner and straightened, hands on hips. "Jay, it doesn't sound great, but what Lorraine said is true. I'm your keeper for the month. I get to come with you and monitor your every move. I'm keeping your ass in line."

"I'm not trying to get out of line, woman."

"Then, you won't have a problem with me coming along."

I sighed. "Fine. The pub is where everyone will be."

She wrinkled her nose. "A pub, Jay? We can't go to a pub. Surrounding yourself with partying is not the way to…"

I stood up to stalk toward her, but my steps faltered when I saw her head jerk back a little. Mikka was always the tiniest woman in a room, but I used to be able to go toe to toe with her. She never cowered, and the skittishness reminded me how very different we were now. I held up both my hands and murmured, "We should lay some ground rules."

Her eyes narrowed at my hands and then, instead of me invading her personal space, she stalked up to invade mine. I towered over her as she craned her neck to glare right in my face. "Fine. First one: I'm not broken. Don't treat me like I am."

I pinched the bridge of my nose. "Come on, Meek—"

"No, Jay. I'm still me." Her brow furrowed. "I might have been through something, but that doesn't make me any different. I'm me."

"And I'm still me!" I bellowed at her, trying to get her to understand she didn't have to be afraid of me. I whipped my arms out to the side. Then I yanked them back, instantly regretting raising my voice at her.

This time she didn't flinch, though. She smiled. "Good, back to you getting pissy and yelling at me. Just where I like to be."

I took a breath. She was going to drive me insane; I already felt it deep in my bones. "Woman, I'm trying, okay? My first instinct is to protect you, even if it's from being scared of me."

"I'm not scared of you. It's just… I can't help it. I'm not used to being around…" She trailed off.

Exposing an open wound hurt like hell. Talking about that wound was like scraping it clean with sanitizer. I didn't want her to feel the pain any more than she needed to, so I poured alcohol on my own wound to distract her. "So, ground rules: I need you to trust me to go out like you did before I went to rehab."

She picked at a nail and then readjusted her blouse.

"I'm serious. This won't work otherwise. You need to trust me to go out alone like you did before."

"I never trusted you." Her words fell out so quick, she tried to catch them by slapping her hand over her mouth. "I didn't mean that. I trust you as a friend. It was just different when you were…"

"High? You can say the words, Meek. I was high and off my fucking rocker. No one can trust someone like that."

"It feels wrong," she admitted, her voice small. "I don't want to rub your addiction in your face."

"There's a difference between talking about my addiction and rubbing it in my face. If I said you were with an abusive guy for years and you learned from it, it's different than saying…"

She held up her hand to stop me. I wanted to continue. My frustration at her situation pushed me to. I needed to shake her from her world, show her that there was something better out there.

I was scared I wouldn't be able to, that there wasn't a rehab for the physically abused. They needed it just as much as any other addict, a place they could go to remember who they were before, a place that would teach them to break the habit and live without the person that had caused them so much pain.

"I'm technically still with him, Jay. We're just on a break."

I breathed in deep. "I know. What's it going to take to change that?"

"It's not that simple. He knows me like no one else. We've built this life together and he's hurting too. Who is going to help him get better? No one understands him like I do, understands that he doesn't mean it."

"What if it ends up being someone else getting hurt?" I tried a different angle. "What if your mom showed up there and he was pissed about something. What then?"

"He wouldn't do that."

"You sure?" I countered, lifting my eyebrows and motioning toward my face where he'd aimed a punch. I saw the look in his eyes, I saw him weighing his options with me in that room. He'd have taken down anyone he knew he could beat. His best option in that moment was to say sorry, though. It was a calculated move on his part and he'd played it well.

She looked down at her outfit: ripped black jeans and a white designer top that hung loosely over a black bra. "I'm sorry you know about all our baggage, Jay." Then she gripped the sides of her shirt as if she could squeeze out the emotion she was feeling. "God, I know I shouldn't even be apologizing for his behavior. It's just… I need time to rework things."

"You mean rework them into working? Sometimes things just don't, Meek. Relationships fail."

Her gaze shot up to me. "I'm not used to failing. I don't. Okay?"

"I said the relationship was failing, not you. There's a difference."

Her manicured fingertips ran over her top. "This okay for the pub?"

"Anything you wear is phenomenal, little one." I brushed off her question fast. "Did you hear me, Meek? Just because your relationship isn't working, doesn't mean you failed. Got it?"

If I didn't push her out of her comfort zone, no one would. No one else knew. And she was making sure that no one else ever would. He'd ruin every part of her before she had a chance to tell anyone else. She slid her small hands over the cotton of her tank top. "What do you want me to say, Jay? Dougie's struggling. He hasn't been able to find a job, he wants to contribute to our household financially, he's lost confidence because I told him about us and…"

"These are excuses for something that's inexcusable," I shot back.

"Do you think some of the things you've done over the past few years have been excusable, Jay?" Her hands fisted at her sides as she stepped back to stare me down, heels clicking against the wooden floor. "You hit on me when you were wasted, knowing I was with another man. That's not what friends do. And you've slept with countless women, degraded them by doing blow off every nook and cranny of their body and wasted a multitude of opportunities because you were too high to follow through with them. You had a problem. So does Dougie."

I nodded at her anger and let her words sink in. She compared me to him and I wondered if she thought I was just like him, if she thought I'd give in again and piss away the opportunity of a lifetime. "Now we're getting somewhere."

"I don't want to do this. I don't want to exchange insults."

"I do. We need ground rules. Number one is us remembering who we are. If you say you're not broken, I'll try to remember that. Two is us trusting each other, and three is honesty. I want honesty and you should too."

"Honesty doesn't have to be mean, Jay."

"In our case, it does." I motioned toward the door to end the conversation. There was nothing left to say. "Let's go before it gets too late."

"Sure. I'll call us a car." I wondered if I should tell her that no car was going to come for us in a town of less than six thousand people, especially when I hadn't booked a service for the trip. She scrolled through her app to look for a driver nearby.

She kept scrolling and scrolling.

Chuckling, I grabbed her phone. "Babe, we aren't requesting a driver from thirty miles away. You'll be here all night waiting. The bar's down the street." I walked out of our room and down the stairs.

She caught up with me, sputtering the whole way. "Jay, wait? Should I bring my bag?"

"No." *Her and that bag.*

She didn't listen; I heard her heels scurrying as she went to get it. "Jay, wait... are you kidding?"

"Kidding about what?" I said as I watched her come down the steps.

She huffed. "You must be kidding. I can't walk all the way there in these shoes. They're purposely made to be uncomfortable. I honestly believe the designer concocted them as a torture device."

"You can't walk all the way there? Woman, you are in shoes like that every day of your life. Why are you always wearing them if they hurt?"

"Because they go with the outfit." She scrunched her face up like she was disgusted that I'd even asked.

I schooled my expression to be as serious as possible. "Do I need to carry you?"

"You're an asshole," she muttered and breezed by me out the front door.

I watched her walk with purpose ahead of me until she got to the end of the driveway. "Which way?" she yelled.

I ambled up to her. "I'll drive us if your feet are going to hurt. Lorraine's got a pickup in the garage if you really don't want to walk."

She breathed in loudly. "I'm just trying to get my bearings a little here. I'm on edge but it's fine. I want to walk. I need to let off steam."

I nodded and slipped the bag off her shoulder and onto mine. Then I slung my arm around her and fit her up against my side. When I did, she sighed into me. I whispered into her hair, "We'll go, you can have a drink, we'll give the town what they want, then leave. Everything's going to be okay."

I made the promise without knowing if it was true. I needed to believe it as much as her though. We were two broken pieces, trying our best to appear whole.

"I'm supposed to be telling you that, Jay. You're supposed to be getting better here, not me."

"Both of us together, Meek. We're doing it together. I'm not letting this movie slip between my fingers and you're going to figure out what you need without your boyfriend. If at the end of the day, you need him..." I shrugged. I couldn't continue the statement because I wasn't sure I could let it happen.

She nodded into my shirt and I hugged her closer as we walked. Her coconut lime shampoo mixed with the fresh summer air that reminded me I was back home.

In my town. And with her. I breathed it in deep.

The walk to the pub relaxed me, even though we bickered over her damn shoes. She insisted she was now comfortable, even after telling me the shoes were a torture device.

When we walked in, the woman beside me stiffened. This wasn't her scene. The low ceilings and dark wood floors matched the mellow feel of the place. A bluesy track played from the one and only jukebox in the corner, and every single vinyl seat in the place was filled with familiar faces.

Some of them I was happy to see; others I could have done without.

Every head turned our way when Ray yelled out, "Jay Stonewood!"

Mikka jerked back, obviously not used to such a boisterous greeting. She knew LA clubs: loud, flashing lights, clean floors, sleek interiors. People might have looked my way but she blended into the crowds there. Here, people were looking more at her than me.

Ray owned this place after his pop passed on, and he hadn't updated any of the design. It was lived in. Loved. Comfortable.

The exact opposite of a big city hot spot.

Ray's bald head shined as bright as his smile in the flickering light over the bar. He lifted the sidebar to greet me. "You son of a damn gun. Get your ass over here and give me a hug."

A few others waved and said, "welcome back." I let him bear hug me, his flannel shirt reminding me that Mikka and I might be overdressed.

"Hey, Ray." I patted his back. "Looks like business is going well."

His belly shook with a chuckle as he looked between Mikka and me. "I'm the only bar within 10 miles. Of course business is going well. Who's this pretty thing? I hear you're trying to keep him in line."

Mikka cleared her throat and shot her small hand forward. "Word seems to travel fast. Yes, I'm Mikka, Jay's PA."

"A PA?" His eyebrows rose. "Whoa, boy. You sure you need it now that your career is about to tank? I read about it in the tabloids."

First dig. I shook it off, ready for thousands of them. This is what I would have to do. I'd prepared for the onslaught of questions. It was the way to face my reality over and over again. I had to be strong enough to handle this and not slip backward. The movie, my career, and my life meant too much. "I hope so. I've weathered the worst of the storm. I'm hoping rehab spat me out better than ever."

He grunted. "Rehab for what? The tabloids didn't say. Is it drugs? Because you know I don't believe in a problem with alcohol."

Ray, to put it bluntly, didn't care if you were an alcoholic. He only cared that you were an alcoholic at his bar.

"Problem is with drugs, Ray. You know I can handle a drink."

"In that case, want a round?" He lifted a shoulder, conversation over for him. One down, thousands more to go.

"I'll still take just a water, and Mikka will want—"

"Vodka soda with lime," she blurted. "And, two shots. Straight. Please."

Ray winked at her and motioned us on. He'd send one of his waitresses to deliver the drinks. "Vodka?" I questioned as we maneuvered around a couple of tables to one farther in the back. Donny and Karen, an older couple that my parents regularly talked with, got up to leave. They waved us over, welcomed me back, and gave up their table.

Her manicured nail tapped on the table as soon as she had sat down and situated her leather bag next to her. She cleared her throat. "Do you need me to do anything, introduce myself to anyone?"

Her tense shoulders, her dark eyes looking more hesitant than I was used to, almost made me reach for her hand. "Meek, relax. It's a bar. We go to bars all the time."

"It feels like everyone is staring." Our drinks arrived and she downed her first shot immediately. She winced and sucked in air through her teeth. "Is it bad that I'm having this in front of you?"

"No. I can drink." I shrugged. Alcohol had never been my problem.

"Okay," she murmured and stared at the next shot like she wasn't sure she should take it.

"The drinking and partying around drugs is my problem, Meek. Cocaine is the problem."

When her hair fell over one side of her cheek, she pushed it behind her ear quickly and looked at me through her lashes. "It's not the right time for me to ask the questions I probably need answers to sooner or later."

"You want to pull out your planner and go down a list, don't you?"

One side of her mouth lifted and she rolled her eyes before grabbing the next shot and downing it too. "Why does it feel like I have more eyes on me than I've ever had in all the times we went out together?"

"Because you do." I shrugged and leaned back into the booth where I could drape my arms along the top. "They know me, they haven't seen me in ages, and they want the latest gossip. They don't know you, which means there is more gossip to be had."

She spun her empty shot glass around. "Can I ask you something?"

I nodded, wondering why she didn't just jump right in. "You can always ask me. Why are you dancing around me like we aren't who we used to be?"

"Do you think we are?" She tilted her head and the light hit her skin in just the right way to make it glow.

I remembered how smooth she felt under my touch, how soft her neck had been when I ran my hand along it. If I touched her now, would she shudder like she had back when I kissed her? Did she think about that night as much as I did?

"Of course." I chuckled and spun my glass of water on the table. "And absolutely not."

She smiled. "Fair and accurate answer."

"I'm trying to be honest. Ground rules, right?" I leaned forward and moved my leg under the table so I could nudge hers. "So, ask me."

"You agreed to come back here to get clean. I get that it's home for you, but do you honestly think it's the healthiest choice?"

I started to tell her I needed to push myself, I needed to get better quickly and test how well I could handle my surroundings. My hometown would push me to my limits in facing my problems. No one sugarcoated anything here.

Before I could blurt it all out, Ray's voice boomed across the bar again. "Another Stonewood and the newest one too," he yelled at no one in particular as he went to hug my brother and sister-in-law. "She's my favorite of them all, folks."

They smiled and said a few hellos to people but I saw my sister-in-law's face. She wasn't here to make nice with anyone. She was blazing through the crowd, glaring people down to get them out of her way.

Aubrey Stonewood, my sister-in-law, and also my childhood best friend, was barreling toward me with fury in her emerald eyes.

I waited. I even relaxed into my seat. The spitfire was about to fireball me and I needed to be ready. Mikka watched in amazement as the most beautiful couple in America—as magazines called them—stopped at our table.

"Do you want me to start or are you going to?" Brey asked, crossing her arms as she glared down at me.

"Brey, meet my friend Mikka," I calmly said.

"I'm not here to meet your flavor of the week, Jay. I'm here because I had to hear from the Greenville grapevine that my best friend is in outpatient rehab at Lorraine's. Now, I find out you didn't bother to dial the number that I know for a fact is on speed dial right when you stepped foot in our hometown."

I looked behind her to see Jax, my brother, smirking like a man on the same damn drug I had a problem with. His drug of choice was just his wife though. He loved seeing her madder than a bat out of hell.

"Jax, don't look so amused. She's going to find a reason to be pissed at you too," I grumbled and sipped my water before I acknowledged her rant.

She snatched the drink from my hand. The woman wasn't going to let me approach this with any nonchalance. She held the drink behind her for Jax to grab. He did so without even blinking. "Don't play games. This isn't a game. This is our friendship. I've cut my heart open and bled for you. How could you not call me?"

Her words finally cut in; I finally felt the impact.

Games.

I was so used to finding fun and games in everything. Had I been skipping over the serious parts of life? Putting my meaningful relationships and friendships on hold?

Brey was right. She'd poured her heart out to her friends, shared some of the darkest secrets about her past with an abusive father.

I wanted to tell her that calling her felt like pulling her down with me, that my time here would be painful enough without them around seeing me struggle through my failures. I wanted to tell her I needed to apologize for not being a better friend to her. I wanted to be the friend she was to me.

LESSON OF THE DAY:
*Every once in a while,
it's good to let go
and let loose.*

CHAPTER TEN

MIKKA

JAY'S GUILT RAN deeper than his fun-loving side, it ran deeper than his charm and definitely deeper than Jax and Brey could see. I suddenly found myself wanting to defend him, even if that meant wedging myself between him and his family.

"So," I announced loudly. Brey's eyes sliced over to me, the green in them a sharp contrast to her dark eyebrows and long dark hair. "I'm Mikka. I'm Jay's PA. Not his flavor of the week or month or year."

"You're Mikka?" Brey asked as if something finally clicked in her head. "You're..." She looked at Jay, then shoved him in the shoulder. "You said she was a 'friend.'"

"She is." Jay balked and then hurried on. "She's not that type... Jesus, Brey. I just got back."

"Yeah, I know. And I hate to assume, but it has always been the norm, Jay."

"It isn't always the damn norm, woman." He looked at Jax. "Is she always this pissy?"

"Watch it." Jax growled, as he wrapped an arm around her waist and settled his chin on her head. He almost swallowed her up and yet she stood there like a freaking queen, her presence so magnetic, I could swear the whole bar was watching her.

She looked up at her husband and whispered something. He smiled and let her go. Then Jax slid right in next to his brother. Those two next to each other in a booth nearly did me in. When Jax wrapped his arm around Jay and grumbled, "Missed you and your dumb ass. Don't make me come out there to LA and babysit you," I about cried.

"Yeah, yeah. Missed you too, man." Jay caught me tearing up. "Let's get you another drink because I can't have you crying before the night begins."

Brey sighed. "I'm normally not this direct and rude, Mikka," she confessed as she curled the ends of her hair, trying to explain herself.

She waited for my response, but I didn't have one yet. She might have been Jay's best friend, but I was protective of him. None of them knew the extent of his addiction. They hadn't found him in the compromising places I had over the years. They hadn't wiped coke off his counter or bathroom or nightstand.

So, I waited for her to continue. Or to not. I didn't have to make the effort. Jay and I were fighting through this month together but I couldn't trust that anyone else knew how to fight that fight with us.

"So, okay." She slumped a little. "I apologize if I came off the wrong way. Before he was ever really my brother-in-law, he was my best friend, the only family I ever really had. I need to know if he's okay, and I expect him to tell me when he's here. We've always been that close."

"Baby girl…" He let the nickname roll from his lips for her. He sounded dejected, apologetic, and simply charming.

I nodded. I scooted over for her, pulled my leather bag to the other side, and patted the booth as I said, "Well, I'm here to organize his priorities. So maybe it's my fault."

I shifted the blame because I felt his thigh tense against my leg. Above the table, though, he was smirking, leaning back and nodding like he was completely okay with her words.

Brey stared at me like she was assessing my intentions, and Jax took that moment to drag his brother to the bar with him.

That left me with her, this phenomenon of a woman who I knew was very protective of my friend. I'd never met her over the years. I knew that was because Jay normally flew back to visit them instead of them coming to us. From what I'd read, I respected her for the life she'd lived. Still, I sat there fiddling with my leather bag instead of making conversation.

As soon as they were out of earshot, she drilled home her point. "If you're taking the blame for him not calling me, I commend your effort but my best friend has fingers. He knows how to dial my number with or without your consent."

I shoved my leather bag more into the corner of the booth so as not to snap at her. I pointedly turned her way and rested my forearm on the table.

Didn't she understand her friend at all? He'd never just call them up and ask for help.

No one wants to be a burden. Yet, sometimes life makes the hardest moments the ones you would never expect them to be. Admitting his failure, admitting his addiction, facing it down over and over in this town would be one of those moments.

"He needs to worry about himself first." I replied and held her gaze.

"Did you discuss his road to recovery with his therapist?" she inquired and I wasn't sure if she was genuinely curious or was about to blurt out that I didn't have a say in what he should worry about.

"I've been updated through our agency on his progress and how well he's done with therapy." I nodded. The doctors and therapists all loved him, thought he would do well, weren't even sure that we needed random drug tests. I filed away their praise as part of Jay's likeability. I had to. Someone had to be strong enough to enforce things for him.

"So." She cleared her throat and busied her hands with scraping at a part of the table. "How can I help? I'm not helping now. I realize that. I'm hurt and it's selfish. I know it but I can't help it. He's always been my rock and to see him crumbling without my knowledge gutted me. And he's going through more. So, I'm only telling you this. I will be strong and I'll do whatever I have to in order to keep him healthy."

I swear the wind was blowing through her hair as she said the words. It was impossible—we were inside—but I felt the earth move with her statement. Her fierceness to protect him knocked down the guard I had up.

I shifted in the booth. "I think we're going to need a lot more alcohol to get through this month because between you and Jax and me and this town, Jay's going to be exhausted. He's going to make it through okay, though. He's Jay."

She smiled. "Isn't he the best?"

"Yeah, he really is." I searched for him at the bar and when I found him, I caught him staring back at me. He didn't glance away, just winked and settled in on his arm as he leaned on the bar. A woman was talking his ear off and he nodded but his eyes stayed on me as he mouthed, "You okay?"

I nodded and motioned at our empty glasses. He chuckled and turned back to the bar. Seconds later, the guys were making their way back over.

"You ready to meet the town?" Jay asked, one eyebrow raised, like he truly thought I might say no.

I wanted to. Everyone was judging me. I knew they were considering my designer shoes, and shirt, and jeans. I almost face palmed when I saw that most of them dressed for comfort, not at all worried about making a fashion statement. The stilettos I wore always made me feel secure in my own skin but in this small town, they made me stick out like a sore thumb.

The four of us downed our drinks and circled the bar. Jay willingly engaged in being welcomed back. If they didn't bring up his stint in rehab, he did. Every single person we talked to knew him and had something to say even if they needed to be prompted.

I pulled him to a corner at one point. "This is like a beating, Jay."

He scratched his jaw and scrubbed up and down like he was trying to scrub away the fatigue. "It's necessary."

"Why?" I practically shouted at him.

"The media can be just as bad," he countered.

"I honestly am doubting it at this point," I replied. One of his high school friends had just asked him how many lines he could sniff in one sitting. The excessive amount of curiosity would have probably caused someone less controlled to lash out.

"That's the thing about this place, Mikka. They say what they mean and mean what they say. If they're wondering, they ask. And then they share. And they will definitely share. So, I'm nipping the gossip in the bud now."

"I just feel like it's overkill at this point."

"It is," he admitted. "It's good practice, though. It's a good way to become desensitized. The media's been doing the same thing."

The headlines about the drugged-out Stonewood Brother had me buying dozens of magazines while standing in line at the drugstore and then throwing them all away. I had called numerous publishers and worked tirelessly in the past two months to curb any news outlet that tried to come for him.

We'd done great damage control. For his movie, though, they wanted more. They wanted him through rehab and here.

I was frustrated for him even though he seemed to be handling it all very well.

Just when I figured the night couldn't get much worse, my phone started ringing. Jay glanced at it before I could silence the tone.

"Don't answer it."

"Jay." I sighed. "He still needs me. I still need him in a lot of ways too."

"I'm not arguing that. You should know there's a time and place to talk to him though. Tonight at a bar with me isn't a great time. You both agreed to getting space."

He was right. I let the phone go to voicemail. I didn't face the music because it was easier to silence it and forget. I was putting a strain on Dougie just by being here with Jay. I'd let my Jay kiss me and, as I stared at him, I knew my feelings for him went beyond friendship. Of course Dougie had a right to be mad, to be prying and calling.

I didn't know what steps to take to make it right and so I followed Jay back to Jax and Aubrey where we let the small town consume us late into the night instead. He caught up with family and friends and let his genuine smile shine through much more than I'd ever seen in LA. I watched him as I drank more and more alcohol.

By the end of the night, I wondered if I was the bad influence on him or he was the bad one on me. He shouldn't have been out this late after just getting out of rehab and I shouldn't have been this drunk, lusting over him.

Had he even had a drink after the first? My fuzzy memory of the night was proof that I needed to slow down.

"I don't think I'm going to be able to stand when I get off this stool," I confessed to Aubrey.

She eyed the mason jar in front of me. "Did you drink that whole thing?"

I closed one eye to try to align my view with hers. I saw more than one jar, but maybe the jar was just swaying a little bit. "I definitely drank some of it."

"Jay!" she yelled over my head. "Mikka drank all the moonshine. She's going to need some help."

"No." I shoved off the bar, and from somewhere Ray's voice said, "slow down." I rolled my eyes. I'd had some of the best and strongest cocktails at bars in California. "A little moonshine never hurt me."

Jay's arm wrapped around my waist and I snuggled in close to him. "You okay to walk home?" he whispered in my ear.

"Are people staring at us?" I asked.

I heard him chuckle. "People always stare at you, woman."

He turned to his brother and best friend to say goodbyes.

They were truly the most beautiful couple in the world.

Aubrey laughed and then hugged me. "You said that out loud."

"Oh, God." I was starting to see the room spin. "I need to go to bed."

"I'll see you soon." Aubrey let me go and then they offered us a ride but Jay must have declined because suddenly the cool Autumn breeze, much cooler than desert air, hit my face.

"Jesus! It's freezing. We should have taken a ride home." I tried to snuggle farther against Jay.

"Well, you need the fresh air. We need to get you some winter clothes too."

"My clothes are fine. I look great in my outfit," I slurred, but I shivered a little and found myself stopping to make a decision. "Maybe we need an Uber."

"Meek, I told you, no Ubers around here."

"Will you be my car then? I'm ruining my shoes." I thought about that for a second. "Or my feet. Probably, most definitely, ruining my feet."

As I was finishing my sentence, Jay dipped to swoop me up into his arms. "I'll be your groom for the night, I guess."

"A groom always screws his bride on their wedding night. Oh my God, that iron headboard would definitely make a loud declaration of love."

He halted mid stride. "Your mind this dirty all the time?"

"Hm." Alcohol had made my lips loose. "I grew up in a porn store. I don't think I'm a nymphomaniac or anything. The ideas are just always in my head or I see them easily because, you know, porn."

He jerked his head up and down like my confession made him uncomfortable.

"Is this weird?" I wiggled a little in his arms. "Put me down."

He didn't. Instead, he stalked forward, much faster than before. "Don't share the ideas in your head with me this month."

Crossing my arms over my chest, I pouted like a baby. "Why not? You said we're being honest and open here. This is the place for it and we're working through it all together. Blah, blah, blah."

"We're working through our problems together, Meek. I don't need your fine ass creating more by sharing your kinky mind with me."

"My mind isn't a problem!" I protested. "I have a healthy sex drive. Did you know the average person is supposed to think about sex eight times a day? Also, thinking about it more is quite possibly good for you."

He groaned. "I highly doubt that in our case."

"What's our case?"

"Our case is us trying to remain friends this month, right? I'm not going to think about anything sexual with you when you're on a break with Dougie."

All of a sudden, I felt the bunched muscles in his arms and chest as he walked. I bounced onto his abs with each stride.

Could he feel my skin heating, my heart starting to jackhammer in my chest? Did he see me staring right at the lips I knew were pillowy soft?

"Put me down," I commanded, our position all of a sudden too much for me.

"No." He smirked. "I'm going to enjoy you up against me for now, woman. Even if it's not the way we both want it."

"That's not a friendly thing to say."

"Sharing how you're contemplating our sex scenes in your bedroom isn't friendly either."

"Who said I was contemplating them with you?" I countered.

"Who else could it be when I'm in the room right next door?"

I scrambled because I had thought about it and it was embarrassing. I should have been focused on other things. "Dougie, a guy in town, anyone really. And quite frankly I have a vast array of sex toys to keep me company for the month. I'm fine."

He didn't respond as we neared the house. Walking up the front steps, I took in the cool air and darkness that enveloped us. The stars above shone brighter than they ever did in the city and bugs chirped like a symphony of nature.

He lowered me onto the white porch but didn't step back as

he let me slide down his body. "The only person you contemplate anything with in this town is me, little one. Stop lying."

His voice rumbled into the cool night air, joining the cold wind in sending shivers down my spine. "I don't lie. I've thought about other men," I proclaimed, sure he wouldn't ask for details.

"Oh, yeah. Let's bet. Name one."

"Wait, what's the bet?" I asked, stalling so I could rack my brain for an answer.

"Don't cheat and delay the inevitable."

"I... Well, there's..." I blanked as I stared into his eyes. They twinkled like the stars in the night sky and lit up my soul. I couldn't finish the sentence because all I saw in front of me was the man I wanted but knew I shouldn't.

I leaned closer and closer to the lips I dreamt about and ran my hand up his chest. He didn't stop me at first. His hand was at my wrist when I lifted on my tiptoes and took his mouth in mine.

He and I both moaned as we got lost in that kiss. The darkness of the night swallowed us up and let us indulge. I didn't worry about who would see us in this small town; I only worried I wouldn't get enough of him.

I gripped him tight and pulled him even closer, nipping at his lip and diving back in. I was feeling brave, like this could work, like we could give in and figure it all out in the morning.

My hand ran over his shoulder, and my core quivered when I felt my leather book bag strap there. He'd always been so thoughtful. I appreciated that about him.

But not when he pulled away.

Not when he said, "Meek, we have to stop. You've been drinking. And I... I can't do this with you right now."

I covered my mouth and stumbled through the front door. "Oh, God. I'm sorry."

"I don't want apologies, little one. I want to make sure that when it happens, you're sober. And it will happen. Mark my words, Little Pebble. That you can bet on."

THERAPIST: *Why haven't you called your best friend, Brey?*

JAY: *I need to make amends with her beyond my addiction. I need to do that face to face. I owe her a lot more than a phone call. I owe her a better friendship.*

CHAPTER ELEVEN

JAY

I HAD LORRAINE LEAVE Advil and water on her bedside the next morning. I couldn't trust myself in there alone with her after her sharing her ideas about the iron headboard, after her kissing me, after tasting her again.

Jesus, she wanted to be ravaged. Was it just me she wanted or would she be fine with anyone giving her the attention she deserved? I'd never considered that she hadn't been loved and cherished, that she might yearn for a touch outside of me or Dougie.

The idea had my heart picking up speed and my gut clenching. And the problem with our ground rules was I had to be honest with myself too.

Mikka wasn't just my friend anymore.

My thoughts had crossed over after that kiss, spiraled and gained as much momentum as a tornado. When she'd thrown into our conversation last night that she'd been considering sex at Lorraine's, I hadn't considered that she was free to come and go without me, that she could bring a man back here, that I would have to hear that iron pounding and know it wasn't me doing it.

The need to seek out a party barreled through me. If this was just the start of the month, just a few days out of rehab, I would have to remind myself daily that some movies were meant to be told by me and only me. This movie needed someone who respected the role, respected the lines and believed them. That someone was me. I had to find a way to stay relaxed. Stress was a trigger of mine. Therapy had taught me that.

It taught me that fatiguing the stress was a combative option too.

I put my running shoes on and bolted out of the house. I burned off the little bit of alcohol I'd drunk and took my frustration out on the sidewalk, on the open winding roads.

Halfway into my run, I turned a corner and saw dark, auburn hair blowing in the wind. "Brey, slow your ass down."

She turned and stopped running. "Fancy seeing you here."

"Running off the grogginess of last night too?"

"The hangover? Yeah, your brother was supposed to come, but he said he was inspired to write some lyrics this morning."

"Huh. He hasn't written in a while." I scratched my jaw.

"He won't sing it. But he said he knows who is meant to sing it already."

"Sounds about right." I nodded and started to stroll up the street. "You two heading back today?" They lived about two hours away in the city. I had a feeling they'd come to check in with me and would be gone soon enough.

Aubrey narrowed her eyes though. "You'd like that, wouldn't you?"

"Give me a break, baby girl. You know I love you; I want you here whenever you can be."

"Then why didn't you call?"

"I'm trying not to bother you or burden you."

"Was I a burden to you all those years ago?"

"What?" I halted my run, scrambling through all the times we'd spent together. Brey was my girl. She'd moved in next door back when we were kids. She was quiet, but quick on her feet. She was polite but had a mouth that could cut down the best of them. She was reserved, but fun and caring. She had needed a friend more than anyone I'd ever seen, and I wasn't one to ever turn away someone in need.

I fell in love with having her around. She accepted my crazy need to enjoy life and I went into every damn scenario with that need. She might have been reserved, but she pushed herself more than any other person I knew to make me happy. She was there for me and I was there for her.

Until the fire. My brother found her house burning down and saved her. After that, their relationship changed. Ours did too. We were still best friends, but something died in her that night and I swear the only person who could fill the hole was my brother.

"After the fire, your mom took me in. Did it feel like a burden having me live with you all?"

"Don't be ridiculous." I screwed up my face in confusion. "We fought tooth and nail to have you there. We wouldn't have had you anywhere else."

"Exactly. You aren't a burden to me either. Jax and I want to be there for you. You have to let me be there for you because I will be whether you like it or not."

"Woman, that's different. You didn't ask for your shit. I asked for mine. I got caught up in the life of it. I was reckless and... I can't lose this role." I shook my head as my voice broke. "It means a lot, so I'm trying to clean up the mess I made."

"I'm going to clean it up too. That's what friends do."

I cleared my throat, not sure how to say the next words that had to come out. They would be the reason I kept avoiding her if I didn't let them go. "You should have lived with us long before the fire, Brey." I sighed and pulled my shirt up to wipe sweat from my face. "There are things I need to apologize for, things I'm not proud of. I'm supposed to deal with my mental instability by letting go of things, by confronting things. I should have spoken up about the abuse going on in your home long before your father set that house on fire. I should have..."

She walked right up to me and shoved me hard in the chest. "Don't you dare put that on yourself."

"Baby girl." I tried to grab her hands but she shoved me again.

"No!" She screamed the word, loud enough for all the town to hear.

No one was in sight, but they were watching. This town leaned in when they heard a whisper and listened extra closely from behind a closed curtain if they heard a stir.

"This, here, this *healing*"—she spat out the word like it was acid on her tongue—"it doesn't work without family. My therapy almost broke me because I wasn't listening to anyone but the voice inside my head."

I wanted to stop her and tell her my situation was different. She'd suffered the loss of her parents, her home, and her life.

I'd just fucked mine up.

That was the difference between me and so many others who survived their addiction. Rehab separated those who'd lived a life much less fortunate than mine and those who'd been given it all. I was in the latter group. I didn't want for much. My group seemed to take their rehab stint as a joke. The other group looked at their stint as a miracle—they'd somehow survived and been given an extra chance.

They were fighters, warriors, champions.

Brey was the queen of all of them. She'd faced her battle and conquered it.

"I don't believe that for a second," I said. "Your voice is the strongest one out there, Sasspot."

"My voice is deranged. Everyone in therapy is there because the voice in their head is off for some reason, Jay. Don't let me or anyone else fool you. We can't set ourselves straight unless we have people helping us steer in the right direction. This life has too many turns to navigate all on our own."

"I'm here with Mikka all month."

"Mikka isn't your best friend." She cocked her head like she was daring me to argue the statement.

"No," I let out slowly and started walking back to Lorraine's with her by my side.

"She's a very pretty friend and an almost too-attractive PA."

I scratched the back of my neck. "Yeah, I'm aware."

"So, you've slept with her?" Brey phrased it as a question but didn't wait for the answer. "I don't see how it's healthy to bring someone like that on a trip to center yourself and heal."

"She's a good PA, Brey. And an even better friend. And the agency wanted her along."

"And your PA didn't fight to stay home? So, what? She have some crush on you that she wanted to be here?" The cynical tone in Brey's voice had me smiling.

"Are you now concerned about me sleeping with my PA? What's the worst that could happen if I did?" I laughed at the notion, brushing off the tiny niggling feeling that came with it.

"She could become attached and when you tell her you can't commit, she could quit, leak information, file a lawsuit, sue you for God knows what, and ultimately have you lose your movie deal."

"Who says I can't commit?"

She rolled her eyes. "Come on, Jay."

For the first time ever, her lack of belief in my ability to commit irritated me. She didn't believe I was capable. Had I never given her reason to think I could be serious about anything?

Did Mikka feel the same?

"Sorry, that was harsh," Brey backtracked.

"It was honest." I turned onto Lorraine's sidewalk and pulled Brey into a hug. "Baby girl, get past me not calling. We're family. I'm sorry, okay?"

She snuggled into my hug and nodded. "Don't do it again. I'm going insane worrying about you. I mean it. Jax is about to flip out on us both for how anxious I've been lately."

"My brother's an asshat. Remind me why you chose to be with him."

"Because you were sleeping with half the cheer team?" she teased me, but we both knew we'd never clicked that way. She was like a kid sister to me, a complete pain in my ass half the time and a necessary person in my life all the time.

"I slept with the whole team."

She laughed and jogged off, leaving me wondering again about my lack of commitment to any of the cheerleaders or other women in my life.

When I walked inside, I found Lorraine and Mikka enjoying tea. Mikka was laughing at something Lorraine had said as the sun streamed in through the windows. Her shining black hair lay straight against her back, and her small frame was dwarfed by the massive wooden table.

"Honeys, I'm home," I announced, sliding off my tennis shoes.

Lorraine blew a raspberry. "We saw you out there hugging other women. We're not at all interested in your arrival now."

I fumbled at her statement. "That was Brey out there."

"So? You left us to go jog with a beautiful woman. I, for one, never did and never will stand for that in a man."

I glanced at Mikka who had a small smile on her face and shrugged at me. I wasn't sure of Lorraine's angle, but I suddenly felt a need to explain myself. "Lorraine, you know Brey's my sister-in-law."

"I know what she is. I've also read the tabloids over the years. Someone like Mikka might not know your history." She harrumphed and wide-eyed me as if I had better explain.

In the span of my jogging, Mikka had won over Lorraine and Lorraine had switched to matchmaker. I saw this for what it was: Lorraine trying to explain away any misunderstandings because Aubrey and I were old news in this town. No one actually believed we had an underlying relationship.

"Lorraine, Mikka knows my history with Brey. She's my PA. She knows the magazines have printed lies for ages. Right, Mikka?"

Mikka waited for a second longer than I expected. "Yeah, I know."

The extra hesitation was enough for me to jump on it. "Why did you wait to answer?" I glanced at Lorraine and she lifted her eyebrows as if to say, 'See, explain yourself.'

"I didn't wait," Mikka denied and got up to put her empty tea cup in the sink. Lorraine joined her and started washing dishes. Lorraine made no attempt to leave the room; she leaned in to make sure the conversation was going her way.

"You did. You know Brey and I have never had anything, right?" I asked.

"It doesn't matter if you have or haven't. I think the press honestly believes you never did now, so that's all that's needed."

I stalked up to her. "No, that's not all that's needed. You need to be aware that I would never have slept with her. She's like a damn sister to me."

"I don't care one way or the other, Jay," she mumbled, but she didn't meet my eyes.

"Well, you should."

Lorraine gasped, and Mikka's eyes snapped to mine with something very close to hope.

"At the very least," I continued, "I'd like you to know I have a better conscience than that. You've been friends with me all this time and wondered if I was sleeping with my brother's wife?"

"No," she blurted and stepped back like she needed the distance. "I don't know. I just...she's beautiful and the pictures in magazines are..."

"Lies," I spat.

She nodded with conviction. "I assumed that. It's just..."

"Well, I put a bug in her ear," Lorraine admitted over the dishes, not at all embarrassed about her eavesdropping. "I told her to look on out that window at the pretty woman and man hugging. Someone needs to lay out all your quirks. Mikka needs to be aware."

"She's aware. Don't stir the pot when there's nothing in there to stir, Lorraine. You know how this town talks," I chastised her.

She laughed and changed the subject. "Are you two going to help me winterize some of my flowers? The autumn air is going to bring the first frost soon."

"Whatever you need, Lorraine." I made my way up the stairs, ushering Mikka to follow me.

She started wringing her hands in the hallway, not able to control the apprehension seeping from her. "I'm sorry. That was weird. You don't need weird right now."

I waved her into my room and shut the door behind her. "Lorraine's just giving us shit. Don't mind her or the whole town for that matter. They're going to throw a lot more shit our way."

She tilted her head. "So, are you going to be helping Lorraine for the next few hours?"

"We"—I emphasized the word and motioned between us—"will be helping Lorraine."

She backed away toward the door. "Oh, no. I don't have… I can't. I don't like plants. I don't have a green thumb and digging in dirt is not something I enjoy."

I chuckled as I pulled my work out shirt over my forehead and grabbed an old t-shirt I'd packed. "You're getting dirty with me, Meek. I'll teach you. I'm good at getting dirty."

LESSON OF THE DAY:
Trying something new means you may find something new to love.

CHAPTER TWELVE

MIKKA

THE SECOND DAY here and I already had a hangover. This was how I knew city girls did not belong in a small town. Moonshine was the devil and it'd thrown me in hangover hell that morning.

I'd woken up in a daze, my ribcage in much more pain than I wanted to admit. Jay carrying me home hadn't been smart because alcohol had made me numb and dumb.

I scraped myself out of bed and tried to chase away the hangover by giving myself a pep talk as I pulled on pressed wide leg pants and a white blouse.

I needed to focus. Jay was off limits and I shouldn't have ever discussed head-banging sex with him. I shouldn't have...

I groaned. I had kissed him.

The head-banging sex in this bed sounded even better knowing that he'd kissed me like I was the only woman in the world. My thighs quaked and my body heated. My pep talk wasn't going to work.

And, of course, when he got me alone after his run, I stood there salivating.

Pep talk be damned.

I knew I was staring and couldn't stop. All I could focus on was the sweat on his body, the sculpted chest, the veins cording his arms. He was a perfect specimen; one I couldn't help but want to lick.

"Meek, I seem to remember you telling me these abs weren't worth the millions they paid me for that movie."

I snapped my gaze away and felt the blush rising to my cheeks. "Give me a break, Jay."

"Why should I? I thought you were just fine with your toys over in your room."

"I am!"

"Then why are you drooling over me shirtless." He stepped closer to me and I stepped back.

"What are you doing?" I saw the look in his eyes. It was the same look he'd given me so many nights ago, like he wanted me again, like he could eat me whole and I'd enjoy it just as much as he would.

When he caught up to my backtracking and met me chest to chest at the door, he whispered down to me, "I'm memorizing this feeling, the one where you act like you don't want this because when you end up begging me for it, I want to make sure we're both aware that I was right from the start."

"I don't need to get off, Jay."

"But you want to."

"Sure." I shrugged. "Like I said before, there's toys for that. And men. I'm sure there are tons of men in this town for me to meet."

His eyebrows slammed down. "Mikka, you don't belong with anyone in this town."

"I don't want to belong to anyone right now either. I just want fun, Jay. I'm finding myself without Dougie so I can figure out if we'll ever be able to be together again. What better place and time to do that than here?"

He sucked on his teeth. "Not smart here or anywhere near me."

"Then, let me go back to LA. You don't need me here. You have friends, family, people that care about you here. I can go back and lick my wounds there while I set up your schedule for you. By the way, have you seen my book bag?" I'd searched my room this morning and hadn't found it. I almost panicked and ran to the bar but recalled Jay having it on the porch last night.

He leaned back. "I'm holding on to it for now."

"Uh, no. I need that back."

"When we both go back to LA, you can have it."

"You realize I don't belong here. I belong in the city. With my bag."

He hummed low and dragged a finger down my arm. "You're perfect here. With me. And without your bag. Let's go repot some plants, huh?"

I narrowed my eyes. "Guessing I should change?"

He nodded as he eyed my clothes. The white blouse I had on cost much more than I was willing to waste rolling in mud. I went to put on some of my least favorite athleisure clothes. Unfortunately, I hadn't packed well. I didn't know if my ass-hugging compression leggings and my zip-up tank with a built-in sports bra were ideal.

I stepped out into the sun and shielded my eyes from the light to observe the older woman hovering over her plants with Jay. Her hands dug into the soil with care. She didn't wince at getting it under her nails, and I glanced down at my manicure, wondering if it would withstand the beating it was about to get.

Jay smirked from where he was crouched. "Come on, princess. I promise it won't be that bad."

"I didn't say it would be bad at all," I countered as I knelt down next to Lorraine. "I'm always happy to help."

I wasn't. I wanted to cringe as my knee hit the dirt, and I was sure there were bugs all around us. Lorraine caught me surveying our surroundings.

"It's a bit nipply for bugs." She cackled at her choice of words and I found myself smiling.

"Should have worn more padding, huh?" I replied.

Her head shot up as if she was completely taken aback that I'd joined in. Then she let loose a smile that showed her molars. "No way, Mikka. If you don't let the headlights out every now and then, the boys down the block won't know where to find you."

Jay groaned. "Lorraine, she's not trying to lead men here."

Lorraine harrumphed. "Even if you aren't, Mikka, it's good to know your options, and the men don't flock to a nest where a bird doesn't show off her feathers, if you know what I mean."

I nodded solemnly as I moved a pot closer to her. She lifted a plant from the ground. When she set it in place, she pointed to a fertilizer bag. I grabbed it and started pouring it in. "I know what you mean."

"She's smarter than most of the women around here, Jay," Lorraine announced, and I felt like I'd just won a freaking award. Why did I suddenly want to make this woman proud?

We worked for some time that way. Lorraine gave unsolicited advice as I filled pots. Jay grumbled about it all while taking the pots and carrying them indoors. I stole more than one glance at his backside, at the way he lifted each plant effortlessly, and at how the veins in his arms popped when he did.

At one point, Lorraine leaned in to whisper, "Now, don't make it so obvious. We all know he's a hottie, but make him work for it. He scares easier than most. Not because he's afraid of commitment."

I tilted my head at her in question.

She continued, "That's what everyone says, but I know my Jay. He only holds back from committing because he doesn't want to be the primary reason for someone's pain. He wants to be there for the good times and to pick you up if you're down."

"I'm not quite sure I understand," I said as I stared off after him.

"His momma's heart broke for his daddy. He was there to pick her up and make her smile. Aubrey went through some things as a kid. She broke down and he picked her up too. He's avoided ever being the cause of someone's pain."

"Why do you think that is?"

"He feels it like it's his own."

I nodded. "I think you're right."

"Don't let him just feel your pain, missy. I know you got it too. I saw it the second you walked up with him. You think you belong back where you came from, but something happened there because Jay's protective of you. So, let me give you some advice."

She waited as I took a breath because I wasn't sure I wanted the advice she was about to give. I nodded then, deciding that someone with this much understanding of me already deserved to give me advice more than most people.

"Don't run back to your problem. I did that with my husband. I went back time and time again. I shouldn't have. I used to dance and sing whenever I was away from him. He dimmed my spirit. I only got it back when he passed not so long ago. It's the happiest I've ever been."

"I'm happy you're happy." Her words made me want to shrink up and disappear because they hit so close to home. Was I throwing away my life, dimming my moments to shine?

"Yeah, well, I should have freed my nips long before then."

I burst out laughing. "Maybe. But you can now."

She patted my shoulder. "You can too. I'll help. Don't you worry."

The sun started to set but I kept working. The dirt would break away from the plants and I could dust it away to find roots long and thick hidden away. Repotting them and positioning them in dark soil to stand straight turned into one small accomplishment after another. They looked alive, new, and like they were thriving every single time.

Lorraine released us so we could go clean up while she made dinner. I showered away the grime but didn't feel at all disgusted with the chore we'd just done. Instead, I felt rejuvenated, reenergized, ready to conquer it all. Especially when I saw some of our work displayed around the house.

Jay even told me I had placed the plants just right. They stood tall, centered, and almost proud. I decided I would water them over my stay and enjoy my newfound skill. Such a small chore reminded me that hard work paid off, that if Jay and I worked hard enough, we could come out of all this ahead.

I jumped when my phone rang.

And my heart sank when I saw Dougie's name on the screen.

Jay walked by and whisked it out of my hands. "Not today. Or this month."

I bit my lip, thinking over what was best. "I should talk to him."

"He should learn to give you space."

"I don't know if that much space will end up being healthy for us."

"I'm trying here, Meek, but you and I both know what I want to say."

"What? That what we had wasn't healthy?"

"Something along those lines."

"Well, there were a lot of unhealthy things we were both doing back in LA," I grumbled because the call had soured the day. It reminded me that this was just a little bubble and we couldn't get lost in it. We needed to face reality: we were both in shitty situations.

"You're right. I'm thinking you'll get a call from our boss soon too. That's the only damn reason I haven't dunked your phone into the toilet at this point."

Normally, Jay would have avoided a business call at all costs. Our agency had a rough time getting a hold of him. They called me for updates, instead. "Your role in this movie is going to be phenomenal because you're holding up your end."

He nodded. "I'm ready for it, I think."

"You were always ready for it, Jay." I whispered, meaning every word.

"You might be one of the only people that believe that, but I'll prove it to the world." He winked at me. "If I have to take my shirt off a few times to win the Oscar for icing on the cake, I'll do that too."

"Oh, God." I rolled my eyes and started to walk past him. He wrapped an arm around my waist to pull me back, chuckling at my disgust with his arrogance.

His arm dug right into the spot of pain, though. I tensed and sucked in air as I grabbed his arm to ward off the pressure against the bruising.

"What?" He jumped back immediately, my sensitivity shocking

him. His hands were up in the air like he thought he was the one who'd done something wrong. "What is it?"

I held the ribs I knew weren't broken but were definitely bruised. "It's nothing."

I sounded defeated, as meek as my nickname, and embarrassed. All the things I definitely was in that moment.

I didn't want to admit to him that I was injured, didn't want to lie either. He scanned me and I must have looked a complete waste hunched over as I breathed in deep, trying to will the pain away.

"I need you to talk to me. I need to know at some point, Mikka." He ground out the words. I looked up to find his jaw working and the muscles across his body tensing.

"What's there to say?" I could search for decades, through every experience ever written and talked about and still not have the right words. Pain and shame couldn't be portrayed accurately. "The stories I have don't need to be spoken any further into existence."

"Fine," he growled and stalked forward. Before I could stop him, he gripped the zipper of my shirt "Can I?"

I stared into his intense azure eyes. My heart beat a mile a minute as I whispered the question I knew the answer to already, "Can you what?"

"Little Pebble, I need to see. You need to show me." One of his hands went to my cheek and he rubbed his thumb back and forth as if my skin was made of fragile porcelain.

Was I that delicate and that worthy of his soft touch? His stare searched deep down within me and somehow I felt like he waded through everything that was insubstantial about me. He got to my heart and rooted himself with my soul.

I rolled my lips between my teeth, trying to hold back the fear of letting someone else I cared about see. I closed my eyes and nodded.

He took a deep breath and ran his hand down my shoulder as the other slowly pulled the zipper down. He slid his fingers under the shirt and my skin shivered at his touch. As he smoothed his hands over me toward the shirt, it fell away.

I didn't look down at myself. I knew from his eyes widening, it looked worse than I made it out to be every time I stared at myself in the mirror.

As he hummed low, I knew he'd seen the dark purple circle on the side of my ribs. The swelling had gone down, but the reddish, purple coloring hadn't faded much.

"Jesus," he blew out, the one word falling from his lips like he was destroyed by it. Then he fell to his knees as his hands ran over my skin. Something was happening as he stared at me, as he assessed the damage. His touch was as delicate as a feather blown over me by a breeze. His azure eyes shined as if they were lone stars leading me back to the safety I longed for.

He leaned in and gently grazed his lips across the darkened skin. He held me like I was cracked glass, like I could shatter under him. And in that moment, I wondered if I would.

No man had ever kissed me so softly, so full of worship, so tenderly.

My body heated, my nipples tightened, and my thighs shook.

Why did something that was supposed to be wrong feel right?

I wondered if the red string of Yue Lao was pulling us together as my arms wrapped around him. I wondered if this was where we were supposed to be.

He unbuttoned my pants and I let him. I was lost in him, oblivious to the idea that I could be anywhere else but with him in this moment.

But then he stopped.

He took a steadying breath and leaned his forehead against my stomach. I combed my hands through his hair and slowly pulled him back. "You're stopping?"

"You're in pain. It's not the way I want to take you."

This man wanted to cherish me. He'd rooted himself in my heart. I'd stopping thinking someone could want to do just that with Dougie. Dougie wouldn't have cared and that had made my heart lose all hope. It had turned cold. But Jay's soft touches and the way he cared for me warmed the heart I thought had frozen over. It turned me on the way I hadn't been turned on in months. "I'll be fine, Jay."

I said the words to soothe him, to have him carry on, but he shook his head. His face was marred with concern.

"When?" His fingers lightly grazed over my bottom rib as he stood back up.

"It doesn't matter," I mumbled. If I admitted it was from two weeks ago, he'd be even more concerned that this wasn't the worst of it. "You were still in rehab, and Dougie and I just weren't connecting."

He lifted my chin so I could look into his eyes as he said, "You. Deserve. Better. Your skin's like porcelain, little one. Don't you get that he should be treating you like it?"

I didn't know if I believed that anymore, and I wasn't sure there was a better man out there who would treat me that way. The only one I knew of stood in front of me, and he'd never committed to a woman in his life. Dougie had. "He's sorry. You know he is. You saw how sorry he is."

"He's scared, not sorry. He'll say whatever to keep you around. Anyone would. You're too damn precious to lose." His hands slid to my waist to hold me steady as he leaned in to study my ribs again. Goosebumps skittered across my skin and my body reacted to him like it never did with Dougie anymore. I wasn't afraid of this man; I wasn't concerned for my wellbeing. There was something in the way he touched me—I wasn't a treasure, but he made me feel like one.

"You get checked out?" He pressed softly over one rib to feel for a break.

I winced a bit and cleared my throat. Admitting it all out loud felt more shameful than experiencing it. "I went to the doctor. Nothing is broken."

"So, you put it on record?"

I stepped back. My head was clouding, getting lost in his touch, getting lost in a feeling that wasn't real, that wasn't an option. "I told them I fell into a railing."

"Dougie's fist that railing?"

I spun to zip my top back up. "It's more complicated than that and you know it. We're the reason for that. Our kiss—that should have never happened, might I add—put stress on my relationship. I failed and I'm trying to fix it."

"That kiss was bound to happen." His stare was hard and glaring. "And a relationship isn't just *you* failing, Meek. There's two people involved."

I narrowed my eyes at him over my shoulder. "Jay, you can't give me advice on relationships."

"Why?"

"Because you've never been in one!" I screamed. I put my hands over my face, trying to hide my frustration. Then I pulled them through my hair and faced him. "Let's just drop this, okay?"

The silence stretched between us. He curled his lips over his teeth, fisted his hand, and clenched his jaw like he had more to say.

I stopped him. "Don't. Please just don't."

"First rule was what?" he asked, holding up a finger.

I shook my head, not ready for any of our rules.

"You're not broken and you need to remember who you are. You don't back down, and you don't cower when I'm about to tell you something. You never have and you won't start now."

I realized at that moment that Dougie had taken a part of me. The part that gave me confidence in myself, the part that told me I could handle anything, was gone.

I'd become a victim, I'd stayed with my abuser, and I'd let him tear apart everything I'd built in myself.

I didn't want to hear more because I was close to breaking. "I'm trying to fix things, Jay."

"Well, stop trying. You're better than all of that, Pebble. Remember when we met?"

I remembered him hitting on me, picking up a pebble and saying I was about as tiny as that. "Yes," I whispered.

"I almost didn't approach you. You had more confidence in your tiny hand than everyone on the whole beach. And when you told me you were only entertaining our conversation because you knew I was an actor, I almost walked away. You didn't let me. You had that fight in your eyes, like you were going to make me see you were the best."

"Yes, exactly." I threw my hands up like he finally got it. "I don't give up and I'm trying not to give up on my relationship either."

"No, Meek. Because what you're doing is giving up on yourself."

I stumbled back at his words. "You're one to talk about giving up when you've been on a self-destructive path for as long as…"

I didn't want to finish. I was throwing insults instead of constructive criticism, and my gut clenched at my immaturity, at my need to defend the dumpster fire of a relationship I was in by tearing my best friend down.

"Going to finish?" he goaded me.

I took a deep breath and shook my head.

"Fine," he grumbled without meeting my eyes. "Then, I'm going to the drugstore. Please ice the bruising on your side." He stalked past me and I started to follow him, concerned I'd pushed him hard and he wouldn't come back, that he'd go do something stupid.

And it was my job to make sure he didn't.

More than that, though, I couldn't fathom that I might lose him again emotionally when we were just starting to build back up what we'd lost.

"Don't follow me, Meek. Your job isn't on the line. I'm not going to do anything crazy."

I opened my mouth to tell him that wasn't the real reason I was following him. He needed to know I wasn't just here for that, but he didn't let me get a word in.

"And if you don't believe me, I'm sure our company will be having you drug test me in a day or two to confirm. Let me be."

I halted my chase. I let him go.

I told myself his wellbeing was more important at the moment than our friendship, that I had to let him deal with his own emotions, not bombard him with mine.

I pulled my phone out to shoot him a text that he needed to be back in time for dinner. I saw my schedule, though. It was the one I'd merged with his phone, and the next event that would sound for both of us was dinner with Lorraine.

Hounding him would just reinforce that I was trying to check on him.

I threw my phone on my bed and paced. My pent-up emotion had me needing a release more than anything. Glancing at the door and listening to see if anyone was near enough to hear what I would be doing in my bedroom, I concluded I was in the clear. I grabbed my mini wand vibrator from a little bag in my suitcase and went to the bathroom that sported a large claw bathtub. I poured soap in, turned the water up to a steaming temperature and slid in right when the water got high enough.

I took the waterproof vibrator and switched it on. Rubbing it once over my clit, I let my mind drift. It went straight to Jay's hands on my waist. In my fantasy, he yanked me close and punished me by devouring my mouth the way he had that night.

I wanted to scream his name, to yank his shirt off, the one he'd been wearing when he'd grabbed me in the club and run my hands over the abs that every girl in America dreamed of. I knew firsthand he tasted like the sweet lollipops he always sucked on; with a sort of masculine finish I couldn't pinpoint.

He tasted of temptation, desire, and my ultimate ruin.

I switched the device to high and slid it inside me, but the thoughts of Jay were what shook me to my core.

When he stared at me like I was the most important thing in the world, when his hands smoothed over my ribs like he'd never, ever hurt me the way someone already had, I was lost to him. I let go of the tension I'd been feeling for days and found a release so high, I wasn't sure I'd ever convince myself that the man in the bedroom next to mine was only supposed to be a friend.

As I dried off and observed the mess I was in the mirror, I catalogued my flaws. My long hair was tangled and needed a good cut, my frame was small and not worked on like most in LA, my almond eyes weren't a good fit in most areas, especially a small town like this one.

Jay and I weren't compatible as more than friends.

The most striking flaws were the spots over my ribs. The bruises were almost healed, but they were still a reminder that I was damaged goods. I'd allowed this to happen. I'd been abused, broken, and beaten down into something I was sure Jay didn't need in his life. Did he just want to fix me like he had so many others or would he want to be with beyond that?

I curled up in bed and lay there waiting.

My phone pinged, and I jumped to see if he'd texted me.

Instead, Dougie's name flashed on the screen.

> **DOUGIE:** I miss you.

I didn't want to write him back, but the tightening in my chest reminded me how much we'd cared for each other for so long. He'd inflicted pain but he'd also been there to soothe it away. He'd stuck with me even when I'd kissed another man and he'd tried to make it work in his own way.

He'd been there and I wanted to be there for him too.

> **ME:** I know. This is hard for both of us.
> **DOUGIE:** Just call me.
> **ME:** We need time apart.
> **DOUGIE:** I don't need anything but you.
> **ME:** That's sweet, Dougie. But if we are going to be together, we need to get back on track.
> **DOUGIE:** If? You aren't leaving me.

My stomach clenched because I could hear him say it, hear the warning in his voice. He'd say the words distinctly. He'd said them before while gripping my arm so tight and shaking me after I'd threatened to do just that. I had bruises hours later.

The reminder had me closing our chat and letting his messages come in unanswered.

I stared at the phone, waiting for a text or call from Jay instead. He didn't do either and he didn't come home. I realized just how much anguish a lover of an addict had to go through. They waited, they wondered, they worried, and they wept as every scenario played out in their head. I knew how strong and smart he was, but I also knew the drugs stole all those things from him.

I had to believe he wouldn't fold under the pressure, under his anger and confusion. All I could do now was wait and hope.

I wasn't good at either of those things.

THERAPIST: *It isn't your job to help everyone be happier, Jay. Do you understand that?*

JAY: *It is actually my job as an actor to provide the audience an experience.*

THERAPIST: *So, when do you turn that off? When do you focus on you?*

JAY: *I don't know.*

CHAPTER THIRTEEN

JAY

I STORMED OFF INTO the night air, trying to rid myself of my anger. Every darkened area on Mikka's ribs had me wondering. Was that a punch? Had he hit her with something else?

I should have broken his jaw, beaten him to within an inch of his life. It was another regret I'd carry with me for a long time.

I roamed around the town I'd grown up in. I tried to forget what I saw, tried to get lost in my own memories and remind myself that she was her own person, that I couldn't make everyone's lives better.

I walked down the sidewalks, took in the homes with meticulous landscaping. Jerry, a man not much older than my father, knelt near some of his mulch and was pulling weeds. He didn't look a day older than the last time I'd seen him doing the exact same thing.

The black paved road beside the sidewalk contrasted with the autumn leaves of the maple trees that surrounded it. It was the same road I'd sped down a million times in high school once I'd gotten my license. I remember begging a cop just two blocks away not to ticket me. He let me off easy, probably because he'd known my parents. Everyone knew everyone. The kids I once played with in the woods near my house were buying up the same homes we'd passed and the same yards we'd ran through.

Sandy fluttered up her sidewalk when she saw me, and I saw the same interest in her eyes I'd seen years ago. I entertained the idea of something with her as I accepted her invitation to dinner, but Mikka lingered in the back of my mind.

I was the friend of a victim, and I didn't know how to do more without pushing her further away. I needed her to see her own value without shoving her face in it, without forcing her acceptance of the situation.

I knew it didn't work that way. Yet when someone you care about is constantly hurting themselves by going back to their abuser, your gut reaction is to rip them away, to shield them even if they don't want the help. The shield warps into a way to repel them from you though.

I was giving her space and letting myself cool down. I needed to distance myself, remind myself that she wasn't a woman I wanted to get tangled in the sheets with. Sandy was supposed to be that reminder.

It didn't work.

That was the funny thing about returning to your hometown. It reminded you of what you had growing up and it served to remind you of what you were missing then and now.

Sitting across the table from Sandy, I missed my Little Pebble.

"Sandy, I've got somewhere to be." I cut our dinner short, folded some bills up to leave on the table.

The blonde woman pursed her lips but didn't push me. She nodded and stood to hug me. "Let's get together sometime soon?"

I nodded and left.

The night sky was dark enough with no city lights that the stars burst out all the constellations. It had me wondering about Mikka's mother's story. Was Yue Lao up there trying to untangle our red strings?

I peeked in on her when I get back. She breathed so softly when she slept, I was reminded of how tiny she was. I backed out of her room fast, afraid I'd lose my control. I wanted to rip her sheets off and make her let me examine the bruising again. I wanted to scoop her up and put her in my bed where I could watch the moonlight dance upon her skin as she slept soundly.

Most of the night I stayed up worrying about the woman that wasn't mine but who I was starting to think should have been a long time ago.

"You were out late." Mikka confronted me as we crossed paths the next morning.

"I caught up with some friends. How are you feeling? Your side still sore? Are your ribs…"

"It's fine. It's almost healed." She turned to the small staircase and her hand gripped the railing tightly. "Our company called, Jay."

With her eyes downcast, I knew what it meant. "If they want to drug test me, I said I was happy to do it. Did the package come with the supplies?"

She whispered, "I hate this. If I was trying the way you were and someone told me I had to check in with a test, I'd be so mad." She ripped her hands from the railing as if the thought burned her. "It's not fair that they're making you do this."

"It is, Mcck. It's fixing the trust I broke so many times with the media. It's proving the point they need me to make to finish off this movie."

"You only have a few scenes left, right?" she asked as she walked back to her room to get the white plastic bag that held the urine cup. The whole process was degrading, a way to put me in my place, and definitely a way to make sure I was serious about promoting this movie the right way. "And you promised to behave through promotion. I'm just frustrated for you."

I leaned against her doorway as she ripped open the package and handed me the cup. "Babe, you might not see it yet, but I've acted the scenes, I've delved into the lead. This movie is it. It's going to propel society into wanting more equal rights. It's going to win awards. It's brilliant. The director knows my mishaps and controversies can't taint that. He's covering his ass and I get it. I agree. This movie needs to shine purely on its own."

Her eyes started to glisten at my words.

"Are you okay? Your ribs hurting?" I hesitated, still worried.

"I'm just really proud of you. You've taken shit parts, Jay." She laughed despite the tears in her eyes. "I knew it when I saw the script too. And I just want this month to work, you know?"

I stepped into the room, a small smile forming on my face at her downtrodden look. "Mikka, if it takes me pissing in a cup in front of you a few times, I think we can get through it."

I started to unbutton my worn jeans as I walked closer to her. Her dark almond eyes widened to saucers. "What? You can't... that's not... Oh, my God! Close the door!"

She slapped her hands over her eyes and swerved around me to rush over to the door and slam it shut. While she did it, I followed through on my word and whipped my dick out to piss in the cup.

"Jay!" she screamed from behind me. "What the hell! That isn't what they asked you to do. When they said you needed to be watched, I'm pretty sure they meant your bathroom door, you idiot!"

"Nah." I screwed the cup's cap on and placed it on the table to zip back up. When I faced her, she was still covering her eyes. "I'm done, woman. Don't act like you haven't seen a million dicks after working in a porn shop."

"Replicas of dicks and real dicks are two completely different beasts."

"Are they?" I countered. "Tell me, which do you like more?"

"You're really asking me questions like this with your pee in a cup on the table?"

I smiled. "I'm not ashamed, baby. Nothing to be ashamed of, according to my therapist."

"I don't think your therapist knows we're talking about porn while drug testing you."

"I was just talking about vibrators and dildos. If you want to go down the porn road, we can. What kink are you into?" I shrugged.

Her face heated, and her reddened cheeks made my dick twitch in a way it shouldn't have. The porn talk wasn't helping matters.

What always surprised me about her was that she never backed down from the challenge. She lowered her chin and looked up at me like she'd been tested this way before. "I don't do porn, Jay. A little BDSM is fun to watch, sure, but let me be honest: a man that can deliver head-banging, screaming good sex and knows that some acting for a video never lives up to the real thing is so much better than porn."

Fuck me. I want her.

With that, she sauntered up to me, grabbed my piss off the table, and studied the cup. "All clear. Not that I had any doubts."

"You sure?" I asked, arms crossed.

She flashed the test lines on the cup at me. "Control strips here indicate that all is working and the T below it is testing your levels of all these drugs. Not one showed up. So, yes, I'm sure. And, yes, I'm sure I didn't have doubts."

"You had them," I shot back. "You tried to follow me out yesterday." I had seen how much it pained her when I told her to stay behind, like she didn't trust me, like she wanted me on a leash.

I tried to understand. Enough bad choices with drugs and the ones you loved, that trusted you, that had provided you support in the past, became the ones that had no trust in you at all, that kept you tethered rather than supported, hoping you wouldn't fly off the handle again.

Everyone had to doubt me at this point. I doubted myself some days.

"No, actually, I didn't doubt you. Me wanting to follow you was because I didn't want you to stay angry with me. I cared that we weren't getting along. I want us to be in a good place. I care about what you think of me. Probably too much. I didn't doubt you." She whispered the last part, but it spoke volumes to me. Mikka had seen me at my worst but kept pushing me to be my best.

A true friend did that, stuck it out with you when you were lying on the ground so miserable that no one else would be caught dead with you. Then they'd pick you up and still believe in you after all was said and done. They believed even when you didn't believe in yourself.

"I appreciate you, Meek."

"Do me a favor, then. Don't pee in front of me again."

She left me just as my phone started ringing.

"Hi, Mom."

"Jay, Lorraine called and said that your friend Mikka is the ray of sunshine her plants needed this fall."

"I told you: she's a good PA and an even better friend."

"Brey said she met her too. And Ray said she's stunning." My mom wasn't going to stop.

"Mom, I realize the whole town is probably talking about the one person who isn't from here. They're all going to have something to say about her."

"Well, you know I don't like secondhand chatter. I expect to meet her soon."

"It's not worth you coming to town."

I shut my eyes as the line went silent. She was navigating uncharted waters with me. My mother and I had always been close. I would take the name of "mama's boy" any day for that woman. She'd stood tall during rough times with my father, given her three growing boys unconditional love as we ran around eating her out of house and home.

She'd given me everything growing up, and I was rewarding her by fucking up. I needed time to make it right, not have her abandon her getaway where she was finally rekindling a romance with my father.

I didn't want to be her burden; I wanted to be the son that made her proud.

And if she came now, the town would bombard her with questions, push her to come to my rescue when it wasn't her fight. I needed to face them, not her.

She cleared whatever emotions she was experiencing from her throat before replying. "I won't come if that's what you need from me."

"Just for a while, Ma. I need space for a while. It'll be easier this way."

"You're crazy if you think that town's easy," she grumbled.

A laugh burst from me. "It's what I need, though."

"You know best." It wasn't condescending—she really meant it, and her words made me wonder how I ever ended up where I was.

I'd been given everything, and she'd never weighed down my road to success.

"I love you, Mom. Stay beautiful."

"I'll try. It's really not easy." Her laugh lifted my spirits. "Love you. Call me if you need me."

We hung up, and I took a moment to reflect before I went down to breakfast. I'd call my therapist later that evening and tell her this was part of the breakthrough every addict needed, a reminder of where they came from and why the drugs weren't worth the destruction of what they'd built for themselves, what their families and friends had helped to build with them.

I was lucky to see my treasure.

And I hoped the feeling of being grateful would become my new addiction.

LESSON OF THE DAY:
*Don't underestimate
something smaller
than you.*

CHAPTER FOURTEEN

MIKKA

LORRAINE, JAY, AND I fell into a routine for the next week. We ate breakfast together, worked on her yard after that, and then went about our day with little to no conflict. Every day Jay would run and Brey would meet him somewhere along the trail. I was usually out on the porch drinking tea with Lorraine when they returned.

I found Brey to be very polite but inquisitive. She watched me closely and always offered for us to get together at a later time. I never knew if she truly wanted that other than for the sake of protecting Jay and learning more about me.

Lorraine told me about a million stories of her life. She'd sat on Liberace's lap while he played the piano, she'd sung at clubs, she'd slept with one too many of the men in town, and she was sure she'd left one of her denture sets at Paul's house. She'd liked Paul but then Rosie from down the street seemed to have whiter dentures than before and she just knew Paul was a dog and Rosie was a thief.

I met both of them when we took a walk to the grocery store together. Lorraine just gave me the stink eye after Rosie smiled at us.

I was still laughing when we got back home and Lorraine pulled a few stray weeds angrily in the front yard.

Jay sauntered out and lifted a brow at my uncontrollable giggling. He took the groceries from my hands and asked, "What's so funny? Share with the class."

I started to tell the story but couldn't form a sentence in my hysterics, so Lorraine jumped in. "She finds it funny that that loosey-goosey Rosie has my teeth. If I had those dentures right now, woof! I'd be the best-looking 80-plus-year-old this town has ever seen. Those babies are much whiter than these. Rosie knows it too and that's why she's smiling as big as she is around town. Did you hear her try to talk?"

"I heard a bit of a slur." I shrugged and covered my mouth when her eyes bulged.

"A bit of one? Now I know you're on the same drugs Jay is because you and I both know she could barely form a sentence."

"Lorraine!" I cut her off, finally comfortable enough with her to chastise her when she got out of line. "You can't throw around Jay's addiction like that."

"Oh, honey, of course I can. Jay, you know I mean less harm than half the people talking in this town and across the United States."

He nodded with a small smirk on his face as he walked the groceries into the kitchen. "I know, Lorraine. Better to talk about it than sweep it under a bumpy rug."

"If you don't talk about it, put it out in the atmosphere and make it known, Mikka, people will make up their own story. And anyway, what's the shame in it? Jay lived a little. Now he's finding a way to restrict that living to a healthier lifestyle. I liked acid when I was his age." She blurted out her confession like Maria from the Sound of Music singing on top of the hill. She stood tall and proud with a smile on her face.

I glanced at Jay, who dropped a bag to hold his stomach as he laughed. The giggle that escaped from me couldn't be stopped. Laughing at their exploits with drugs wasn't something I ever thought I would do, but on Lorraine's sidewalk, after a week of spending time with them both, it felt right. It felt like I was shaking off problems, dusting off burdens, and lightening my mind of unnecessary worries.

I wiped my eyes. "I never, ever thought I'd laugh about that."

"Says the woman who grew up in a porn store," Jay tossed back as he righted himself to stare me down.

"You grew up in a porn store?" Lorraine asked, completely intrigued. Then she slapped her thigh. "Well, why have you been keeping that a secret? She's a locked box, Jay. Such a quiet little thing."

Jay stared at me for a few seconds, his eyes roaming over me. Then he murmured, so softly we barely heard him, "She's the tiniest she's ever been, Lorraine."

"Well, start bringing her meals," Lorraine threw out, not at all concerned with his statement.

I wasn't either. The last couple of months had taken a toll on me. I'd eaten less, done more meditation and yoga at night than ever before, and dropped weight because of it.

Jay nodded like he was putting together a puzzle, but Lorraine was stuck on one thing. "So, I need to know: what's the best vibrator?"

"Woman, have you no shame?" Jay snapped out of his thoughts to bump his shoulder against hers, teasing her.

"I don't need shame at my age. I need orgasms. Which is it, Mikka?"

"Hmm." I tapped my chin, actually wanting to give her the best information. It was something my mother ingrained in me. People should always be able to make themselves feel good, and we'd provided the tools. It was something to take pride in, not be ashamed of. "Depends on what you like. I like a slow build, and the mini wand has tons of different speeds and features. I have to say the longevity of it has been superb also. But if you're into a quick build-up and are ready for something that can hit everything all at once, including your a- and g-spot, go with a dual vibrator with clitoral suction. I can give you our porn shop's card to order if you want and..."

"Whoa." Jay held up his hands. "Why the hell are you open to giving her advice on toys but not me?"

"Because you didn't actually ever ask for advice, Jay."

"I'll genuinely ask if I can have you talk to me like that. I want more details, though, and say it slowly, seductively," he said and then winked at me.

I rolled my eyes at his antics.

Lorraine's eyes sparkled and crinkled at the corners as she said, "You want more because you got a pretty lady talking sex. But she's your friend, not your lover." Lorraine patted him on the back and gave him a look I couldn't quite put my finger on. "Anyway, Mikka, I've decided I'm never letting you leave. You are now my best friend and sexual advisor. I need to get dinner on the stove for us. Do me a favor, both of you, and look to see if any peter rabbits have been munching on my garden, will you?"

"Like Mikka's going to look for rodents here, Lorraine."

"Mikka should be looking for those varmints. She needs to learn what it means to be in a small town. Don't you want to be cut out for the town, Mikka?"

I wasn't sure how to respond to Lorraine. She'd cloaked her assessment of me in a dare and I wanted to prove to her I could do anything but looking for small animals that could bite me sounded insane. I was a city girl through and through. I would call pest control or something.

"Oh, forget it. Jay, get the rabbits out of my garden if they're in there." She slammed her screen door.

Jay left the groceries on the porch and walked around the side of the house where Lorraine had planted lettuce and tomatoes. He grumbled, "So much for this being a nice, relaxing bed and breakfast."

My heart started beating a little faster as I rounded the corner too. I'd never encountered a bunny in the wild. I tried to be brave, though. "So, one time our porn shop had a snake in it."

"Really?" Jay sounded interested as he walked through a row of small tomato vines. "You kill it?"

"Well, no. I called pest control."

He scratched the scruff of his face to hide what I am sure was a condescending smile.

"It was huge. And poisonous."

"Well, then, a bunny won't be too much for you to handle. Not that we should be working at all."

"Honestly, I'm surprised I'm actually having a good time at Lorraine's Little Lodge," I admitted as I followed him.

He nodded as he touched a plant that looked like it had been chewed through. "Hard not to love her and her crazy ways even if we are sifting through plants to find rodents."

"Are there really bunnies that come to—" I gasped and grabbed Jay's arm, pointing. Right in front of us was the smallest, cutest, furriest brown bunny with tiny ears that were tilting towards us.

"There's Peter Rabbit," Jay murmured.

The bunny stared at us.

We stared at it.

I could do this. It was the least I could do to prove myself to Jay, to Lorraine too.

I took a deep, steadying breath and did what any sane person would do if their garden was under attack. I launched toward the creature, arms wide, fully confident that I could outrun the little thing.

It darted like a lightning bolt, faster than a cheetah, I swear. It moved just out of my reach as I landed in a pile of wet soil.

The rabbit scurried toward Jay, too frightened to realize there was another opponent to outmaneuver.

"Jay! Get him!" I scrambled up, full of mud, but completely rejuvenated when I saw we could have him if Jay just dove in like I did.

"Get him?" He lifted his eyebrows and tilted his head.

I zig zagged as I saw the bunny, now darting back and forth after spotting Jay. "Yes!" I ran toward him again. I pointed toward Jay's feet. The rabbit was running straight toward him, obviously scared beyond comprehending that it was heading straight into danger. "We got him, now!"

I launched myself toward the bunny but ran into the legs of my infuriating friend. In all the commotion, Jay had decided not to move, not to make any attempt to catch Mr. Peter Rabbit, and the bunny proved to be much smarter than I expected. It took out its two opponents in one sprint as we both toppled over from my momentum.

Doubly dirty and empty handed, my competitive spirit a little hurt, my temper ignited. "What the hell, Jay?"

I was lying on top of him, and I sat to straddle him and slap him in the chest. I followed it up with some poking. "We could have had him! What were you doing?"

For a beat, he held a straight face. I'll give him that much. Then his stomach shook underneath me and he grabbed my hips as he shut his eyes and laughed his ass off.

"Are you freaking kidding me?" I growled and tried to get up.

His hands held me there, though, and I crossed my arms over my muddy chest to stare death lasers at him.

"Meek, you dove like you were in the Army and there was a landmine. For a bunny..." He cracked up again, unable to finish his thought.

"Lorraine has wanted to catch that rabbit for ages. It's been eating her garden for years, Jay!"

His eyes got wide and he looked at me seriously as he nodded along with my statement. "Yes, you're right. That one rabbit has eaten her garden for years even though I promise you these bunnies reproduce at an alarming rate and all of them look the same."

"No, but she said..." I sputtered out, unable to accept that my mission to win over the town and Lorraine was shot to shit.

"She just wanted us to shoo them away, Meek, not try to catch them."

"You acted like... didn't Lorraine say to catch him?"

He started laughing again.

I'd been through a lot in my life, I decided. I could talk porn for days to anyone. I could turn up at Jay's parties to shut them down. I could even sit at the doctor's office discussing bruised ribs.

But this—this was embarrassing. I'd misinterpreted everyone.

And him laughing under me didn't just frustrate me, it enraged me.

He blubbered out a half-ass "sorry" while trying to catch his breath.

"You're an ass," I told him.

"And you're a great bunny catcher." He shook his head in the dirt at his joke, completely happy with himself.

I couldn't help myself. The mud was right there. He deserved it. I grabbed a handful, one so big it got under my now ruined manicured nails and shoved it in his face. I even smeared it in for good measure.

"Meek!" He let go of my hips to scramble and wipe the dirt from his eyes.

He looked precisely how he should.

Ridiculous.

It was only fair; he normally looked like a god among gods. His chiseled jaw had a clump of soil caking it, and his blue eyes shimmered brightly to contrast the brown covering his face. His hair still curled a bit at the longer ends but had a sort of chocolate gel look now.

"You deserve it for making fun of me," I replied, holding up my dirty hands, not sure where to set them now.

His nod was slow, calculated, and just when I had decided it was definitely time to get up, he grabbed my hips again and spun us around.

As I screamed his name and we flipped over so that Jay was hovering over me, I knew I was in trouble. He didn't look worse than normal. He actually looked better. He was dirty and a little irritated. He looked like a man who'd done hard labor all day and was now ready to take me in the dirt.

The look he gave me was one I'd dreamt about, one I wasn't sure I'd ever see again.

The humor in his eyes bled out slowly, like he was realizing the same thing I was.

Our bodies fit like they'd known each other forever and had been waiting for this moment. I didn't know if we'd avoided what could have been for too long or if our energy had just shifted over the past few months, but I knew I wanted him.

I wanted him more than I'd ever wanted someone. Maybe Dougie and I weren't meant to be. Maybe our red strings weren't really connected. I didn't want to fail at our relationship but I didn't want to fail at experiencing real love either.

"Meek, I'm trying to find a reason not to kiss you. Give me one."

"We're friends?" I whispered, staring at his lips.

"Friends who've kissed before."

"We're just starting new lives?" I tried again, knowing that was true. We were both broken, both trying to get healthy, both completely unhealthy at the moment.

"What if I want you in that new life?" he said, his lips a whisper from mine. "I need to know that Dougie knows you two are done, Meek. Tell me that he knows."

I winced at his words, pushed myself farther into the mud, away from the only man that had ever made me feel completely safe. He'd wiggled his way through all the nonsense and found our weakness: Dougie. I hadn't fully cut him off. I'd told him I needed time, and time was only proving to solidify what I was scared of.

We were done.

I couldn't love a man who didn't keep me safe or that put me in harm's way, who inflicted harm upon me.

I closed my eyes and said the words I didn't want to say. It was admitting defeat, admitting I couldn't conquer something. I'd always believed that if you buffed something hard enough it would shine. If I studied hard enough, I would ace it; if I put in the work, I would accomplish it.

My relationship hadn't worked that way. I'd done something wrong, and Dougie was the first to pinpoint what it was.

"I need to call him," I murmured, eyes closed to hold back the tears.

Jay was working through what he wanted to say to me. I wished for a moment that he wouldn't say anything, that he'd just give in to what I wanted.

I wanted to kiss him again. I wanted to feel what I only felt with him, to disappear under him and escape to the place where everything felt right, felt safe, felt secure. My hands were at home on him, and my knees lifted on their own so he was wedged between them.

He groaned and then pushed off the ground to kneel next to me. The whoosh of air between us was immediate, a cold reminder that I wanted him close to me always.

He reached a hand out to help me up. "Let's keep figuring our shit out, Meek. No need to make more problems than we already have."

I nodded but felt my stomach contort like someone had squeezed it and then twisted it, trying to drain me of all my feelings for Jay. It was painful, uncomfortable, and definitely concerning. He'd said the thing I kept repeating to myself: we didn't need more conflict; we were a load of complicated problems already.

Jay needed to focus on his movie; he needed to stay sober. And I'd done a terrible job so far of making sure he had less stress so he could do just that.

Still, losing his body on mine, thinking of him drifting further from me or going on a date with another woman, had me thinking I'd do just about anything to have one more conflict in my life.

Which meant I had to suck it up and accept one of my first fails ever.

I'd failed with Dougie, and I knew that loss was going to be very, very difficult to swallow.

LESSON OF THE DAY:
Sometimes strangers have the strangest way of knowing you better than you know yourself.

CHAPTER FIFTEEN

MIKKA

"**I'M NOT GIVING** up, Mikka," his voice rasped over the phone. Hearing it for the first time in about a week and a half jarred me. I'd never been away from Dougie this long and when he called again after all the texts he'd sent, I knew it was time to answer.

"I don't like to think of it as that," I replied. I actually hated thinking of it like that. It made me want to fly back to LA and claw my way through the relationship just because the sheer frustration of not being the best at something crippled me.

"Then don't. You've been the best at everything. You were top of your class, you took a job with a top agency and you PA for a top actor, baby. You never once gave up when you were pushing through college and working. We've been through it all and giving up on our relationship now..." He paused for the full effect and sighed.

"That's not you. You and I can do this. This is a rough patch, and I need you home to get through it."

His words fueled something in me. They reminded me that Dougie knew me, inside and out. He knew how to manipulate me, mold me, and sculpt me into what he wanted.

I hated that I'd let it get this far.

"I can't come home, Dougie. I just can't." The first tear slipped. For him. For us. For the life we'd had and the life I'd dreamed of us living.

"You need to get your ass home." The deep, guttural command he spat into the phone shocked fear straight back into me. It flew through my veins like ice, freezing over my confidence at handling everything and frosting up my mind so that I couldn't think straight.

"Dougie, please..." I pleaded with him as if he ruled over me, and my body believed it. I even went to stand over my suitcase.

"Please, what? I let you stay there for a fucking week. You keep acting like you're out there fixing something. If you don't get your ass back here, I'll make sure you're so broken, no one will be able to fix you."

His threat hammered home the last nail in the coffin that held our relationship. He'd reminded me of the rules I had with Jay: I wasn't broken. I was strong. I'd always been strong.

And maybe I was stronger after having to survive him too.

"No." One word. It quaked out of me, but it was a resounding declaration that gained momentum in my soul.

"No?" His voice went up ten octaves.

"No, Dougie. I'm done with us. I'm coming home in three weeks to move everything, but we can't go on like this. I'm unhappy, and so are you."

"Look, baby. Be reasonable, okay? This is stressful for both of us." He paused. "I won't hurt you again." He said the words low, like someone might be listening, like he was ashamed to speak the situation into existence.

Truthfully, I was. I looked around as if someone might hear the conversation.

"I know you won't hurt me again," I whispered back.

I didn't know though. I didn't remember when I'd lost faith over the past month because I'd believed him the first time he'd said it wouldn't happen again.

I believed him the second.

And the third.

Somewhere, my belief died. I was only realizing now that I had accepted his violence as a part of our relationship I would just have to cover up.

It was unhealthy.

And I was far enough away that a small amount of light shined through, making everything clear to me. I didn't have to live this way, nor did I want to. There were other men out there, other possible futures that I deserved to see. The cloud that hovered over us had been blown away by distance, and I saw so much more clearly now.

"I'm sorry, Dougie. I love you, but I can't be in love with you anymore."

"Is this because of him?" His voice turned; the edge was back, cutting our cordial conversation short like a sharp knife slicing through a tender heart. As fast as a conman switches personalities, he warped into the man I feared. Him jumping back and forth from sweet to vicious was a clear sign that he wasn't controlling his abusive tendencies. It was a sign I'd missed for so long. My heart sped up as if he was in the room with me, as if I was physically in danger again.

I heard a creak from the next room and took a deep breath, reminding myself that Jay was just in the room over, that I was about to have dinner with him and Lorraine half a country away from Dougie.

"No. It's because I've come to terms with what I need. That isn't you." My voice shook along with the hand holding the phone.

"I'll make you see that it is. We haven't come this far so you can fuck it all up, Mikka. You get your ass home now."

I glanced at my suitcase, lying empty in the corner of the room. The urge to listen and do as I was told was there. I shoved it down, pushed it away.

"Please pack your things. I'm cancelling our lease."

He started to yell something into the phone, but I hung up.

I silenced and threw the phone away from me like it was a hot potato. Then I collapsed on the bed and listened to the fall bugs outside my window. I'd started to enjoy the sound, so different from city cars. The scent of vegetation coming through the open window was much richer than in LA too.

Did small town life fill everyone's bones with a sense of relief? Could I fit in here, stay, and become part of a place that was a blip on everyone else's radar but was becoming everything on mine?

"Mikka!" Lorraine's voice carried from downstairs. "Delilah wants some help down the street. We need to go."

Of course Lorraine didn't ask if I was available to go. She expected my help, and for some reason my heart warmed at the idea. She'd taken me under her wing and was spreading me around the community like I could fit right in.

"I'll be right down," I said loudly and jumped from the bed.

When Jay asked if he could tag along to help, Lorraine shook her head, saying she needed him to watch dinner.

Out on the sidewalk with the light of the setting sun on our skin, she glanced at me. "I heard your phone conversation."

"Excuse me," I stuttered, my world tilting. What had she heard? Would she tell others?

"Don't look at me like I'm a gossip. Of course I'm not going to share your business." She smiled at me, the wrinkles crinkling on her face. "Yet."

"Lorraine—" I started.

She cut me off. "I told you my husband died. He died nice and slow, might I add. And I didn't enjoy any one of those excruciating moments of him screaming on his deathbed."

"I'm so sorry," I murmured, not knowing where she was going with the conversation.

"You'd think I would have, considering how he threw a good punch every time he drank or got mad at me."

I halted midstride. I grabbed her hand without realizing and squeezed. The woman wasn't much bigger than me. Her kind eyes and high cheekbones were still absolutely stunning, even with her gray hair and hunched over figure. She tried to keep up appearances by curling her hair every day and wearing gold studs. She was the fabulous embodiment of life and the wisdom you gained by surviving it.

"I'm sorry you had to go through that, Lorraine," I said softly. "It's not right and, quite honestly, I don't understand how anyone could ever get mad at you."

"Oh, really?" She cackled and pointed toward Delilah's shop. It smelled divine right outside the pink doors and cotton candy colored letters to match read above, "Delilah's Treats."

Lorraine pushed through the doors and yelled toward the back door, "Delilah! Mikka here is confused as to why my dead husband used to knock me around."

A woman not much taller than me but about the same age pushed through a white swinging door smiling. Her rosy cheeks and big doe eyes along with her wider hips and the apron sitting atop them made her the picture-perfect owner of the shop. She stood behind a window counter filled with intricate chocolate truffles and swiped at some melted chocolate on her face. Her loose bun was the same color as her treats.

She shook her head at Lorraine after glancing at me. "Lorraine, that man would have knocked you around even more for putting this woman here on the spot."

"You're scolding me?" Lorraine asked, placing her hand on her chest as if affronted. "Mikka deserves it. She keeps trying to hide secrets from me while staying in my house. She thought I wouldn't listen in on her conversation with her now ex-boyfriend."

Delilah's eyes grew even bigger as she put both hands on the clear counter. Then she glared at Lorraine. "You're intolerable at times!"

"Yeah, yeah." Lorraine waved her off. "Meet Mikka, porn shop aficionado and Jay's mediocre PA. She can stir chocolate while I do the frosting."

Delilah came around the counter and stuck a hand out. "Sorry for her. I'm really happy you're here to help. I pay in as much dessert as you can eat."

"Pleasure to be dragged around town by this lovely woman." I returned her handshake and instantly felt warmer from it.

Delilah proceeded to walk me through the steps of melting different chocolate chips and mixing them so they had the right colors and flavors. She wanted peanut butter added sometimes, or molasses, or caramel, or vanilla. She dropped lavender in sometimes even and my mouth watered through the whole evening.

When we finally took a break to rest, I moaned into a lavender and caramel one that she'd frosted with gold tips. "This is so, so divine."

"Not as divine as leaving that abusive lump of a man behind, I bet," Lorraine grumbled around her own truffle.

"Lorraine!" Delilah yelped at her.

For a moment, I didn't know how to respond. Not one person had guessed Dougie's behavior except Jay. I wondered if it was because I had hid it so well or because no one had cared enough to notice.

Lorraine stared at me. Her eyes dug deep like she was trying to shovel out all my secrets. Then her wrinkled hand with two turquoise rings on it grabbed mine and squeezed like I had hers. "Don't worry. I know how hard it is to admit the first time. You'll remember soon enough you're not the one who should feel ashamed."

I shook my head at her and then at Delilah who moved in to hug me. I didn't realize I was crying until Lorraine lifted her hand to wipe away my tears.

LESSON OF THE DAY:
*Be honest with
your feelings and
they will be honest
with you too.*

CHAPTER SIXTEEN

MIKKA

THE NEXT NIGHT, I threw on a pink blouse that cut low in front and squeezed into some dark jeans for dinner. I finger combed my hair in the mirror, wondering if everyone would be able to see my failed relationship on my face.

I didn't hide losing well. I remember crying in my bedroom for days when I found out Sarah Bell had gotten a better grade than me on a test in 8th grade. My mother didn't comfort me; she told me that if I couldn't be the best in school, I should find something else to be good at. So, I doubled down to prove to her I could do it. I passed up opportunities at friendships, underage drinking parties, and maybe even a boyfriend or two in order to stay at the very top of my class.

My relationship had been somewhat the same. She'd told me I should find the best in a partner and that Dougie wasn't it. So, I doubled down on him. I pushed us so hard, we broke. At first, I only saw myself as the one to blame. But Jay kept saying there were two in a relationship and Dougie had become the slacker in ours.

Still, admitting we'd lost was something I didn't know how to do. I just didn't know how well I would be able to hide the feeling of having failed either.

I made my way downstairs and heard not just Jay but another man's voice. When I turned the corner into the dining room, I looked toward the kitchen but couldn't see past Lorraine busying herself at the table.

"Grab these napkins and set them next to the plates, please," she said.

I counted four place settings. "Who's joining us for dinner?"

"Well, I'm trying to do us all a favor." She set down the last glass and poured large amounts of red wine into each.

"What kind of favor?" My voice held skepticism. Lorraine had done a lot of little things lately to push Jay and me together. Two nights before, she'd made a candlelit dinner and thrown rose petals on my bed. Jay and I had laughed, but I'd felt a tension between us building. I didn't want awkwardness in our friendship and knew we'd crossed too many lines for it to disappear overnight. Still, Lorraine's blatant attempts at matchmaking were worsening things.

"You've been quiet in your room for most of the day. Moping around with your tail between your legs." She walked over and smoothed down a piece of my hair as she studied my face. "You're not healing, missy. And so we have to do something about that."

"For an 80-plus-year-old, you seem to be very perceptive," I countered.

"You bet I am." She gave my cheek a good pat before she turned to busy herself again. "Brady lives in town. He's the hottest guy I know your age, I promise. You helped me and so I'm helping you."

"Helping me with what?"

"Helping you get laid. Get an orgasm. Something to loosen the tension in your shoulders, girlie. It's making me uncomfortable." She leaned over the table to whisper to me, "He gets around. He'll go for you. I promise. I'm sorry that Jay's being so uptight. I thought the roses would work, I swear."

She mumbled her last sentence as she walked back into the kitchen, leaving me with my mouth agape.

Jay and Brady walked out of the kitchen laughing before I could recover.

Brady stood as tall as Jay and had a chest as wide as his friend too. Their laughs rolled through the room, rich and warm, like hot chocolate for the cold soul. I grasped the back of a wooden chair to keep from falling over as my knees buckled at all the testosterone floating around.

Brady's hair was much lighter than Jay's and curled a bit more too. His blond locks were full, ready to be mussed, and they framed his face well. The man gave Jay a run for his money. I had to give Lorraine that.

When I glanced her way, she winked so dramatically the whole room probably caught the old bat's antics.

"Do I want to know?" Jay asked.

I shook my head and grabbed a glass of wine. I handled it slowly because Lorraine had filled it to the brim.

Brady eyed it. "She use two or three bottles to fill all these?"

I held back a smile and shrugged. "I'm Mikka. Nice to meet you."

"Ah, yes. You're the beautiful Asian woman everyone keeps talking about."

I lifted a brow. "That how they describe people here?"

It was a good jolt of reality, letting me know I didn't belong in this town.

"By ethnicity? By appearance? Sure, but honestly, they describe you as a million different other things too. You just have to have more than a one-sentence conversation with them. I can't be bothered to do that."

"A man of few words?" I asked coyly. Had I really said that? I felt like Brady could handle it, that it was the type of communication he responded to.

"A man of few words for gossip. I figured, instead of that, I'd stop by and see for myself."

"Good thing you did too," Lorraine yelled from the kitchen. "I made your favorite: Chicken noodle soup for the cool night."

She brought the soup through and ladled out a large helping for each of us. We sat and made small talk, mostly Brady asking me questions and Jay sitting silently as he sipped his wine and took in our conversation.

"So, you're Jay's personal assistant? What does that entail?" he asked.

Jay jumped in, his tone much more serious than it had been before. "Everything and anything you can think of."

I shifted a little in my seat and folded my napkin. "I'm not sure if it's everything. I know his schedule, handle his endorsements, and attend meetings with him to make sure he's taken care of. That sort of thing."

"Seems like a lot," Brady said into his food.

"It is. And she's downplaying it. The woman has been my crutch since I moved to LA," Jay replied and his tone was genuine, like I meant the world to him.

I smiled. "We've been there for each other."

Lorraine killed the mood with a loud cough that was completely fake. "Mikka probably should have had more of a handle on Jay's partying or they wouldn't be here. But the cat's out of the bag and I'm sure even with you not gossiping, Brady, you've heard. Jay's in recovery and Mikka's stuck here with him. You need to take her out so she can get some fresh air away from the boy."

If I could have kicked the old lady in the shin under the table, I would have. As Brady laughed into his napkin, Jay's face got more and more red. "Mikka's not gonna just go out with some stranger, Lorraine."

"Stranger? Man, you've known me since high school," Brady tossed back. "When you were in high school, I brought a damn ladder to Sandy's so you could climb out her window when her parents showed up. I was the only one there to bail your ass out."

"Jax should have come to help me out," Jay grumbled.

"Yeah, but instead, the stranger came." Brady crossed his arms and stared down Jay.

My friend sat there struggling with something. I didn't know if he was frustrated that Lorraine was making me look like his keeper or if he just didn't want me to go. "You're a stranger to her. Plus, knowing your damn antics makes it even worse. She's not interested in going out on the town with someone like you."

"Why? You just told me you took Sandy out the other night. We all know she's willing to go out for just one thing. If I wanted that, I would have called her. Instead, I'm trying to get to know the new city girl. No bad intentions."

"Your intentions are always bad, dumbass," Jay threw back. The name flew off his tongue like they tossed it around casually, and Brady didn't even flinch when he said it. He actually smiled like they'd done this dance before. "Mikka's here to work, not play."

I couldn't believe he was sitting there speaking for me as if I wasn't in the room and was just an employee that he got to control.

Lorraine let out a "woo-ee" under her breath and I felt it deep in my soul. Maybe more than I ever had. I was finally without Dougie, without someone trying to control my every move, and didn't need another man doing just that. "Um, hi, Jay." I waved and snapped my fingers at him. "I'm right here. I can speak for myself."

"Don't entertain his bullshit, Meek. You're not going out with him. He's trying to piss me off by sniffing around where his damn nose shouldn't be."

I read into his words more than I should have. My stomach rolled at the thought that just days before another man had tried to control me, tried to tell me exactly what to do and take away my say. "Who says I'm not? I need a night out."

"Yeah, Jay, who says she's not? She needs a night out." Brady mimicked me, and his white smile spread so far across his face, I swear it would have been the width of the room if he could have made it that way.

Jay studied me, like he couldn't quite read my thoughts.

Good because they were all bad.

I needed a night out because my body heated all day at the idea of his proximity to me. It'd only been two days since I told Dougie we were over and every minute, I wondered when Jay would ask me again if I was with him.

Maybe we'd just been in the moment. Maybe this wasn't what he wanted.

I was fine with that. More than fine. We wanted to protect our friendship anyway by not indulging in anything more.

That meant that what Brady proposed was perfect. I needed a distraction from Jay and the relationship I'd just ended.

Brady was tall, built like an athlete. He knew how to hold a conversation and seemed as interested in me as I was in him. There wouldn't be any strings. He knew I lived in LA.

Jay's hand was on my thigh under the table before I could think of anything further. The shock of it flew straight to my core. "Babe, if you want a night out, I'll take you out."

I stared at him, the look in his eyes so full of concern, I almost gave in. This was Jay though, the man that would do anything for his friends.

I was falling for a man who'd put me back in the friendzone. We were both sober, we weren't drinking and losing our inhibitions.

I crossed my legs so that his hand fell away. "I'm not looking to go out with a friend." My words implied exactly what Brady and I wanted.

"I know the night scene in this city isn't much but there's a festival in a few days. I can take you, we can go through the fun house, have some funnel cake, see if Lorraine's pie wins the blue ribbon this year. Spoiler alert: it wins every year."

As if on cue, Lorraine waltzed back in with an apple pie in a brown bag. She set it down and ripped the bag from it to present us with a pie that had caramelized spun brown sugar arching above it like a carriage holding a delectable treat. It smelled like cinnamon and apples, like autumn in the warmest way. "I win because mine's the best."

"I'm not arguing that, Lorraine. Rosie might because she knows Paul is sweet on you. Either way, I like yours best." Brady blatantly sweet talked the woman as she cut him a massive slice. He winked at me as she set it down on his plate. The warm feeling of having an admirer was back, like I wasn't whole yet but I could get there. I knew it would take time, but having his attention might push me a little further on my way.

"Well, the festival sounds nice," I said as I cut a piece of pie.

"You should all go, then," Lorraine chimed in. "Brady can swing by and help us pack up some of the pies."

"I'll do that," he said around a mouthful of pie.

Jay was unusually silent. Restraining myself from glancing over at him, I took my first bite of the pie. My concerns of whether or not Jay was frustrated with Brady coming melted away. My concerns over Dougie and my relationship ending melted away. My concerns about going back to LA and finding my own life melted away.

All I could wrap my mind around was the sweet taste of fall on my lips. It was like I'd disappeared into a place where colorful leaves floated through the sky and the scent of caramel apples filled the air while someone wrapped me up in a comfy blanket.

"Well, I know Mikka will vote for my pie too." Lorraine chuckled. "It sounds like you think it's as good as your mini wand."

"What's a mini wand?' Brady asked.

"A vibrator."

"Oh, jeez," I mumbled.

Lorraine continued. "Mikka grew up in a porn shop. An official one. I looked it up on the world wide web."

I smiled because I knew my mother's site was a precise representation of how pristine and perfect her shop was. She and I had spent boatloads of time and money working with web designers to make sure her store was represented correctly and that people had a great online shopping experience.

When Lorraine offered to pull up the site on her phone, I was surprised at how savvy she was. She announced that she'd favorited the site. Jay snickered next to me and nudged my leg with his.

He sat there, completely relaxed and I wondered if I'd imagined the tension between Brady and him. He even jumped into the conversation to poke fun at my mom's shop. Then he concluded with saying it had shaped a fine woman and was a really lucrative business.

Coming from any Stonewood, I knew that was a compliment. Brady nodded too, like he didn't take the statement lightly. When we wished him goodbye, he hugged me and whispered in my ear, "Looking forward to getting you to myself for a few hours at the fest."

I thought I heard Jay grunt but when I turned around he was waving goodbye to his friend and wishing him well.

We helped Lorraine clean and I got a phone call soon after.

Our company wanted another drug test.

After Lorraine excused herself to go to her downstairs portion of the home, I rinsed off and knocked on Jay's door. It was cracked, like his life was open to the world but I didn't want to invade his privacy. Movie stars didn't have that much to begin with and his last name earned him even less.

"Door's open."

I stuck my arm in with the drug test package in my hand. "I come out of obligation to my job."

I was pretty sure I heard him sigh, but when his door swung open, any frustration had disappeared. He looked like he had in his first movie. It was a rom-com where he and the actress cozied up with him shirtless in every other scene. With just some sweats on and no shirt, I knew I needed to get the test done quickly.

He took it from my hands without really meeting my eyes. "Bob call you?"

The mood between us was different. Jay didn't crack a joke or try to ease the discomfort of the situation. The question hung in the air as he tore open the bag.

"Um, yes," I said quietly. "Just a minute ago."

"Talked to my therapist just a minute ago too."

I waited for him to elaborate because he wouldn't have said it if he didn't mean something by it.

"She thinks I have to let my emotions unfold sometimes without worrying about keeping those close to me happy. Sometimes I have to make myself happy."

I narrowed my eyes. What was he trying to say? There was something deeper there. He wanted me to understand that something was coming. I just didn't know what it was.

He turned to go into his en suite bathroom.

When he returned, the cup was full and the test strips showed that it was clean.

I put my hand on his shoulder. "You're doing amazing."

I wanted us to get back to who we were before the kiss in LA. I wanted him to smile like there weren't twenty different things on his mind, a rollercoaster of feelings, none of which we would want to experience ourselves.

He nodded, put his hand on top of mine and squeezed. "I'm getting there."

He grabbed the cup and took it to the bathroom to dispose of. I glanced around to see what he had been doing. His script was on the bedside table and some of the takes were on the TV screen.

Working.

Jay had always, always worked harder than he played. I had wondered when he was getting it done because he hadn't ask me to read the last part of the script they would be filming. The main actress would be flying in soon, and the film crew hoped to get their scenes taped in two weeks' time.

When he walked back in, I pointed at the pages. "You're working?"

"On the scenes we'll do here."

"I should help you." I grabbed the packet and looked over the lines. I'd read them all. I knew the movie inside and out. I hadn't provided much feedback because the script was better than anything I could have written. I was in awe of it.

"Not giving me an option?" He chuckled a bit. "You love that script."

"It's a good script." I acted nonchalant as I sat down on the bed and reread the part they were filming here. "Do you think Lela can handle this?"

"She's more brilliant than people give her credit for."

"God, this scene is going to wreck people."

"'I'm going to kill him.'" Jay paced back and forth, and his whole body morphed into a man on the brink of rage, so different from the type of character he usually played. I felt the edge in his voice, the intensity in his walk, the urge to inflict bodily harm.

I immediately knew women would react to him in a whole new way after seeing him as this character.

"'You don't have any ground to stand on.'" I glanced at the paper. "'I want your love. Not your protection.'"

"'You get both. Always.'" He walked up to me, pushed himself between my legs and lifted my chin. "'I'll die for you.'"

He paused to stare down at me with a look of love, of complete sacrifice, like he was giving his whole heart to me.

He was just acting. They were lines from a movie, a movie written by someone else. He was repeating words he'd memorized, looking at me the way he would look at the actress.

Still.

I got lost in them. I found myself swimming in the blue, blue color of his eyes, treading through all the emotions he felt. Being on the receiving end when he opened up the amusement park of his soul was like being pummeled by a waterfall of pain and love and determination. He pushed all those feelings onto me with just a look.

Then he whispered, "I'm going to die for you. You and I already know it. I intend to take that man with me when I do."

He was Brad Pitt in Fight Club, Denzel in Training Day. He was bordering on crazy, definitely lethal, and hotter than he'd ever been. A dangerous man ready to protect the woman he loved.

"I literally can't look away from you," I whispered.

He held my gaze for a moment, looked down at my mouth, and then stepped back to wipe a hand over his face. He relaxed after a few breaths, and then a real smile flew onto his face. "You think I got that line?"

I could see that line going down in history; I felt it in my bones, and goosebumps spread over my skin just thinking about it. "You crushed it. Oh my God!" I shivered. "It's going to be so good. You have to make sure they film it from the woman's point of view, camera angled up at you."

"You can be on set and tell them yourself." Jay waved me off like it wasn't a big deal.

I slumped onto the bed and stretched my arm out, shaking the script a little for him to take. "You know it doesn't work that way. I'm your PA."

"You're more than that. You need to step in at some point. This is the best opportunity. The director will be there. He wants this movie to be the greatest."

I shrugged, suddenly feeling like Jay was peeling back my skin to see the blood that gave me life. He was seeing my vulnerability. "PA's don't offer advice. But you need him to portray your anger and sexuality from her point of view. And when she takes control when you have sex that night, it needs to be from your point of view, the camera angled so that she's the one finally dominating. It will be an amazing display of her controlling him, him submitting to her, but also him masterminding everyone else. So, in the end, she's the one who controls through him."

Jay stopped writing. "Our director is going to love you. I'm not writing that down. You can tell him."

"Jay." I rolled my eyes and got up. "I love you for trying."

"I don't just try," he growled.

"Fine." It wasn't worth arguing with him. "I'm going to bed."

"Don't want to go to Ray's?"

"Do you?" I asked because I would go with him if he wanted to. It wasn't so that I could watch him either, I admitted to myself. My intentions had turned selfish.

"Mikka, you don't have to come with me every time."

"I know," I rushed to say. Then I took a breath. "I know. You just went out the other night and I...I wondered where you were. It's easier for me, not you, if I go when you go."

"I didn't go to Ray's that night. You know that now."

I nodded, starting to back away from the conversation and retreat to my bedroom. I didn't want to hear that he went to dinner with Sandy. My words came out more accusatory than I intended. "Right, you went to see Sandy."

"You jealous, little one?" He sat down on the bed and leaned back on his hands, his arms straight to hold up his muscular chest.

"Of course not. In the past couple years, I've seen you in just about every position and cleaned up plenty of your one night stands."

"Doesn't mean you enjoyed it. Did you wish you were one of them?"

"I never wanted to be a one night stand of yours, Jay." I meant those words too. His friendship was so much more important, and every one of his conquests of the night ended up never talking to him again.

"I never wanted you to be one either," he shot back. "Sandy would only ever have been a one night stand if I'd done anything with her. You're a million times more important than that."

I didn't know if he meant that I was his friend and that's why I was important or if I could potentially be something more. I shouldn't even have been thinking about it.

"Good. Friends should be more important than the women you leave behind."

He laughed but it was hollow. Something else was on his mind as his eyes tracked up and down my body. "Yes. I wonder if friends should be as jealous as I was of Brady tonight."

"Jay," I whispered to stop him but he didn't let me.

"He better not be more than just a one night stand, Meek. That idea alone makes me want to shut that door behind you and lock you in here with me until the fest is over. Does Dougie know you're going out with him?"

"I'm going to the fest with all of you, not just Brady." I was skirting around answering his question. I'd already told him I was breaking up with Dougie, but I didn't want to admit the failure again. I was free but I wasn't sure about anything anymore. Being free meant floundering around for what I really wanted. It meant I wasn't on a set plan ahead.

Jay was the last person I wanted to admit that to. He saw me as someone who overcame every battle and I told him I would overcome this one too. "Same difference, Meek. We both know what Brady wants. Mostly to irritate me, I'm sure."

"Are you saying he's merely hanging out with me to irritate you, that I'm not good enough for his attention on my own merit?"

"I swear if you weren't tied to a man right now, I'd show you how easy it is for you to have any man's undivided attention. Shit, I'd probably have committed my noncommittal ass to you a long time ago had you ever been available."

I waved his comment away, trying not to hear it or let it spark hope somewhere deep down where I didn't need hope right now. "You don't commit your ass to anyone. Let's be honest, your attention was definitely elsewhere with Sandy the other night." It would ground us both to say the truth out loud.

He licked his lips and nodded slowly. He got up from the bed and took a step toward me. "When's the last time you talked to Dougie?"

I stepped back toward the door. This line of questioning was going to get us in trouble fast. "It doesn't matter."

"Oh, it matters."

"Why?" I took two more steps back as he took another toward me.

"Because you're stalling. Are you scared of us, Meek?"

"I don't know what you're talking about."

"You do. You're one of the smartest people I know, and I come from a long line of smart businessmen. I'm starting to realize that Dougie was a lot of horrible things, but he may have served as a barrier between us the past couple of weeks."

"Why would I ever need that?" I threw back at him. He couldn't possibly know what I'd just figured out: Dougie had been a tool to help me keep Jay at arm's length, to stop myself falling over the edge like so many before me I didn't want to love him and his charm. I could not let a kiss or two turn into something more.

Because I didn't know if I could handle losing more.

I worried that the loss of Jay would hurt more than the bruises Dougie inflicted or the failure of our relationship. If Jay didn't fall for me as I knew I would fall for him, the wreckage would be catastrophic. Epic. Devastating.

"You and I both know why. We've always worked well together. We're always in sync. The day I met you on the beach should have been the day I made you mine."

"I had a boyfriend."

"Had or have?"

"We shouldn't be having this conversation right now," I mumbled as I looked away.

"Woman, you don't make mistakes with words."

"I definitely can make mistakes with words," I countered, but it wasn't true. My mother had taught me Chinese and English and hired speech pathologists to make sure no one would be able to tell that I was the daughter of an immigrant. It was another way to ensure I'd be the best, and she told me daily that she expected that.

He shook his head like he couldn't believe I was trying to lie to him. "When did you end it?" he asked softly.

Maybe I felt the need to cry because he said it so delicately or maybe because he rested his forehead on mine before I could answer.

Why was this the part that hurt so much?

My throat burned as I took a deep breath. My voice shook along with my chin as I answered, "He called me. I answered."

I didn't say the words. I didn't admit the failure just yet.

"Is it over?"

"Jay, can we just…"

"Answer me. Yes or no?"

"Yes."

JAY: *I've never been ready for a relationship. And now that I'm considering one, I wonder if that's a sign that I am.*

THERAPIST: *Is she filling a hole for something else?*

JAY: *Yes, but she's not a drug I plan to quit if I start.*

THERAPIST: *Then, be sure before you do.*

CHAPTER SEVENTEEN

JAY

THAT ONE WORD. I saw how it broke her to admit it. Even if they weren't meant to be, even if the guy was a complete asshole who'd hurt her more in the last couple of months than any other individual she'd ever met, I knew how hard it was for my little pebble to admit to what she thought was a failure. She needed to see it would be one of her greatest accomplishments, instead.

I didn't hesitate any longer. I took her mouth in mine. I should have waited—she needed time to heal—but I realized I'd been waiting since the day I'd met her.

Three years was a long-ass time to wait.

She tasted even better than she had the first time I'd kissed her. This time, she tasted free and right and like the sweet ChapStick she always rubbed on her lips.

We explored each other's mouths and she gripped my bare shoulders like she was holding on for dear life. I did the same with her waist.

I knew it was life and death for me now. Mikka was my new addiction. One I wasn't going to get over or give up.

I pulled her shirt from her body. That porcelain skin was my perfection now. I ran my lips along every inch I hadn't touched before. I worked off her pants and panties before she even considered stopping.

Our stars had finally aligned; the string that tethered us had finally untangled. "Yue Lao did tie you to me," I murmured into her ear as I carried her to the bed.

She shook her head but brought my lips to hers again. Nothing outside of the room mattered anymore. We tasted each other and explored every sensitive spot between us.

I dragged my hand over her stomach and ran my thumb over her clit. She moaned, as if she'd been waiting for me to do that for as long as I'd wanted to.

"I'm going to have to do this with you every night," I murmured into her neck. She gasped as I slid two fingers into her. "Are you on birth control?"

She rode my fingers and nodded. I curled them inside her and she arched under me. Her long, silken hair was spread over the pillow as she screamed and threw her head back.

The iron headboard banged against the wall and I smiled down at her, watching her orgasm take over.

My control snapped as I felt her core tighten around my fingers. I slid them out, told to her that I was clean, and slid into her in one swift motion.

Our eyes met. Our worlds collided.

If it was an old man on the moon who'd put us together, he'd done it right. The feeling of being in her, having her around me, and being one with her almost did me in with one thrust. My heartbeat was as wild as my need for her.

We moved together, taking each other to a place where no one else would ever go but us. It was our small world in that room and we were on lockdown away from all our problems.

I reached a high I didn't think existed as I came and she screamed my name.

Afterwards, I wrapped us up in the blanket and we lay there in silence as I held her to me.

When my phone vibrated, Mikka jumped and shot up, a sheet still wrapped around her chest.

I smiled at the look of fear in her eyes, like she was a deer caught in the headlights.

"We're friends, Jay. This was... oh, Lord. A friends-with-benefits misstep? Neither of us are ready for anything new."

I turned my mouth down and shrugged a little. "Sure. Nothing new, but you're not new to me, Pebble."

"A relationship between us would be new," she clarified. "We both need to just back off and focus on ourselves, on being healthy."

"Sex is healthy," I pushed back, happy to irritate her. I knew this wouldn't be just sex between us, I knew she was going to be much, much more. "You of all people should know that. I think it even says that on King Chang's website."

"Fair." She narrowed her eyes and slid from the bed to find her clothes. "Sex is healthy. Sex with random people for fun is very healthy when you aren't healthy enough to commit to someone, which is why going to a festival tomorrow with Brady is a great idea for me."

It took a minute for her words to sink in. I'm pretty sure that by the time they did, my jaw had dropped. "Are you insinuating that you're going to go fuck around with some other guy after what we just did?"

She shrugged into her shirt after pulling on her pants and crossed her arms like it would ward me off. "I'm just saying neither of us can commit to anything right now and you're right: sex is good. It's a way to release stress. So..."

"So, you'd be fine with me inviting Sandy?" I sat up and threw her game back in her face.

"That would be a great idea." Her voice was high with her retort.

"Bullshit."

"Jay, let's just focus on having fun over the next few days. We'll help Lorraine make her pies and forget about this, okay?" Suddenly, she looked so tired. I wanted to wrap her up and pull her back into bed with me. She needed to unwind and I knew more than a few ways to get her to do that. "Baby, look at me."

When she did, her dark eyes held mine with determination in them, but behind it was fatigue. "Yes?"

"We're not forgetting."

She sighed and I had to tell myself it was with relief.

"You're doing great, little one. It's only been two days since you broke things off with him. Breathe and know it will get better. We'll get better together."

"And you know this how?" she whispered.

"Because the first few days without using were the hardest. Then it got better and better. Addictions fight you; they claw at your insecurities. Then they become these rabid, feral, fucking vicious monsters when you try to ignore them. It's their way of fighting their hardest before they die. If you're hurting, it's because your addiction to saving your relationship with him or your addiction to being with him—I'm not sure which—is dying."

She wrung her hands and then nodded. She made her way out the door, but before she closed it behind her, she turned to say, "It's the first. It was always the first. I figured that out the second you kissed me. I've never felt with him what I do with you."

She closed the door before I could reply. I started after her but then stopped. We needed the night or a couple to work things out.

I already knew what conclusion she'd drawn.

We were addicts, and addicts didn't overcome addiction, they just found new ones. If someone could find a new habit, a new healthy obsession, they'd found their way out. There were the thrill seekers who would find a new adrenaline rush: rock climbing or swimming with sharks. There were the holistic ones who obsessed about their new organic lifestyles. There were the ones who even found their niche to be healing. They'd been healed and they could now heal others.

Then, there was me, the one who found myself obsessing about another person.

I didn't commit to much in my life, especially not women. Mikka, I was going to commit to. She'd always been the one, even when I thought she wasn't. I wasn't going to be able to quit her even if I tried.

Since the moment I'd kissed her, she'd intoxicated me. She would be my new addiction, and I was never ever going to rehab for her.

THERAPIST: *You're an addict.*

JAY: *And I'm not ashamed of that. Not anymore. I'm accepting who I am.*

THERAPIST: *Why?*

JAY: *My town, my people, the ones that matter never stopped accepting me for who I was. So, I'm learning from them.*

CHAPTER EIGHTEEN

JAY

MIKKA WANTED TO act like nothing had happened. She passed me in the hall with a look of uncertainty in her eye. I pinned her up against the wall and took her mouth in mine. She relaxed immediately and let me taste her.

"I'm going to be doing that a lot lately," I said. "Get used to it."

"Jay, we're jumping into uncharted waters," she said, smoothing my t-shirt on my chest.

"That's where I want to be," I grumbled and then walked away.

She'd warm to the idea. We had time. Another two weeks in a small town with me pushing her would change her mind. I had no doubt.

I would make sure of it.

Lorraine sent us to the grocery store. I massaged Mikka's thigh the whole drive. "You game for pulling over and making out on the side of the road, Little One?"

I saw her lick her lips, saw the blush rise to her cheeks. She shook her head, but she was smiling. "Absolutely not, Jay. I'm not doing PDA around here. You know everyone in Greenville will talk."

I shrugged and pulled over anyway.

Her mouth tasted as good as it had just hours before. I wondered if this was what being committed was. Or being committed to who you were meant to be with.

When we pulled up to the small parking lot, Mikka gasped. "Why is everyone here? There's no parking spots left."

I chuckled. "Greenville Village Fest starts tomorrow. Everyone's buying last minute supplies."

"Oh my God. We should have come earlier. This is why I need my planner."

"How would your planner have helped?" I asked as I relaxed into the seat, waiting for the ridiculous answer she was about to conjure up.

"I could have added in the dates, made note of what we needed over the past week."

"You wouldn't have known to get it early. Your planner wouldn't have told you that."

"I need the lesson of the day!" she countered, grasping for any reason.

"I'll give you Jay's lesson of the day."

"Oh God." She sighed, pausing for dramatic effect.

"Don't overthink it. I got you."

"That's so stupid. You don't have anything! No groceries whatsoever." She yanked open her car door and hopped out on a new mission. "We have to hurry. We aren't going to get everything for Lorraine's pie with everyone else buying up all the stock."

"You don't think they bought all the pie crust, do you?" I asked with pretend trepidation in my voice.

She didn't even look back at me. She just grabbed my arm and yanked me toward the shop. "I bet they did. I can't believe you guys didn't think of this. We are going to have to drive to the next town or something."

"Meek, I got it, it's fine," I said to her back.

"You don't have it. I hate when you do this, Jay!" she yelled, frantically grabbing a cart and pushing forward.

I decided she was too cute in her futile pursuit to stop her now.

She power walked through the store, and her face fell every single time an item on her list wasn't on the shelf. Most of the things we needed for Lorraine's pie were sold out.

We got to the checkout counter and she grumbled, "How can a store not have any sugar left? I mean, that's ludicrous. They should have stocked extra, Jay."

I couldn't hold in my laugh as we neared the counter.

"You think this is funny? We are going to spend all day chasing down these items, and if you'd planned better, we would have saved hours."

I'd heard this speech from her before. She was my PA after all. I could admit that there had been a lot of times in LA when I didn't remember something. My mind would be on a scene or foggy from a night of partying. She'd corrected me more than once, righted the ship when I partied too hard and didn't show up. I was notorious for flaking on our one-on-one meetings too. It wasn't something I was proud of.

Before partying, I'd been a stickler for punctuality and found that after rehab, the habit hadn't died. I knew what we needed and I knew we would be fine.

"Relax. I'll take care of it." I patted her back. I had it under control.

Her cheeks reddened, and I knew she was frustrated with my lackadaisical attitude when she stomped a foot. "Are you trying to be patronizing? Because you are. You always say that in LA. 'I'll take care of it.' No. *I* take care of it. And it won't be fine if Lorraine doesn't have the local flour to put in for her pie crusts. When did she ask you to get them?"

So, frustrated was an understatement. She was pissed.

I shrugged because answering her would have raised her blood pressure well beyond what it was now.

She whipped out her phone and started typing.

"What are you doing?" I asked.

"Finding the nearest grocery store with sugar and pie crust in stock."

Her brow was furrowed and her onyx hair fell over one shoulder as she clicked away at the speed of light.

I should have stopped her. I should have told her again it was all taken care of, but this was the Meek I knew. The one who barreled through every problem, even ones this small, with a clear plan for how to fix it in mind. I was surprised to find it was something I'd missed. It was a small victory to see her this way again but a victory nonetheless. She was getting her footing back.

We inched forward in line and, just my luck, Sandy ambled over. The tall blonde from my high school years looked good and yet I had no interest in her. Not even after I'd had dinner with her.

She curved her red lips at me and waved. "You ready for the festival?"

Mikka glanced up, and her eyes narrowed a little. She didn't engage, though.

"We're ready. Probably going tomorrow," I answered, not caring to converse with her.

"I'll see you there, hopefully? Maybe we can meet up?"

There wasn't a chance in hell, but I shrugged anyway, not wanting to hurt her feelings. "Yeah, we'll see."

As the words left my mouth, I saw Mikka look between the two of us. Sandy walked off and I let the encounter go, sure we didn't need to discuss it.

Dex, a scraggly-haired kid brother of a friend in town, started to check out our items. "Dex, can you tell Al we need the rest of my order?"

The kid mumbled into the mic that was attached to his headphone. Two seconds later, Al came around the corner with a cart of local flour, along with sugar and every other item we needed.

The old man was smiling under his white beard and started packing the materials into a bag and then into our cart. "Lorraine started the pies?"

I nodded. "She and Delilah are whipping them up over at the bakery. We're going to take this there and help them."

"Can't wait to get my hands on one."

As we walked to the truck, Mikka punched me hard in my shoulder. "You're an asshole."

"I told you it would be fine."

"I nearly had a heart attack."

"No, you were nearly just yourself," I retorted as I pushed our cart to the truck bed and started loading the groceries. "You needed a reminder of who you are. You were about to track down everything missing on that damn list and it would have taken all day, I promise you. But you would've done it."

"Well"—she shrugged, trying to hold onto her anger even with me complimenting her—"Lorraine needs to deliver the best pies." She grabbed the empty cart as I packed in the last bag. I watched her shove it into a row of others. When it didn't immediately roll into the other cart, she shoved it harder.

I chuckled as she made her way back. "Sure you can handle the cart?"

"Oh, shut up." She yanked open the truck door but, before she could hop in, I lifted her by the waist like the tiny little thing she was and set her inside.

I waited for a thank you, but she glared down at me from her seat.

"You're welcome, Meek."

"I can climb into a truck by myself."

"Barely," I muttered under my breath, but I made sure it was loud enough for her to hear and slammed the door before she could respond. Antagonizing her was becoming a habit of mine. I saw her confidence resurfacing, the fight in her returning. When her eyes sparkled with the drive to put me in my place, she didn't hesitate. This was the friend I'd missed and the woman I wanted to have in my life forever.

When I jumped in the driver's side and turned the ignition, she was ready. "I'm not that small, Jay. I'm probably stronger than half the women you've met."

"Hmmm." I thought about it for point two seconds. "Definitely not."

"Are you kidding me?" She scrunched her nose in irritation.

"Meek, you haven't worked out once since you've been here. I know you don't own a gym membership. You're a tiny little thing. You look good, you know it, and I promise you no guy is complaining. But"—I held my hand up—"you got good genes, not a good exercise drive."

"You're so rude. Of course I work out."

I laughed. "Mikka, an exercise video here and there where they tell you to hold a plank for five seconds doesn't count."

Her lips thinned and her eye twitched. I knew that look; it was the one where she was going to prove me wrong. "Pull over."

"You want to make out again?" I winked at her.

I turned the corner into the village and came to a stop sign.

She opened her door and jumped out. "I'll bet you whatever you want that I can hold a plank for longer than you."

"What the hell, woman?" I looked in my rearview mirror and saw none other than Brady in his pick up behind me. "People are waiting for me to drive!"

"Then, turn the corner and pull over."

I didn't have much of a choice. And of course, instead of my asshole of a friend driving away, he smiled like a damn kid in a candy store and pulled over right behind me.

"Mikka, this man bothering you?" he asked as he unfolded from his driver's seat.

Fucking Brady. I wanted to punch him square in the face for even looking at her. He eyed her up and down again right in front of me.

He knew exactly what he was doing. He'd always been one to stir the pot in high school, and he had a thing for women who were taken.

Or near taken.

Damn, I need to make Mikka mine.

"Go home, Brady," I growled.

Mikka smiled like she'd won the lottery. "Oh, no. We need a witness." She walked up to Brady and said hi as he leaned in to hug her. The fucker smiled over her shoulder at me.

"Oh, you're going to get more than one witness." I waited for her to notice that Lorraine and Delilah had already come out of the bakery to see why we'd parked so far down the street.

And Ray walked out of his bar as if he wanted some fresh air. He waved when Mikka saw him.

She smiled and then turned back to me. "I don't care who sees that you're out of shape."

Her drive to win practically radiated off her. She glowed with it.

"Alright. I'll play. I'll bet your festival night with this idiot here."

"Hey!" Brady said.

Mikka nodded. "It's okay, Brady. I won't lose our date. And when I win, we'll make Jay pay for all our festival food. He and Sandy can follow us around, considering he'll be with her."

What the fuck? I hadn't agreed to… what did she think happened between Sandy and me in that grocery store?

She didn't even wait for me to agree. She got on her knees right in front of me, baiting me with the look in her eyes. I couldn't tell if she'd meant to stare up at me from that position or was just showing me how easily she could get up and down, even in stilettos. Even in a tight little black shirt. Even in jeans that molded to her ass.

Either way, I wanted something completely different from a competition in that moment.

"Come on, big boy," she purred. "Show me what you're made of."

She was definitely fucking with me. Maybe because I was fucking with her. But I dropped down next to her and whispered in her ear before we got into our planks. "Don't think I won't remember that. You learn that from a video at King Chang?"

She licked her lips slowly. "Maybe."

My dick twitched, and I considered whether or not I needed to adjust my jeans before we started.

She smirked and then turned to yell at the crowd. "On three, we see who's in better shape. One. Two. Three."

We both got into plank position and I was surprised at how languidly she did so, like a kitten just stretching out.

I studied her form and found it was as good as mine, if not better. And she was wearing those heels.

A minute or so passed, and I felt the first bead of sweat form as my stomach started to quiver just a little.

With more of a crowd forming, I wondered how long she would last. I didn't need all of Greenville knowing I'd beaten her, but I wasn't going to give her the satisfaction of a date with Brady.

I had a freaking eight-pack that the world had seen on the big screen, and she never worked out.

Another minute passed and the new chant in my head was that she never fucking worked out.

I glanced at her. She wasn't shaking at all. She wasn't even sweating. She smiled sweetly at me, her hair pooled on the ground next to her arms and her shirt dipping low enough that I could see a little more than normal.

"I can see down your shirt," I whispered, hoping to get a cheap win in.

"Nothing you haven't seen before," she shot back.

Fuck.

I was going to lose.

I was going to collapse and she was going to get this damn date with Brady.

"Woman, what type of work outs are you doing in the darkness of the night?" I dropped my head to focus on maintaining my stance.

"Wouldn't you like to know?"

I snapped it back up to look at her. Her eyes were shining with mirth, and she looked like a damn yoga goddess. "You do yoga or something, don't you?"

"Jay, I'll be happy to give you my workout routine if you ask nicely." She waited a beat. "After I win this."

Brady started to chant her name and, as others joined in, I knew I was done for. I whispered one last desperate plea. "Don't make me lose in front of my entire town."

"You started this," she whispered back. "And don't try to win by guilt-tripping me."

My stomach muscles surrendered, and I crumbled to the ground, laughing my ass off.

The crowd that had formed cheered. As she folded one leg up to lunge back and stand over me, Ray ran over and patted her on the back. "Good work. I'll bring you a vodka soda with some lime, my dear. That's your drink, right?"

She blushed and nodded. My damn town was choosing her over me. I saw it happening plain as day and I couldn't have been prouder.

Brady stuck his hand out to help me up. I grabbed it as he said, "She must really want to go out with me, huh?"

I pulled him close so that I could pat him on the back and whisper in his ear, "I know where you live, man. You try anything with her, I'm coming to break down your door."

"I thought you said she's just your PA," he remarked snidely.

"She's definitely something of mine and it isn't just that."

LESSON OF THE DAY:
*Don't dim your light
just so someone else's
can shine brighter.*

CHAPTER NINETEEN

MIKKA

I SHOULDN'T HAVE MADE a scene, but my blood was boiling over. Sandy was the perfect woman to catch Jay's eye and he hadn't even turned her down in front of me.

Not that he should have.

We hadn't established anything between us. I knew that. I knew we probably never would.

Still, I deserved a little respect. And maybe my heart wanted a bit more than that.

Add to it that he teased me all through the store and then had the audacity to compliment my Type A nature after.

I was getting whiplash and he deserved to lose because of it. The audience was icing on the cake.

And, man, it felt good to win, even if it was something so small. The clapping and whooping and chanting of my name had me smiling. One person even let out a whistle, as if this was the best entertainment they'd had all week.

"I knew you were amazing even in stilettos," Delilah announced. She hugged me while Ray went to get me a celebratory drink.

"We were just fooling around," I mumbled, not sure how to take the compliments for such a small victory, one that was really just a joke. I'd been first in my class, won a state spelling bee, and graduated with two majors and a cumulative 4.0 GPA. My mother might have patted me on the back. We didn't have a crowd. There was never cheering or clapping.

Delilah leaned in. "No, Mikka. This is your official initiation into the town. Maybe it doesn't feel like it now, but you just became one of us by putting a Stonewood in their place."

I brushed the grass off my knees and acted as if her words didn't shoot straight to my little lonely soul. I knew I was leaving this small town soon. So, fitting in here shouldn't have meant anything. Yet, it meant everything. "If you say so. We got all the materials for the pie in the back of Jay's truck. We should get to it, right?"

Delilah nodded and waved Lorraine toward the vehicle. "We better start baking if we're going to feed this town."

"My pies aren't going to be the only eats at the festival, Delilah," Lorraine said, but it was through a knowing smile.

We hurried over to the truck, and I picked up a few bags. Jay met us there and grabbed the rest quietly. I lingered so that I could walk with him. "Sorry I had to beat you in front of all your friends. But if it helps ease the pain of losing, I'm happy to help you open a jar or two here and there in the next few weeks if you're ever having trouble."

He chuckled, not at all the sore loser. He appeared to look even happier. "All in good fun, right? Not like you're really going on that date with Brady, right?"

"Of course I am," I replied. "He was nice enough to ask and I'm not cancelling now."

"You're kidding me."

I shook my head and smiled at his jaw working and his biceps flexing. "It's just a date, Jay."

"God damn, just a date," he grumbled and then tilted his head to the side so fast his neck cracked. "You're driving me insane. You know you're not supposed to be doing that. You're supposed to be helping me."

I shrugged. "You wanted to push your boundaries and see what you could handle."

He glared at me, but I saw the hint of a smile crossing his lips. "You're ruthless, Little Pebble. When do you work out? I never see you doing a damn thing."

"I do it at night before bed sometimes. Mostly yoga," I admitted. "I need it to relax. I used to get really bad anxiety when I was at school. In high school, I started to have panic attacks. My mother researched what I could do about it and called enough therapists in. We found yoga worked for me.

"You're mom always pushed for what was best for you, I see." He said thoughtfully.

I nodded. "And I'm thankful she did." I knew for a fact it was a good thing. "I don't say it much, but she's shaped me into who I am. I have a lot of flaws, but I'm proud of what I can do. And you never know what you can do until you push yourself hard enough to break."

It was true. I was still standing next to Jay, still walking down the village sidewalk, smiling from ear to ear, even knowing I'd survived a terrible couple of months with Dougie.

Jay slid his hand around my elbow to slow me down and rubbed the inside of my arm as he said, "Sometimes you need to know when to walk away from the pushing through, Meek."

I turned my head from him, let my hair act as a curtain to hide my face. I didn't want him to see that I struggled with the fact that I was leaving Dougie for this very reason. "My mom always taught me that you fight, bleed, and remain strong enough to conquer whatever you're afraid of or it will conquer you."

"I know." He dropped his hand from my elbow and I felt the loss immediately, but then he pulled me close by my waist and didn't let me go. "I'll have to show you that sometimes the strongest thing you can do is walk away, love. It's not always your job to be the best or make something perfect. And once you figure that out, you'll be even more wonderful than we all think you are now, which is already pretty damn close to flawless, woman."

What he said dug down deep into my bones and burrowed there, making a home in me, making me want to build myself a better foundation than before to prove those words belonged where they'd set up shop. "I appreciate you, Jay."

"I love your little, strong-as-hell ass too, Meek," he mumbled into my hair. As we walked to Delilah's, I laid my head on his shoulder, finally feeling like Jay and I were back to our old rapport. This was the friendship I couldn't live without, the man I couldn't live without, the relationship that would withstand basically anything.

I hoped I would find that in my next boyfriend, but I was happy to at least have found it in a friend.

Ray jogged over to us just as we were about to walk into Delilah's. "Here's your vodka soda."

"Thank you." I took it from his hands. "No one is judging me for drinking this early, right?"

"Of course not. They'd judge you if you turned down a drink from me in this town." He winked. "Are you helping Lorraine bake all those?"

Jay held up the bag of extra pie crusts. "We'll be there all night."

"I'll bring more drinks over later," Ray announced loud enough for Lorraine to hear as she pushed the glass swinging door open for us. He smiled brightly at her and she returned it with a sultry look. I swear the woman had every older man in the town wrapped around her finger.

She waved us in. "Delilah already has the first batch in the oven and is working on mixing spices into the cinnamon. Jay, we need you to fill the crusts and pass them to me. I'll work on the pie top and caramel topping."

The woman buzzed about the industrial kitchen as if it was hers. Delilah let her own it too. They worked well together, moving around one another like they'd done it for years. "How long have you all made these pies?" I asked.

"Delilah's mom used to do it with me here when she first opened the shop. How old were you, Delilah?"

"I think five? My mom thought this town could use a bakery and I was her pride and joy. So I got the name." She smiled fondly to herself as she stirred some nutmeg into a large metal bowl. "Somewhat fitting since I inherited the shop when she passed."

Lorraine didn't let us dwell. "Right. So I told Delilah she better let me make my pies here. We've expanded a few times with our earnings from the pies and her treats in shops throughout the state. The festival is the most fun, though. We have to make enough to feed an army."

On that note, we worked hard for hours. Lorraine had me stir brown sugar in three sauce pans until it melted. A dash of cacao was added right before the concoction changed color. Then I was to watch it brown as I lowered the temperature. At that point, I called Lorraine who would dash over and grab it right as it turned a golden color every time.

It was masterful and almost scientific how she worked so precisely. Every single one came out smelling as fantastic as the one before it.

And Jay kept us upbeat while we worked, sliding in next to me every now and then to bother me. He'd ask me a question like, "What do you think I should wear tonight?" or "Do you think Bob is still hung up on that secretary at work?" or "Remember the time we were listening to that song on the way to the beach? What was that song?"

I responded with one-word answers. I could barely concentrate.

He kept on. "Do you really think the scene where I dive into that lake needs to be shot from under the water? It might be better from behind me."

Normally, I was extremely good at answering questions like that. I could multitask with the best of them. I prided myself on it.

But the caramel was finicky, so finicky that I'd burned one batch when he'd taken my focus from it ten minutes earlier. "I don't know, Jay," I huffed.

"How can you not, woman? You study every angle when you read it." He was leaning against the counter, his hip brushing mine. And just when I thought I would be okay if we were only friends, if he went on his date with Sandy, he dipped his finger in some of the cooled caramel that had been set aside and wrapped his mouth around it to lick it off.

I should have scolded him but I was distracted. My eyes were laser focused on one thing and it was him being so close with his soft, pillowy lips sucking sweet-as-heaven caramel off his calloused finger.

"Meek," he whispered.

I hummed, still in a trance.

He turned toward the saucepans and put his hand on the small of my back as he took the spoon from my hand. He whispered in my ear, "You keep letting your mind go where it's going, you're going to burn the caramel again."

I jerked back from him and glared. His lips were pursed in an attempt to hold back a grin. "I don't know what you're talking about." I swiped back the spoon. "The caramel's fine."

"If you say so." He shrugged. "So, what do you think?"

"About what?" I practically yelled. He was distracting me on purpose, I knew he was. I stirred the caramel faster, trying to defuse my frustration at not being immune to him. "Can you please back up?"

This time he outright laughed at me. "Woman, I haven't gotten near as close as I want and you're already quivering. Village Fest is going to be a riot."

"At Village Fest, I'll be standing as close to Brady as I can get," I threw back at him. "Just like you'll be next to Sandy, I assume." If he wanted to irk me, I'd do the same to him. "I haven't gotten anything *good* in weeks and I'm sure he'll give it right up."

"You baiting me, Meek?" he growled.

"Would you classify what you're doing to me as that?" I shot back.

"Only if it's working." He quirked a brow innocently.

"I'm contemplating pouring this hot caramel on you," I said under my breath.

"I'd take it if you promised to lick it off."

That time, my stomach clenched along with my thighs and I felt my body practically beg me to give in to him. Goosebumps skittered across my skin and Jay dragged a finger along the ones up my arm. "This is just the start of us, little pebble. Don't think I'm going to bed you and then let you forget about me. Not after the night we had together."

I glanced around to make sure Lorraine and Delilah weren't listening. "We got carried away. Neither of us was ready for something serious. We saw that when you didn't shoot down Sandy at the grocery store."

"Is that what all this is about? Woman, it was so far from my mind, I didn't think to shoot her down. It was never an option. I got you in front of me. I don't see anyone else."

"Jay." I sighed, his words melting me just like the caramel in front of me. "You might think you're ready to commit, but I think we need to play it by ear. See how things go. I can't have expectations this early on. I'll push you too hard. I'll ramp up my Type A drive to make it the best relationship and I—" My hand shook as I lifted the back of my wrist to push my hair from my face. "I can't fail again."

He crossed his arms and shook his head at me. "Little one, it's not a failure when you get out of a bad situation. It's a win. And you really think 'friends with benefits' is going to work for us?"

I shrugged. "Why not? You don't have to commit and I get my iron headboard banging."

"What about Brady?"

"It's just a date."

His eyes narrowed. "I'm beginning to hate you saying it's just anything." He sighed. "You want to play the game with Brady, fine. I'll play. And I'll win."

He pushed off the counter and called Lorraine and Delilah back in before I could respond.

He resumed his charismatic attitude and charmed all of us the rest of the night as we worked.

At one point, a rap song came on the radio and he actually danced and sang every single word to Lorraine like she needed them enunciated to her.

"I looked up this song," Lorraine told us. "I wanted to know what a WAP was. Guess what, I have one and every man who has been with me loves it."

Delilah's cheeks turned pink and her eyes bulged. "Lorraine! Mikka is going to think you are..."

"What?" Lorraine asked. "She worked in a porn store her whole life. Haven't you heard?"

"Lorraine!" I mimicked Delilah's tone. "Didn't you tell me you weren't a gossip?"

Jay chuckled as he took some pie bags out. "She lied."

"Proud of it," Lorraine retorted and went back to pouring caramel. "And speaking of whores, because Delilah was about to call me one, Sandy wants to come help set up the pie stand at Village Fest tomorrow."

At the mention of her name, I turned the stove burner up a bit. We all knew why she'd jumped on the bandwagon to help.

"She's excited to be all over Jay," Lorraine continued, and Jay turned his back on me so I couldn't see his reaction. "And Jay, I'll have you know that she is spreading around her status with you like wildfire. You intend on doing anything more than you already have with her, you better be prepared for the town to get a play by play of it the next day."

He carefully pulled pies out of the oven and didn't look up or respond to her at all. I wanted him to acknowledge her words, to say he didn't want anything to do with Sandy, to shut down the gossip mill about him with anyone other than me immediately.

He didn't do any of that, though.

I wasn't sure if this was part of the game.

And I wasn't sure I wanted to play. It was dangerous, potentially catastrophic. I was starting to realize Jay had a piece of my heart and it was the piece that didn't compete well. It was the piece I wasn't sure could withstand seeing him with someone else.

It was the piece that loved him more than I'd ever loved anyone else before.

As I curled up in bed that night, I considered my toys and thought about Jay licking caramel off more than just his fingers. All the fun from the day died, though, when my phone rang.

Dougie's name flashed across the screen, and I silenced the ringing. I'd silenced it more than a few times over the past week.

A text came through.

> **DOUGIE:** You know I hate the silent treatment.
> **DOUGIE:** I'm getting impatient.

I laid there for ten minutes, not responding. I got up and started my exercises, carefully breathing in and out. I stretched to the sky and tried to push the negative energy away from me. After it seemed like he'd given up, I turned on my yoga app to start working through a routine that would get my blood flowing.

As I hit the start button, another text came through.

> **DOUGIE:** What do I have to do to get some of your time? I'm sorry I'm being pushy and I'm sorry to be reaching out. I miss you. Please tell me you miss me too.

He was trying so hard and pushing all my buttons. He wanted my guilt to override my decision to end us.

I'd given in to him for so long that I almost texted back.
Almost.
Much later, I wondered what would have happened if I had.

THERAPIST: *Sometimes letting things play out and letting them come to you is a healthier path.*

JAY: *I'm a Stonewood. I fight for what's mine, for what's worth it, and I win.*

CHAPTER TWENTY

JAY

> **BREY:** Sandy is spreading around the town that she has a date with you. Do we need to go for a run before festival so that I know what to expect?
> **JAY:** Expect all women to be fawning over me at all times.
> **BREY:** Seriously, Jay. The town's talking.
> **JAY:** It always does, baby girl. I'm not worried.
> **BREY:** I am.

MOST PEOPLE DIDN'T like the town gossip. It was like a small wind that built a tsunami that descended on whoever was the target. I knew Mikka and I had positioned ourselves as potential targets.

I was accustomed to the risks after being in the public eye for so long. Mikka was a different story. In LA, she could stand to one side of me and not be noticed. Here, she was the center of attention, and her every move was examined under a microscope. I didn't know if it was fair to put her in that position, but I couldn't have her anywhere else.

The moment I saw her when I walked out of rehab, I knew I wouldn't let her go anywhere without me. The woman had been broken, and I wasn't about to have her shattered any further. She needed time to find herself again. And for some reason, Greenville's small town nosey magnifying glass was allowing her to do that.

She emerged from her room in ripped up jeans, bright white tennis shoes, and a sweater that hung off one shoulder. Her hair fell in soft waves down her back and I knew it would slide through my fingers like liquid. Something in my gut twisted at seeing her dressed down like this. She usually wore her stilettos with red bottoms and a designer fitted shirt that looked lethal.

Tonight, she'd gone for an "autumn in a village" style, and thinking of her cozying up to another man in that relaxed look... it didn't feel at all right.

She wrinkled her nose and pulled at the dark sweater. "This okay?"

"You've finally figured out you aren't in LA anymore," I murmured. Her bare shoulder and exposed thighs teased me into contemplating dragging her back into her room to show her how the night was really going to go.

She wasn't going to be cuddling up to Brady, and I wasn't going to have men eyeing up every part of her exposed skin all night as if she was completely available. It looked too smooth, too enticing, too damn good for anyone, especially Brady.

I knew it deep in my bones. I was a good actor, but no one was that good. This woman wasn't going near anyone but me tonight.

"You look good," I mumbled and cleared my throat. "The shoes should work for the walk."

"Why can't we drive?" she whined just as the doorbell rang.

Knowing it was Brady, I didn't hurry to the door. I lingered in front of the stair's landing instead. "Because there's no parking from here all the way to the festival."

She peered out the window down the street and her jaw dropped at the line of cars past the lodge. "Where did they all come from?"

"People come from all over for this. The pies, the music, the nostalgia, the memories—it's the big event of the year here."

"You didn't come back for it last year." Her rolodex of a mind was trying to figure out where I was instead.

"We had back to back shows scheduled for my newest movie."

She rubbed a hand over her shoulder as she put the pieces together. "I made you do those shows. You didn't want to. You wanted to go home."

I shrugged. "It all worked out." Mikka knew what was best for my career. I let her line things up and sacrificed things like this because of that. I'd made up for it by visiting my brothers in the city for a Halloween party later that year. It hadn't mattered much.

"You should have told me you wanted to come back to be with your family, to be a part of this."

"It's not a big deal, Meek."

"Sometimes I wonder if you realize that not having anything be a big deal is a big deal. When you roll with everything to make it all good for everyone, do you ever feel as if you've made it bad for yourself?"

My therapist had asked me that once before. "I don't intend to roll with everything tonight."

Just as I was about to tell her we were done playing games, that Brady wasn't taking her anywhere, that we needed to discuss our friendship being not just a friendship anymore, her phone rang.

The sound made her jump and I knew right then who it was.

She dug in her purse to silence it.

The name on the screen reminded me we had even bigger issues than Brady. "He calling you a lot?"

"No." She sighed and pushed a finger to her temple. "Yes. Sometimes."

"Are you answering?" Could I break her phone without her realizing it was on purpose?

"Not as of yet. But he's persistent and he's texted me a few times about wanting to stay friends and all that."

"He's trying to get a reaction."

"Maybe, but also, maybe not. We were friends for a long time, Jay. I spent most of college with him. He knows me—"

"—well enough to use what he knows to get you to talk to him," I finished for her. "You know I'm right."

She shifted from one foot to the other and slid her phone out of sight. "Let's just focus on the festival, okay? We have a ton to do tonight."

"I know, Lorraine. I promised Mikka I'd drive her though." Brady practically whined in his collared shirt and dark jeans. He'd gotten dressed for the date I didn't want them to go on.

"Nonsense. She can walk. Your truck is bigger than mine. I just need you all to help me load the pies in there. It'll only take fifteen minutes for you to drive with me and unload."

He sighed but conceded because we all knew that if you lived in this town, you did what Lorraine said.

After we'd filled Brady's pickup with the sweet smelling apple pies, she announced dramatically. "I wish you two could fit in the pickup with us. It'd be so nice if we could all use my reserved parking spot at the fest."

No one bought her acting especially when she winked big at me and smiled.

I patted Brady on the shoulder as we all chuckled at her antics. "See you there, buddy. I'll keep Mikka happy on our walk."

Mikka whined the whole damn walk. "I'm not made for small towns and the amount of gravel and dirt I have to trek through to get to these events."

"Coachella is just as dirty and you walk just as much."

She hummed. "True, but I belong there with the amount of potential celebrity clientele I can rake in."

I grabbed her and pulled her close. "You don't get to PA for anyone else for long, Meek. I'm supposed to get you full time."

She laughed and fell into step with me. "You forget that I gave up a month for you. I'm losing clients because of it."

"Good. I'm trying to make damn sure you lose all of them."

"Jay, you could probably get a better PA than me." Her step didn't falter, and the small smile as she said it made my dick twitch. The woman knew her worth—her competitiveness would never allow her to give me up to someone else.

"No, I couldn't, and we both know it. You're invaluable." As we came up to the village, her eyes lit up like she was at a more extravagant event than Beyonce at Coachella, and I muttered more to myself than her, "Invaluable in more ways than one."

LESSON OF THE DAY:
And sometimes the reward is greater than the risk.

CHAPTER TWENTY-ONE

MIKKA

JAY GRUMBLED UNDER his breath, surely annoyed with my workload back in LA. He didn't understand that I couldn't rely only on him, even if I wanted to.

Except for now. Right now, I had dropped everything to go with him and get away from my problems. They would catch up to me, to both of us. Dougie's call was a reminder that we needed to face them eventually.

I looked toward the festival and let the lights and crowd swallow up my worry. The folk music mingled with the rustling of the trees, like they were harmonizing. They whispered to me as though they knew every secret I had, like they'd blow them away in the wind and we'd never have to speak of them again. It was comforting.

Soothing.

Addictive.

Delilah ran up to us with her wholesome smile and bright red cheeks, so happy to see me that she basically hit me at full speed to give me a hug. I stumbled back but caught us before we fell, something I wouldn't have been able to do without my new sneakers on.

We both laughed at her enthusiasm. "Is the pie stand that bad already?" Jay asked as he looked at us.

"It's crazy. And Rosy tried to sprinkle cumin on top of Lorraine's pies." Delilah's eyes were wide like she couldn't believe it. "I didn't think she'd go to those extremes."

Jay pulled her in for a hug. "Lorraine would go to the same extremes, I'm sure."

I stood up for her because she couldn't speak for herself. "She absolutely wouldn't."

Jay chuckled. "She would, and you would too. This is the biggest competition of the year. You wouldn't let someone else beat you."

"I wouldn't cheat." I stomped my foot. "I would win, though. Just like Lorraine is going to because she put in the damn work."

"That's right, I did put in the work. And that wrinkly old hag is going to hear from me about that cumin." Lorraine and Brady walked up behind us, no pies in hand. When she saw me looking around, she said, "We already parked the truck, and Ray's unloading the pies."

"Ray does a lot for you." I leaned in to say as we all started weaving through the crowd. Brady walked up next to me and mumbled another hello. Jay eyed the two of us like he had a claim on me as his friend or employee or something more, I wasn't sure which.

"Of course he does. He never got over the fact that I left him after he looked at another woman. He's hoping I'll gift him with my presence again." She tapped one red nail against her chin as she thought about it. "I might. He was good in bed."

Delilah groaned, and Brady took that moment to tease her. "Delilah, come on. You gotta hand it to Lorraine—she's getting more than most of us."

Delilah glared at him, and I saw her face get redder than usual. "Lorraine's generation of men is much better than ours in Greenville, Brady. This town is full of duds our age."

Jay stumbled at her proclamation. "Are you kidding me? I'm a gentleman."

Delilah nodded. "Sure, but you left me in Greenville with men like him." She sighed and now it was Brady's face turning red. "Maybe I should move."

As she said the words, Sandy strutted toward us and I almost groaned. Tonight was about to turn into something I knew I wouldn't like. Delilah leaned over to whisper to us before Sandy was within earshot. "Another dud. Brady, you and her would be perfect together."

Jay laughed. "He's been there, done that."

"As have you," Brady threw back, but Jay shook his head. Brady shrugged. "Alright, well, we know what's in store for you tonight then."

Part of me wanted to remind Jay this wasn't a partying scene. Kids nipped past our legs and families were playing carnival games for stuffed animals down each dirt aisle we walked. As Sally slid her hands around Jay's waist and pressed her whole body to his to whisper in his ear, though, I knew I couldn't. They weren't drinking or doing anything illegal. They were on a date, just as I was with Brady, not doing anything wrong.

It only felt wrong in my heart, in my gut, where the ball of jealousy grew and festered into something ugly, competitive, and mean. I wanted to lash out, to accuse Jay of making me feel like I meant more to him than I did.

I turned to Brady, grabbed his hand, and announced, "I want to ride the worst ride here and then go vote for Lorraine's pie. Who's with me?"

Delilah and Lorraine whooped like I'd made their day. I didn't wait for Jay to answer because I wasn't going to let him and Sandy ruin my night. Sure, I was his PA, but I wasn't his keeper and I needed to enjoy this night just as much as the next person.

Lorraine's eyes jumped between Jay and me and, before I knew it, she was speeding ahead, telling me to go find a ride and then come to her pie stand. "The pie tasting isn't ready yet, but they'll all be good. You'll enjoy them, I promise. Some of those women cook almost as well as me."

Lorraine complimenting others meant one thing: she was distracting me.

The tightening in my stomach, in my soul, in my heart was there.

I shouldn't look back.

It was going to hurt. Jay was a friend, but my heart had placed him in another category too. The competitive person in me, the one that wanted him for more, needed all the facts. I needed to catalogue everything, even if it ripped me apart.

I glanced back as our group left Jay and Sandy behind. She was kissing his neck, the spot I knew smelled just like him. It was the place I wanted to nuzzle in, the place I felt safe always. My only safe place.

Maybe the way I looked at him broke him, or maybe it was just his way, but his blue eyes poured out sympathy and pain as if he wanted to take away mine. "Meek!"

I spun around and gripped Brady's hand tighter. "You better find me the best ride, Brady. I need some fun tonight."

"Don't worry. The Twirling Fury is either going to make you hurl or scream. Either way, I got you." He winked at me, and a little spark of hope flickered. His easygoing way along with his classic good looks could entertain me through the night, better than a mini wand, although mine was a workhorse. And his company was much better than Jay's with Sandy on his arm.

Lorraine split off from us and Delilah went with her, quiet and reserved as she glanced back at me and Brady.

"Is there something between you and Delilah?" I asked.

Brady tilted his head as he steered me toward a stand with a baseball and bottles stacked in a pyramid about fifteen feet away. "She's the one that got away, I guess."

"How so?"

He paid the man who then handed him five balls. "I dated her one summer in college and didn't really commit." He shrugged and pointed at a bottle pyramid. He threw his ball and knocked them all down. "Two more to go."

"So, you cheated?" I pried.

"Not really. We never set those boundaries, but I hurt her. I'm not proud of it. She's all I ever wanted, but I didn't know it at the time. I was young, stupid, and reckless. Lesson learned."

I smiled at his candor. Brady and I would get along, even beyond whatever type of date this was. "And that lesson is?"

"Grass isn't greener anywhere unless you work at it and make it flourish. We would have been good together, but now she won't come near that idea with a ten foot pole. She's too nice to act like I'm a leper, but I see the way she looks at me. She wants nothing to do with me." He threw another ball and knocked down all the bottles but one. He winced. "You're distracting me, Mikka."

"By asking you a serious question?"

"We're supposed to be on a date. Not talking about a woman I used to date."

"It's not a date," Jay said from behind. I jumped at his voice. "Mikka said we were all just going together. So, here we are."

Turning to face him, I noticed how good he and his date looked together. Jay clearly belonged in a small town with his worn jeans and faded t-shirt that hugged his chest. He only had to throw on some boots and kick up a corner of his mouth and the whole female population swooned. He made millions in rom-coms because he'd been born with that charm.

Sandy fit the beautiful blonde bombshell stereotype, leaning into him like she belonged there. Her jeans molded to her long legs, and her white blouse billowed out in the breeze, making them as picturesque as a small town romance movie.

Together.

Without me.

A couple of screaming kids approached Jay and Sandy. A teen girl asked for his autograph, and it was a stark reminder that, while most of the time in Greenville, Jay was just Jay, he was also an international celebrity.

I didn't belong here, not with the magical rustling wind, the hyper kids, the autumn air, and the townsfolk who knew each other inside out. Greenville was an exclusive little town, and I felt like an outsider again.

Brady pulled me close. "Of course it's a date. She just has to be convinced of it. I'm willing to work on our grass, Mikka."

Sandy squinted. "I don't get it."

"Because it's an inside joke, Sandy." Brady rolled his eyes and lifted his chin at Jay. "You going to let me throw or you going for it?"

Jay walked to the bar that separated us and the bottles. He didn't stop to aim or focus on the target. He wound up on his last step and let the ball fly straight into the other bottles. They all fell.

The stand employee smiled. "Sorry. Your friend missed this one, so no stuffed animal today."

"All good, Johnny." Jay put down an extra tip on the stand's table. "Thanks for letting us play."

"Well, I messed that up," Brady murmured to me. "I'll get you something by the end of the night. Want to head over to the Twirling Fury before the teens come out and it gets too busy?"

"Sure." I looped my arm in his and tried my best not to make eye contact with Jay. His presence as he followed behind us niggled like a tiny little insect that shouldn't have been so detrimental to my fun but took all my attention. It buzzed around, and if I tried to wave away the idea of him with her, it buzzed back more furiously.

The Twirling Fury lit up as we approached, and the little carts attached to some flimsy-looking chain spread out as the spinning got faster. Then the cart started swirling with the couples caged in.

"This is a joke," I whispered.

"No, this is Greenville, love," Brady responded. "It's fun. I promise."

"I don't think those chains are that secure."

Sandy shrugged beside us. "Mr. Herman has been running this little rollercoaster for years. The chains are old but unbreakable."

The little man stood by the gate and pushed a lever that made the spinning death traps start to rise up over our head. The music was loud, bouncy, and a little psychotic. You had to be crazy to go on it. Or on drugs.

I turned to Jay. "No."

His smile was slow, like he'd been waiting for me to look at him. "Baby girl, you got this, and when it's over, I got you." My heart dropped so fast I almost lurched at the shift in weight. A part of me knew right then that Jay was all I wanted that night, but I tried my best to ignore it.

I closed my eyes and clutched Brady's arm. He was supposed to be the one I was here with. "Let's go."

Mr. Herman, balding and frail, smiled one of the liveliest smiles I'd ever seen as I walked up with Brady. "You're new. I remember all my riders."

I nodded. "I'm new to town."

"I know. Mikka Chang, PA to Jay, and a few of us think you might be a little broken too." His assessment and intense gaze caught me off guard.

"I... I'm not broken."

"No. Someone broke your spirit, though." His dark eyes squinted at me and then he lifted a knobby, wrinkled finger. "Ah, yes. I can see the guilt. Don't worry; Greenville will fix you. This ride might break you, though."

He cackled as he lowered the carts and slowed their spin. Clearing my throat, I tried to ignore his cerily accurate assessment. One of the couples that passed us on their way out looked especially pale. "Maybe this isn't such a good idea."

Brady pulled me along. "I'll take care of you."

Jay grumbled from behind us. "Watch your hands, Brady."

Tunnel vision was setting in, my palms were starting to sweat, and I wasn't thinking about Jay's words properly. "What can happen to our hands? Do they need to stay inside the cart at all times? Oh, God. Do I want to know any of the horror stories?"

Mr. Herman came up to check our seatbelts, which pulled tight over the waist. "There's not one horror story, little lady. But, yes, keep those hands inside the cart. I don't want a horror story tonight."

He laughed at his own joke and slammed our cage shut.

Just Brady and me. Jay and Sandy went into their own enclosure. "Any last words?" the man sitting across from me said.

"This isn't safe. If we die, everyone should mark my words. There should be a vest seat belt or one of those bars that go across you at amusement parks."

"What's the fun in that?" Brady practically vibrated in his seat; his adrenaline was getting the best of him. As the music started up again, I wondered if I could die of a heart attack before we even started spinning.

He gripped my thigh and said, "Scream your head off."

The spinning started, and then the cart started flipping. I saw all of Greenville whip past as my hair flew everywhere. The ride raised us so high that if we flew off we'd all die.

Lights and trees and screaming, so much screaming. Then I realized it was me screaming. I was sure those were my last moments.

I closed my eyes and spun away to where all my problems disappeared, too scared to really grab any of them and hang on. The beauty of sheer fear, of being whipped around on a metal chain, was I realized I was so damn fragile but so amazingly strong in the same moment.

My life was like that. Dougie had shown me strength and weakness.

And I had survived it.

As the ride started to slow and we lowered to the ground, I found I had survived this too.

"That was…" I waited for Sandy and Jay to come over as we left the ride. "Amazing!"

"The fact that you could scream that long is amazing," Jay retorted.

Sandy laughed as if he was making fun of me, but his blue eyes twinkled as he looked over her head at me.

He lost his smile when Brady's arm went around my shoulder, pulling me close so he could kiss my cheek. "You're a hell of a date, woman."

I nodded and looked away from Jay. Just my "friend with benefits," I reminded myself.

Next, Brady insisted we get funnel cake before pie because I'd told him I'd never tried the fried mess of dough.

"Jay, you think my mom would have raised me to eat funnel cake?"

"No. Well, maybe if Wren offered, but I'm guessing he didn't."

"Exactly." I sighed. "I'll have one piece."

Sandy grew on me when she smiled and confessed, "I promise you won't be able to stop with just one bite."

It looked like fried brains but tasted like a warm donut doused in oil and sugar. "Oh my god. Why didn't you get this for me earlier, Jay?"

"Because how was I supposed to know you hadn't eaten carnival food? Dougie wronged you."

I nodded, suddenly more solemn than I wanted to be. "He did. But not anymore."

Jay's jaw ticked as I said the words, and when I licked the powdered sugar from my fingers, something in his eyes shifted. "Brady, I'm calling dibs on my friend for the fun house. It's my favorite little part of this festival and I'm dragging her through it."

Brady shrugged. "Sandy, guess you're on my arm behind them for it."

Sandy whined, but Jay had already grabbed my hand and was pulling me along. He murmured something to the employee that was manning the fun house and then we were walking through it.

"Jay, you know I've been in a fun house before."

He grunted but continued pulling me through.

We passed a room that had contrasting colors swirling around and then one where we walked on uneven floors. "We're not even enjoying it." I pointed to a wall that was painted in swirly colors but didn't seem all that astonishing.

He continued to pull me through a room that had a mirror every which way and I saw the determination on his face, like he wasn't going to stop. Yanking my hand back and stopping both of us, I ground out, "Jay. I'm not even seeing the fun of the house."

He spun on me. "That's not the point of me bringing you in here."

"What's the point, then?" I put my hands on my hips, ready for him to say something ridiculous.

"Do you see yourself in all these mirrors?"

I turned my palms up as I shrugged. "Sure?"

"Do you see what I see, though?"

I waited because I wasn't sure I wanted to give an answer.

"I see you, the girl I wanted but could never have. I see you, the woman I had that I'm never letting go again. I've never committed to another woman because no one is like you. You had me on that red string since the day I met you. And now we're walking around as if 'friends with benefits' is going to be enough? As if Brady is going to be enough?"

"Jay, it's just some fun with Brady and I don't expect anything more from you. You shouldn't expect more either. We're both in delicate states. I just got out of a relationship and you just got out of rehab."

"The timing may be off, but I'm not letting you slip through my fingers again," he growled.

I groaned. "We're not ready. We've done well the way we've always been. You and I are—"

"Don't say friends." He stepped up to me. "Don't you dare."

"Aren't we, though? We always have been."

"I should have taken you the first day I met you on that beach, Dougie or no."

I shook my head, trying to shake away the idea. "Don't be ridiculous. We don't work, we never would have and Dougie was—"

"Dougie is gone, and Brady's not going to stand in my way like your last boyfriend did."

"I'm not looking for anything, Jay. I want fun and we're too complicated, too close. Brady is—"

"Brady is NOT an option. Do you know that since the night I kissed you, you're all I think about? I don't want other women. I don't want a party. I want you."

I stepped back again, came up against a mirror, and knew there wasn't anywhere to hide. My breath came faster as he cornered me like he did the night he kissed me.

He gripped my jaw and lifted my face as if it belonged to him. "I just want you."

Maybe I kissed him then. Maybe he kissed me.

But with ourselves as witnesses on every single mirror surrounding us, we devoured one another. He tasted like sugar and devastation, like dreams and nightmares all mixed into one. I moaned when his tongue tangled with mine, not sure I would ever be able to forget his kiss, forget the way he felt against me, forget the idea that I could have him to myself like this.

I shoved him and tore my mouth away. "I can't do this with you. You're my place, Jay."

And he was. My mom pushed me to be everything; Dougie had made me feel like nothing. LA swallowed me up until I had to claw my way out, and this small town gave me the illusion I was something even though I may never be anything to them. I didn't have close friends. I didn't have any place to feel home.

Except for Jay.

"You're my friend," I whispered and dragged a finger across his lips because I knew I'd miss them, that they deserved to be treasured, and I wanted to be the only one to do that.

He gripped my finger and dipped it into his mouth. He wrapped his tongue around it and sucked off what little bit of sugar may have been left as he closed the gap between us. He pulled me from his mouth and pushed his hips against me. I felt the length of him, knew I was a goner as he said, "More than friends, Meek."

He dove in to kiss me again, but I made a last ditch effort. "Brady and Sandy are going to be coming up behind us very shortly. We need to stop."

"I paid the man in charge. No one comes in the fun house. Except you. You get to come in the funhouse, baby, and I'm going to provide the fun." He grabbed my hips and dipped his head to suck on my neck. The spot was so sensitive, it hardly registered that his hands were unbuttoning and lowering my jeans. When his fingers touched my bare skin, I didn't hesitate. I kicked off my shoes and pants.

"I'm going to hell for doing this with kids waiting outside," I mumbled as I gripped his dark hair.

"No one'll know. The electricity goes out on this thing half the time anyway. That guy shuts it down for maintenance most of the festival."

"Brady and Sandy will know, Jay." I yanked at his hair so he'd stop for a second to consider what we were doing. He lifted his head from my neck. His lips glistened, his smile popped with a dimple, and his voice held confidence as he replied, "I'm aware. Brady can go fuck himself. Or Sandy for that matter. I don't care."

There wasn't a way to stop myself if Jay didn't have any restraint either. I unzipped his jeans and grabbed the whole length of him, ready for him to work me better than any man ever had.

Biting my lip, I lifted my leg to wrap around him. "So, we're doing this?" The question was a last ditch effort to save what was left of our friendship. We'd fallen over the edge into something more and I knew we couldn't go back, but fear festered in me.

I could lose him.

But the fighter in me, the competitor that knew I didn't lose, told me I would never lose him. I'd fight harder for this man than I'd fought for anything ever before.

"I want you, Meek. You ready for me?"

Maybe it was my vulnerability that made him ask, but I didn't want him to treat me as fragile. Dougie would do that after a fight: cherish me like he hadn't thrown me around just moments before.

"Don't you dare hold back and make me ask for it, Jay. If you want me, take me."

He pushed into me before I could get any more words out. I gasped at his speed, at how he switched from the charm he showed everyone else to the ferocious desire he only had with me.

"No more obstacles, Meek. I'm finding that even a small one like Brady is making me crazy."

He slid in and out of me, and I closed my eyes, nodding as he did. With his large hands on my hips, holding me to his rhythm but not giving me any room to hesitate, I couldn't reply. Time stopped, planning stopped, my heart stopped. I was his and didn't know what else existed as I clawed at his back and moaned his name.

Nothing made sense. I was supposed to be in the big city getting ahead in the film industry, not starting to enjoy small town life more than I'd ever enjoyed any other place I'd lived. It felt like my life was in a snow globe and Jay was shaking it all up.

Purposely.

Deliberately.

And with an end goal in mind.

I wasn't sure I could handle the outcome, but getting there was getting me off faster than I'd ever imagined. I screamed his name as I climaxed, and he pounded into me more swiftly, finding his release a few moments after.

Our breaths came rapidly, but his smile was even quicker as he pecked my forehead and cheeks and then bit my bottom lip. "You taste as sweet as I remember, and you fuck better than I could ever imagine. And I imagined it, Meek. Many. Times."

Lowering my legs, I tried not to let the compliment bring a smile to my face. "We need to get back out there."

"Sure you don't want another go? I paid good money for this fun house."

My mouth about dropped as I glanced down to see he was ready to go again. My eyes widened. Before I could even think to be nervous about what we'd find outside the fun house, I started laughing. "You're crazy."

"You're hot, and that little home you got between your legs for me is damn near impossible to stop thinking about." He waggled his eyebrows like he was going to get some.

Even rumpled and completely disheveled, Jay looked like he belonged on a magazine cover. Maybe more so than usual. And the fact that he was still trying to charm me into sleeping with him after we had done just that proved he was the same old Jay.

He started forward, but I shook my head at him. "Put it away, Jay. Think of something else. We have to get through the night before we do anything else. Think bad thoughts."

"I am." He chuckled but zipped his jeans back up.

The post-high of my orgasm had gone to my head. A curl fell over his forehead as he straightened his shirt and pockets. Running my hands through it now would have been asking for a repeat. One I wanted but was sure I shouldn't.

Jay Stonewood had finally cracked the shell of our friendship and broken through to something more. I wasn't sure if I should cry for the loss of that safe little haven the shell provided or be elated we had the freedom to finally explore the world of our lust. I knew I had to try, though. I knew I'd try just about anything for him.

THERAPIST: *Happiness is sometimes hard to find. It's okay to feel down some days.*

JAY: *Sure, but I also think we've just programmed ourselves not to look for happiness. If we stop to take a second, joy is all around us. And if we work for it, we'll be the happiest we've ever been.*

CHAPTER TWENTY-TWO

JAY

"OKAY." **MIKKA LOOKED** frazzled, and I loved that I'd done that to her. She wiggled her ripped jeans back and forth a few times. "Let's go try Lorraine's pie and get this over with. We're still on dates with other people."

"Wait." I halted while she continued walking over some wavy floorboards. They creaked under me like they were sighing at my weight as I rocked back on my feet, trying to roll back the instant anger I felt at her words. "I'm not going back to my date, woman."

She wiped a finger over her mouth when she looked back at me, still trying to get rid of the evidence that I'd had her in the fun house. "I'm not going to tell Brady we did the dirty in here and now I can't continue the night with him."

"Why the hell not?"

"Because!" Her arms flew up as if I was crazy. "It's weird and..."

"And what?" I followed as she spun and stalked out of the room toward the exit. We walked down a colorful ramp with shimmering strands of rubber hanging from the ceiling. The accordion music bounced all over the place, a little like my emotions.

"And I don't think the town needs to know about us right when they are just starting to accept me."

"Who cares if they accept you or not? You're here with me."

She stopped, the exit door in front of her. She didn't look at me, but I knew she wanted to. After years of knowing her, years of watching how she handled things, I'd begun to see what I really enjoyed about her. She was headstrong as hell. She didn't show weakness, not even when she felt it.

But Mikka was honest. She could admit fear to me because she knew the strongest thing you could do with fear was overcome it. "I want them to like me, Jay. For some reason, I really, really want everyone in this town to like me."

Her voice broke as she confessed, and I wrapped my arms around her from behind. I whispered into her soft hair, "You have to know it's impossible not to like you."

She sighed. "I wasn't likeable in my hometown and I wasn't in college either. People respected me. They didn't like me, though."

"What's not to like?" I asked.

"I was the little Asian in a white neighborhood with big glasses and big dreams. I didn't let anyone outdo me, and I learned quickly that most of my friends had nasty things to say behind my back. I stole a lot of people's thunder."

"They were jealous."

"Yes. And malicious. Still, it makes me want to have a place where people enjoy me for who I am, and I like to think I'm getting that here, even if it's for just a little while."

My arms slid off her, and I walked around to face her. "I'm going to agree to not saying anything. I won't agree to him touching you."

She lifted that bare shoulder that I wanted to bite and then lick better. "Fine. Same goes for you and Sandy."

I slid my arm around her waist and yanked her to me. "I'm tasting your mouth one last time before we face the music."

I kissed her again, and this time I worked her lips so well, they looked a little bruised when we came up for air. She was panting like she wanted me, like I was her oxygen, and her eyes ate me up when she glanced down at my crotch.

"Woman, I swear to Christ, you look there again and I'm going to check to see how wet you are for me. Then, we won't be going anywhere at all tonight."

"Oh my God. Go!" She shoved me in the shoulder and pushed out of the exit doors before I could.

Brady and Sandy started a slow clap. Lorraine whooped, and then I glanced around. Practically the whole town, including my brothers, Jax and Jett, were there slow-clapping with them.

I swore low and soft, and Mikka followed suit. Her string of curses was longer and much more fluent than mine.

"Leave it to you to beat me at a damn swearing contest too," I mumbled to her.

She smiled at the crowd, but the blush rising to her cheeks made me wonder if she really felt comfortable. "This is completely and utterly embarrassing, Jay," she said through her teeth.

"Okay, everyone," I bellowed. "Can we get back to the festival? We're not here as entertainment."

Brey and Jax shooed a few people away, and my oldest brother stood with his new wife, looking unamused. We all hugged, and Jett mumbled that I needed to think about my actions before I executed them. I laughed at him and told him he needed to loosen up.

Brey whispered in my ear, "Way to kill the rumors about you and Sandy. Now they're going to name the fun house after you and Mikka."

"Baby girl, keep your mouth shut," I muttered as I hugged her. "You going to manage to stay out with my brother more than an hour tonight?"

"Probably not." She flipped her dark hair over her shoulder and smiled at my brother. Those two always had hearts in their eyes, like they could seriously hole up away from the world together and still be completely fine because they had each other.

Brey had always been my best friend, but I'd known she could live without me. It was my brother she couldn't live without.

Lorraine strolled up to Mikka, and I watched the older woman straighten my PA's hair. There wasn't a real reason to hide anything now. We'd just got a standing ovation, one that the town wouldn't have given had they not accepted her as family. Lorraine fixing her hair was just another confirmation of that.

I wondered what it would be like to be back, to fall back into step with the people who knew you most, knew your background and what shaped you. Hundreds of people had gathered for the festival, and many of them knew me beyond my acting career. They didn't care about that status, though. I even glanced around to see if anyone had filmed me coming out of the fun house. No one had. No one cared.

I was just Jay to them.

It made me wonder if I wanted to be anything else to anyone else. "Do you ever want to move back to Greenville?"

Brey didn't answer immediately. She stared over at Mikka like I did, taking in Lorraine introducing her to Jett and Vick. Jax stood near but didn't take his eyes off Brey much. She smiled at him and nodded once before she looked at me and said, "I think I'm pregnant. So you'll be an uncle soon. And I've considered it. But what I went through here is very different to your childhood."

"You..." I stuttered and then stopped. I hadn't known she'd wanted a baby, never really considered it. The idea plowed into me and caught me so off guard I found myself not being able to school my shocked expression.

"A lot to take in?" She smirked. "I'm only eight weeks along. And you'll be a godfather obviously."

I scooped her up and spun her around. Jax practically barreled through the crowd to get over to us. "Put her down," he growled.

"Relax." I winked at Brey because we were both used to him being overprotective.

"He's ten times as bad now that I'm carrying our offspring," she grumbled.

"I'm about to be a million times as bad if he doesn't put you down, woman."

I spun her one last time just to piss him off and then set her down. "I'm happy for you guys."

"I'm happy you finally know," Brey said. "I never thought keeping a secret would be this hard. It's still really early, but I had to tell you. Vick and Kate know too."

I almost gave her shit for telling her other best friends before me, but I understood. She'd been tiptoeing around, navigating new waters with me, feeling me out on our runs.

"Shit. Should you be running?"

Jax said, "No."

She said, "Yes," then glared at him like he was a maniac. "The doctor wants me to continue my normal exercise routine. He's just ridiculous."

"I'm not ridiculous, I'm careful. You've got precious cargo…"

Jax trailed off when he realized I wasn't listening. Instead, my eyes had cut to Mikka laughing behind us all. I could swear Brady was smiling down at her like she was the magic lamp he'd just recovered too. Jealousy flooded in and washed away all my other emotions. I wasn't used to it nor did I know how to handle it.

"And finally we see my brother giving a damn," Jax mumbled, "Guess we don't have to worry about her signing an NDA. She might be signing a marriage certificate instead."

As Brady's hand went to the small of her back, I tried not to bare my teeth. "Fuck off, Jax. You barely look away from Brey, let alone let another man touch her."

"So, you're saying she's as important to you as I am to Jax?" Brey asked, catching on to something not even I was ready to admit to myself.

"She's as important as something," I mumbled and nodded to them. "I'm happy for you both. I'll take you out for dinner soon, baby girl. But now, my woman needs saving from a man she's not supposed to be with."

Brey didn't ask any more questions, didn't push the issue. She stared on like she knew, and maybe she did. She'd known me most of the time I'd been into girls. We'd had our share of talks about who was worthy of each other's time. I'd known her time was priceless, that no one deserved her, but Jax made her happy. She'd felt I deserved someone who wasn't just a roll in the hay.

"Be happy, Jay," she whispered, and I knew her words meant for me to be careful, to do what was right, and not fuck it up if that's what I wanted.

"Meek!" I yelled her name louder than I needed to, but people already knew what we'd done in the fun house. I stalked over to her to remind her in case she'd forgotten. "I'm about to buy you the best pie you've ever tasted. Brady and Sandy can find their way around the rest of the festival, right?"

Mikka had the audacity to look embarrassed, like those two weren't some of the most promiscuous people in town. Glaring at me, Brady ground out, "You realize you're stealing my date?"

"Man, she wasn't ever your date to begin with and your ass knows it." I pointed toward the pie stand in the distance. "I can smell the warm apple from here. Lorraine needs our votes. Let's go."

Weaving through the screaming kids and throngs of families had me smiling. Our fun house experience solidified where this woman should be.

By my side.

LESSON OF THE DAY:
Finding someone that loves you more than they love themselves is hard and necessary.

CHAPTER TWENTY-THREE

MIKKA

JAY TOOK ME home on a belly full of funnel cake, pie, beer, and fried food.

The tennis shoes had provided me with comfort when he spun me around while a local played the banjo and dipped me in front of almost everyone in the town. They'd cheered us on like they'd accepted me. They'd smiled at me like I was one of them. They'd hugged me goodbye like I'd always been a part of their town. I fell for the love they gave me that night. I found something I'd always missed growing up and didn't ever want to let it go.

As the texts rolled in from Dougie, I hit ignore. I found my concern was overpowered by the sudden comfort that there may be another place for me to belong.

Jay held his arm out for me to take on the walk home, and I stared down at my white sneakers, now dirty from the dust of the festival. "Shouldn't we wait for them to crown Lorraine the pie queen?"

"It's not a pageant, Meek. She gets a ribbon, not a crown." His bicep flexed under my hand, and I squeezed it like it was mine to do with as I pleased.

"Are you correcting me?" I was about to tell him to shove it when my phone pinged again.

"You should turn your phone off," Jay said. He didn't follow up with an explanation, and my body heated, wondering what he might have in store for me, wondering if he wanted to continue what had happened in the fun house as much as I did.

"It could be the job." I shrugged, knowing that it wasn't.

"If it's the job, they can wait until tomorrow. If you want, give me a cup and I'll piss in it tonight so you don't have to worry about them bothering us," Jay said like the test was the easiest thing in the world.

"You say that like it's a piece of cake." A breeze blew over us, reminding me of how cold it got here and how quickly the seasons changed. "You're doing it, Jay. Recovering like so many can't. It's freaking amazing."

He stopped on the sidewalk, and the streetlight shone down on him, tinting his dark hair golden and bronzing his skin. His hands slid under my sweater and grazed the skin at the small of my back. His feather light touch and the wind in my hair, the way the light spotlighted him and me—it made a feeling I couldn't put my finger on rustle into my heart and snuggle up there.

"Woman, I'm not doing this alone. I have therapists and you. You do all the hard work. So, I appreciate you being here with me."

Most of my life had been spent pushing to be the best, and Jay didn't push for that at all. He never took the credit unless it allowed for someone else to step onto the pedestal with him. "Appreciate me being here with you because of the fun house or…"

"Oh, the fun house is what I'm most appreciative of." He folded the arm I was holding in and pulled me close enough to tickle the crap out of me. "I'd appreciate more of that too in the future rather than you dragging me out on dates with other men."

I wiggled under him, and he finally let up so that he could hold me close. We walked in silence the rest of the way to Lorraine's. When we headed up the stairs, my heart pounded with each step. I wanted him to follow me into my bedroom and keep me in the bubble we'd created.

Somehow, here, in this little town, we worked. We lost our baggage, our jobs, our expectations of what we should be, and held on to what we were in front of one another. I turned abruptly and pressed my body to his. "Sleep with me?"

"Pebble, no sweet talk?" he teased me.

"I can use my mini wand if you aren't interested."

"Brought to my senses by a little device put up against me." He motioned toward my room. "Lead the way."

I backed up to my door, keeping my eyes on him as I turned the knob. "This doesn't have to be any more than tonight. It doesn't have to mean anything."

"It means something," he said matter-of-factly.

My heart pitter-pattered and I couldn't shake the feeling that I was falling for him and this town too quickly. I'd failed with Dougie, and if I failed with him, I wouldn't recover. Dougie had been the man I thought could be my forever, but Jay was the man I *wanted* to be my forever. The devastation of losing him would be much worse.

"No," I corrected and spun to try to weed through the mess we were going to make by doing this again. "I'm trying to tell you it's okay. I just want the night and let's not worry about the repercussions. We can go back to being friends tomorrow." The wind nearly whooshed out of me as I said the words like someone had grabbed my soul and ripped it away with the thought.

"No, we can't," he said again, so dispassionately that I wondered if he was really taking in what I was saying.

"Jay." I snapped my fingers at him because his blue eyes had darkened and perused my body like he was contemplating which piece of clothing to take off first. "Are you really hearing me? We need boundaries. I don't want to lose our friendship."

"There are no boundaries. We annihilated them in the fun house."

"Well, then, we need to establish new ones." I crossed my arms and popped out a hip. "Until then, we shouldn't be doing anything. I don't want to ruin—"

He stalked toward me and started to unbuckle my jeans before I could complete the sentence.

"I... You... I don't want to ruin our friendship," I stuttered out. He nodded but slid his hands down my lace panties and pressed a thumb to my clit as his fingers worked out how wet I was for him. "I'm listening, Meek. Set all the boundaries you want."

His middle finger slid so far into me, I grabbed his shoulders to keep from falling. "Oh, God."

He dipped his head to suck on my neck.

"Jay, wait." I tried to form a thought about boundaries, to find some semblance of logic, but everything was melting away.

He dragged his nose up my neck and murmured, "I'll wait forever if that's what you need."

I shook my head. "Don't. I need you." My hesitation had rolled away. The light kisses on my skin were like whispers that my body leaned in to hear more of. His touch against me was like a fire lighting my coldest night. He was bringing me back to life.

His hands slid up under my sweater to lift it over my head. I stared at him as I slid my jeans off, leaving me standing there in lingerie.

The smile he normally had was gone, the charm, the laid-back side of him nowhere to be found. He took a step back and drank me in.

His jaw tensed. "You're perfect, Meek."

"I'm just me," I whispered back.

"And that's all I want you to be. Always."

He reached out to grip my ribs where the bruises had faded but where he knew they'd been. He rubbed his thumbs over each bone. "I'm going to show you how you should be cherished, Little Pebble."

My breath quivered as he knelt down and kissed each rib with a feather light touch. "Jay, you don't have to—"

"I do."

He picked me up by my hips, and they automatically wrapped around him like they knew this was my home, this was safety, this was where we were supposed to be.

I stared down at him, my arms atop his shoulders and my hands in his hair. "This is going to ruin us."

He shook his head as he leaned his forehead into my neck. "Nothing can ruin us, little one. This is where we're supposed to be. New ground rules?"

I waited for him to tell me.

"No boundaries. You're mine. I'm sure of it now."

His words shined a light on a dark part of my heart I didn't know existed. My hands drifted to his cheeks and I crashed my mouth to his, not sure where we were going from here but sure I was going wherever it was with him. I kissed him and felt the light dim on every other love I'd felt before.

Everything he did felt new, like smelling a flower for the first time, like silk across your skin when all you'd known was sand. He laid me on the bed and threaded his fingers through my hair. Over and over he combed the strands as he ran a finger up and down my stomach.

"Jay," I whispered, not sure I could hold back the buildup of emotion.

The only time I had ever been cherished like this was when Dougie beat me so badly he felt the need to make up for it.

Jay did it without being prompted, like I was worth it always, like I deserved it for just being me.

The first tear slipped as I realized he was right.

I lifted up on one elbow to grab his neck and pull him down to kiss me. I wanted to taste the man who did this to me, to memorize his lips, the way his tongue curled around mine, how he held me close as I moved under him.

I pulled his shirt over his head and undid his jeans. He kissed down my neck and across my chest, his hands finding their way to the back of my bra and undoing it with ease. Just as my hand dipped into his boxers, he lowered his mouth to one of my breasts.

I hissed when he grazed his teeth over one nipple. I gripped him tighter, feeling how thick he was in my hand as he brought me to the edge of ecstasy.

"Meek, you ready?" His azure eyes searched mine, mouth wet and jaw tense like he was holding back.

I wasn't sure I could respond, but my body did for me. My legs spread, willing and wanton for him. He slid a hand down my stomach and rolled each finger over my clit before he tested how wet I was. "You have no idea how long I've waited for this."

I stroked him as he did me, keeping his pace. "I'm sure I have an idea." I moaned and arched my back when he sucked a nipple into his mouth.

"Jay, I'm close," I admitted between panting and moaning. I warned him so he could take me, so we could go over the edge of oblivion together. Yet, he worked me faster and grabbed my wrist, pulling my hand out of his boxers. He lifted it above my head and continued to trail kisses over my chest.

"Let go, little one." His words were so soft I almost didn't hear them. My orgasm hit like a wild animal that had been caged forever. The way he made love like he worshiped me, the way he took his time to bring me to the edge, the way Jay was Jay roused something foreign in me.

I thought I knew love. I thought I'd felt butterflies in my stomach. I thought Dougie had shown me what there was out there.

I was wrong.

Jay watched me with adoration in his eyes, with something new sparkling there. "I think I found my new addiction."

I shook my head, trying not to fall down the rabbit hole of love without at least grasping for a handhold. "It's just different when you do it with someone you know, Jay."

"Is that all, Meek? This just like being with someone else you know?"

I tried to tell him it was. I tried to keep a level head, but the smile that spread across his face was a challenge. Then he dove down to kiss me like I was all he could ever be addicted to. He kissed like he was a junkie and I would deliver the fix, the high, the rush.

Except I felt it too. He was bleeding into me, pumping into my veins to intoxicate every part of me. He slid his hands to hold my jaw open farther, so he could taste every part of my mouth.

It wasn't soft anymore. His hands were rough, his touch desperate, he was everywhere as he wedged himself between my legs and pushed into me.

I arched and took all of him in. I hissed out his name; I clawed at his back; I bit his shoulder, not sure what marks I would leave. I wasn't nervous about the repercussions; I wasn't thinking about how he'd react.

With Jay, I was safe. With Jay, I could do anything.

We fell over the edge together, and the fall was just like the moment you drop from the top of a rollercoaster ride: you scream for your life, wonder if you'll survive, and then experience the ride of a lifetime. There isn't a feeling more invigorating in the world than the moment you think you might lose yourself, only to come out of the experience hands shaking and adrenaline pumping. I felt like I could do anything, and as I came down from our rush, I realized that was because he believed I could too.

And that pinpointed the shift from what I was before to how I would be going forward.

Jay's forehead leaned onto mine. "I misjudged you."

"Huh?"

"I thought you were just a pebble, but you're a wrecking ball. I'm wrecked for other women now."

I chuckled at his automatic charm, but his mention of other women shattered the idea of having something more with him. I started to sit up. "Jay, I need to shower and you need to go to bed."

"For what?"

"I don't know. I mean, you can't stay in here," I stuttered out.

"Why not? What if you need some more fun tonight?" He rolled onto one of his elbows and dragged a hand up my stomach.

I quivered, and my nipples stood to attention.

"You might need more fun right now," he said, staring at them.

I jumped up and grabbed the sheet to wrap around myself. "I don't. You need to go before Lorraine gets home."

"Lorraine would love to know we're fooling around in here."

"Jay!" I stomped my foot. "Come on."

He slid out of bed, languid as ever, and I noticed he was growing hard as a rock again as he grabbed his clothes and pulled on his jeans. He bunched up the boxers and shirt and put them under his arm before grabbing the sheet to pull me close. "I'll be sneaking back in tonight."

"For what?" I asked but tilted my head to give him access to my neck as he leaned in.

"For you, Wrecking Ball." His lips tickled over me. "I want to be destroyed, and you're the woman to do it."

"Jay, this probably isn't a good—"

My phone went off and we both jumped at the sound. Everything in me tensed. The safe place we'd created in this bedroom was gone with that sound.

I shook my head as Jay started to say something. "Go to bed, Jay. We've had enough fun for the night."

He snapped his mouth shut. His jaw ticked as we listened to the ring over and over again. "I'll break that phone one day."

"Not tonight." I grabbed his arm and shoved him toward the door. He narrowed his eyes but let me steer him out.

After picking a few things out of my suitcase to wear to bed, I walked to the shower, trying my best to ignore the call. I jumped about a foot when the text message notification beeped. I don't know why that sound brought tears to my eyes. Maybe I wanted to forget what I had back home, or maybe what I'd done with Jay finally brought it all to the surface.

I grabbed the phone to see a text from the man I didn't want to hear from.

> **DOUGIE:** I thought about you tonight.
> **DOUGIE:** I thought about how good it was to have you home. And how you're ruining everything.
> **DOUGIE:** I want to show you how I've changed. You owe me that. Can't you at least have the decency to let me show you? Or don't you have the strength? I thought you could do it all, Mikka. Why can't you do this?

THERAPIST: *Is it healthy, Jay?*

JAY: *Most things in life that are worth it aren't healthy.*

THERAPIST: *It's not a time to risk sobriety.*

JAY: *You don't get to pick the time. You just get to pick whether or not you take the risk.*

CHAPTER TWENTY-FOUR

JAY

LEFT HER WITH that time bomb of a phone, knowing that it held a potential explosion. I went to bed thinking about how she'd unraveled in front of me, relaxed into the woman I knew her to be, and then wound up like the woman I always knew she could be.

Mikka had been a friend for far too long. I should have taken her on the beach the first day I met her and never looked back.

Tossing and turning in my bed, I pictured Dougie texting her. I wondered how long he'd continue pursuing her, how long I'd be able to keep from ripping him apart.

Mikka didn't know it because I hid the frustration growing in me, but I held back rage at knowing he'd harmed her. Things were building between us, and I wasn't sure either of us could handle the consequences.

I got up to run before the sun rose. I skipped hanging out with Brey and trying to de-stress. I showered and waited outside her door when she opened it the next morning.

"Whoa! What are you doing?" She jumped when she saw me in her doorway.

I stalked in and crowded her right into the dresser. I grabbed her hips and lifted her onto it so I could wedge myself between her legs. "I want your phone."

Her face fell. "For what, Jay? I can't—"

I grabbed it from her back pocket where I knew she kept it now that I had her book bag. She snatched it back and glared at me. "I'm your designated babysitter. I need this for check-ins."

"Fine. Then, block him so that you don't turn into a bundle of nerves every time your phone goes off."

"I..." She hesitated.

"What the hell are you hesitating for?" I bellowed and then recoiled at the fury that roared out of my lungs.

She didn't. She poked me in the chest and said, "You can't throw stones at him, and I can't either. We all have our problems, Jay. What if he ends up needing me? What if he gets into some type of trouble? I owe him a lifeline."

"What?" I whispered, my stomach knotting at her words. "How could you possibly think he deserves anything after the pain he's put you through?"

"It wasn't all bad," she replied, rubbing a hand over my chest as if the motion would soothe away the pain of her words.

"I only saw the aftermath, Meek. It was bad enough." My hands automatically found her ribs where there weren't any spots anymore—I'd checked the night before—but I still saw them every single time I looked at her. I still saw her strength, her spirit as she sat there like nothing had ever been wrong.

"I promise you, Jay. It looked worse than it was." Mikka embodied everything I respected in a woman. She plowed forward into uncharted territory and no matter how gritty she survived. Women didn't complain, that was for men. Women didn't find the wretchedness in the evil of the world, they found reason to still believe and hope for one drop of good. Even when she encountered the nastiest fucker, she still doubled down, willing to keep searching.

I didn't know what it would take to convince her. I just knew I had to.

"One mark on your body is bad enough, little one. He put dozens there. I can't begin to imagine what fucked up logic makes that okay or makes it not so bad."

"Jay." She sighed. "It's complicated."

"Uncomplicate it for me, then." I leaned forward and put my arms on either side of her. I stared into her dark eyes, trying to see into her soul and dig down deep enough to find the root cause of her belief. I needed to pinpoint it so I could cut it from her, dispose of the faulty seed that had somehow been planted there.

"He'd never ever hit me before like that." She whispered the words and hunched over to shield her face and maybe her embarrassment.

I tilted her chin back up. "Don't hide from me. You're a wrecking ball, remember? You don't have to hide from anyone."

"But I do," she blurted out. "Don't you get it? We were the tipping point. Me and you. Us together because we couldn't keep away from each other. I told him and it crushed him. He turned into something ugly. I cheated, Jay. There was going to be a price for that."

"Oh, bullshit, Meek," I threw back. "I could have fucked you in that hallway and it still wouldn't have been equal to the price you've been paying."

"Oh my God!" Her eyes widened, and then she looked behind me at the closed door.

"What?" I said, not looking over my shoulder as I continued loudly. "You nervous Lorraine is going to hear about our sexual encounters?"

"Could you please be quieter?" She tried to keep a straight face, but I saw the corner of her mouth lift. This little town and all the people in it somehow boosted her spirits even in the darkest moments.

"Quieter or louder?" I said even louder this time.

She put her hand over my mouth and shushed me.

I smiled before I nipped it.

Her eyes bulged. "What are you doing?"

"Seeing if you still taste as good as last night." I waggled my eyebrows. "Don't worry, you do."

I saw the blush of anger creep up over her cheeks, and when I glanced lower, I saw it on her chest too. The conversation was taking a turn and so was my libido.

She yanked her hand away. "You're so immature."

"If you put your hands down my pants and repeat that with a straight face, I'll do whatever you tell me."

She glanced down. No one would ever call me that with their hand wrapped around my dick.

Her eyes narrowed. "It might be big, Jay, but it doesn't make you any more mature. I've seen bigger with men even more immature than you."

Her insult shot straight through me, effectively deflating my ego as she shoved me back so she could hop off the dresser. I couldn't stop myself from asking, "You've seen bigger?"

"That's all you took away? Really? I retract my statement. He definitely was more mature than you."

I followed close behind her as she turned to go check herself in the bathroom mirror. "How many men have you slept with?"

She spun around and poked me in the chest. "You have some audacity asking me that. You want me to ask you?"

"Sure. And I'll be honest. Too many to count."

Her mouth snapped shut into a thin line and I saw the worry creases between her eyes. She didn't have to say a thing for me to know she was working through her odds, figuring out if she was a good competitor. It was her nature, her drive to succeed, and I mostly respected it.

Here, it pissed me off. She wasn't comparable to any of them. She was beyond them, and this wasn't a competition.

It was just us.

"Look at me." I grabbed her chin and got her attention. "Stop thinking. I promise you none of them compare to us together."

"It doesn't matter." She shook her head and turned back to the mirror.

I watched her in it over her shoulder. "It does because we matter."

"I'm your PA, Jay."

"You're my everything, woman." Her brow furrowed like my statement troubled her, but I wasn't taking it back. She needed to know where we stood. "That means I need you to be nothing to Dougie back home. I need you to trust that this is a good thing."

We both glanced down at the phone outline in her pocket. "If I give up on him, I'm—"

"It's not giving up when the assignment ends up not having a right answer, Meek."

She nodded but blinked rapidly. I was witnessing her overcoming her own addiction, witnessing the denial, the withdrawal, the acceptance, and the anger of it all as she pulled up his name. "I tried so hard."

"You did, but a relationship takes more than one person trying. There's no inadequacy in knowing what you're worth. You've fought countless times for a bigger paycheck or role for me. I'm pushing you to fight for a better life for yourself too."

A tear escaped and fell to her cheek where I swiped it away. She blocked his number quickly and then slammed her phone down.

"Take my mind off this, Jay," she demanded as she hopped up on the bathroom counter.

I didn't hesitate for a second. I took her on the counter, in the shower, and in her bed.

I took what I knew would be mine for the rest of my life because I wasn't letting any man near her ever again.

LESSON OF THE DAY:
Sometimes you should be selfless.
Other times you need to be selfish.

CHAPTER TWENTY-FIVE

MIKKA

BOB CALLED WHILE Jay was lying next to me, running his hand up and down my arm. Completely naked. I'd turned into the worst PA.

And, for once, I didn't care.

"Hello?" I shoved his hand away to try to maintain some semblance of professionalism. Jay rolled over to get out of bed.

Bob bellowed into the phone, "Director's requesting another test. Seems he's actually feeling pretty good about things, though. The paparazzi didn't follow you there and there's been no news, which is good news."

I heard Jay rummaging and sat up to see him in my suitcase, looking for something I was sure I didn't want him to find. "Yes, um, it's great. Everything's great here. I'll get the test for you right away." I wriggled over and tried to shove Jay away from my things without losing the sheet wrapped around my body.

"He seem like he's recovering, okay?" Bob sounded concerned as Jay whipped out my purple mini wand like he'd found a freaking treasure.

"Uh, yes. He's doing well. He runs every morning and has been very healthy."

Jay pulled the sheet back and slid onto the mattress.

"I'm just concerned. That boy is like a son to me." I heard the vibrator turn on, and Jay licked his lips as his eyes roamed up and down my body. I shoved him, but he didn't falter at all. He pulled back the sheet and kissed his way down my stomach.

I hissed at the contact, my body so sensitive already to his touch. I pulled at his hair, but he didn't come up for air. Instead, he inched down farther and rubbed the wand up my thigh.

"You okay, Mikka?" Bob's voice sounded far away. I'd almost forgotten about him.

"Yes. I...I'm so good." I dragged out the word, arching when Jay slid the wand up so that it shook right at my entrance. "I should go if you want this test completed."

"Oh, no rush. Director wants it by end of day. I'm also thinking we should schedule some interviews with TV shows and see if Lela's PA can work with you to put some couple events on the calendar for them. You have your planner on you?"

The answer should have been yes. I used to have that leather book bag stuck to my side. I was the best at what I did, but Jay was the best at what he was doing.

The mini wand slid in and out of me, and he sucked on my clit like it was his favorite piece of candy.

"Bob, I can't..." I gasped. "I'm going to have to call you back."

I hung up.

On my boss.

Then, I wrapped my legs around Jay's neck and rode his mouth and that wand like I was an equestrian. I screamed his name and wondered if I'd ever had this much fun with a toy before.

I hadn't.

When I finally came down from the ride, he slid the wand out of me and waved it around with newfound love. "Well, this little device is useful."

"I can't believe you did that," I huffed. "So unprofessional."

"Would it be unprofessional of me to tell my PA I want to fuck her after I piss in a cup, too?"

I groaned. "You're hopeless, Jay."

"Nah, just honest."

"Back to our ground rules?"

"They were damn good ones, woman. Now, get up and get ready. We have to make an appearance downstairs."

I searched the room for my clothes and slipped into jeans and a sweater. "Why? Have you gotten a text already saying they heard we're trying to conceive up here?"

"No. But I'm sure that's coming. I need the cup too."

I grabbed a drug kit package from the closet and handed it to him. "Bob said he doesn't think the director will ask for many more."

He shrugged. "Don't care if he does."

"Can I ask you something?"

He tensed before he crossed over into the bathroom, cup in hand.

"You don't have to answer, but does it get easier? Do you still have the craving?"

"I miss the habit of the partying scene, Meek. But I like to think I wasn't that bad."

I didn't know if he believed it, if he knew what bad meant. "There's bad in everyone, right? And maybe a little addiction too."

"Right. But I stumbled a little farther down that path than most. So I did my time, and I've got a better handle on things now."

I believed him. Who wouldn't? He was Jay Stonewood. He could charm anyone into believing anything.

He closed the bathroom door and emerged a minute later with the glorified cup that held his results.

I took a photo and sent it to Bob. "I need my planner to—"

"No planner for the month. We already discussed this. Your plan is to hang out with me."

"I have to plan past this month, Jay," I whined.

"We do? For what?"

My jaw dropped. "You're baiting me, right? You can't honestly think we're going to wing this whole movie premiere. You have to get on Good Morning America; you need to be seen out with Lela and the crew. You need to schedule radio interviews, more talk shows, and we'll need to ramp up your social media."

"Mikka, you had that all planned months ago. Your planner is filled with shit we're doing all of next month."

He was right, but the more I talked about it, the more I felt the need crawling its way back in. "I need my planner!"

"Or what?"

"Or I'll hold out for the rest of the time we're here," I blurted, like I could hold that over his head, like he couldn't just go get some from someone else.

"Woman, you couldn't hold out if your life depended on it."

"Excuse me?" I narrowed my eyes. I wasn't thinking about the book bag anymore. All I saw was the dare he'd thrown at me.

He walked up to me and pushed his chest into mine. He cupped my cheeks and peered down at me. "I'm not betting on it. I want you too much and you'll make it your mission to prove you can."

"I can," I retorted.

He chuckled and pecked me on the lips. "I know, Meek. You can do anything you set your mind to. Should we go bother Lorraine with our presence?"

I shrugged, not sure I was completely happy with the turn of events. "I still don't have my planner."

"And you won't until the end of the month. Lela and the film crew will be here next week. It'll be our last week here. We should enjoy this, little one. We won't get the time back."

It was true. Time would be against us. It would whittle away at our little bubble and remind me that we were only here to work temporarily in this small town where I didn't belong anyway.

I sighed and nodded.

We both deserved a moment of peace, a place to rest our heads, and a safe haven for our bodies. We'd treated them poorly for long enough. And it wouldn't be long before the movie released, before we parted ways so that Jay could be larger than life again.

Larger than this small town and definitely larger than being with me.

THERAPIST: *Stress of a job is a trigger for a lot of people.*

JAY: *I'm always going to struggle, aren't I?*

THERAPIST: *It's what makes addicts some of the strongest people you'll ever meet.*

CHAPTER TWENTY-SIX

JAY

WE WERE DAYS from the film crew getting here and my body wanted an outlet. I scrolled my phone's contacts and knew I was searching out the people I'd got my drugs from before. I would have used. I would have partied.

The reality was I'd always done it at this point in the film. They took my mind of the script, off the pressure, off the depth. Swimming in someone else's emotions, encompassing their whole self for days on end, fatigued a person, even a person like me who loved doing it.

I was about to give in to the exhaustion, and I needed a lifesaver. Mikka provided that.

"Jay!" Mikka snapped her fingers.

She was standing in my room holding my script and glaring at me as she played Lela's part. "Focus."

I nodded.

Her eyebrows slammed down as she looked over her lines. She threw her hair over her shoulder and tensed to play the part. She vibrated with anger, her hand shaking at me as she screamed, "I don't want my love to be our ruin. I want to love someone that doesn't have to risk their life to be with me."

"That's not the way love works." I murmured the words and knew how truthful they were. This story was one of racial injustice, of interracial marriage and the systemic racism that plagued our nation.

It would leave audiences raw, hurting, wondering, I hoped, about their complicity in the discrimination.

"In this town," she whispered, tears springing to her eyes, "our love doesn't work at all."

I grabbed her wrist and pulled her close. I ran a thumb right under her ear and leaned in to whisper, "It'll work anywhere because love overpowers hate."

"Promise me you'll remember that."

I nodded and leaned my forehead to hers as I bled the next words. "I promise."

They would flash back to this scene when two men beat me to death. My body would be the sacrifice that a small town needed—a white man dying for the love of his black girlfriend while she wept beside him.

It was a racial Romeo and Juliet of sorts.

Those two words had to carry impact, had to show he'd die without fighting back, had to show every sliver of love a man had for his woman.

Embodying all that and speaking those words to Mikka was easy.

She whooped beside me. "You do it better every time."

"I do everything better every time."

She laughed so hard her cheeks turned red. This was Mikka in the film industry, though. She had the eye for a good script and knew how to make it even better. Like me, she loved how powerful a movie could be. "You're so arrogant."

"Confident."

She rolled her eyes. "Confident enough to get all these lines in one take within two days?"

"A challenge?" I lifted an eyebrow at her. "What do I get if I win?"

She shrugged. "I don't care. I want my planner back and a promise that you'll do every meeting on the calendar for the next two months with no fight. We need you out there for this movie."

I narrowed my eyes and leaned back on the dresser as I stared down at her. "Fine. I want you to move in with me."

She giggled like I wasn't serious. She even waved her hand at me like she was shooing away the idea. When I crossed my arms and didn't say another word, her eyes widened. Then she plopped onto the bed as her jaw dropped. "You're not serious?"

"I am. I wasn't lying when I said I wanted no boundaries."

"When did you say that?" She rubbed her forehead.

"The other night."

"When we were screwing?" she asked, voice so high it probably echoed the wheels screeching into overdrive in her head. "That wasn't real!"

"What do you mean?" I schooled my expression. "We're as real as ever, woman. Why do you keep pushing the idea of us away whenever we aren't tangled in each other?"

"Because we do tangled together well. Outside of that, outside of this small room, we can't work."

"Oh, we can, we do, and we will," I said, my voice low and final. "You can't stop it now, Wrecking Ball. We probably committed the day we kissed each other. It all started there. We just didn't know it then."

She shook her head. "You're a movie star, Jay, and you grew up in this quaint little town where everyone loves you. Those are the places you belong. I don't belong beside you in either of them. I'm just your PA."

I pointed toward the doorway. "You think Lorraine's going to tell just anyone about her dentures and that Delilah's going to let anyone cook in her kitchen? Ray carried a drink halfway across the village for you, just because you beat me in a contest. They love you here, and they love you in LA too. Probably more than they love me."

"You're crazy," she whispered. "You've never even been in a real relationship."

"You're right. I was waiting for you, Wrecking Ball. I needed you to come in and destroy my lack of commitment. You did a damn good job. I'm committed and I'm not going anywhere." The words rang true, so true I realized this is how my life would be. I might need an outlet but I'd find one with her.

"I'm not moving in with you," she proclaimed and shot off the bed.

"Wanna bet?" I followed her out of my room.

"Fine. Get every shot in the first take, Jay. I'm excited to get my scheduler back."

LESSON OF THE DAY:
*Reality is only
what you perceive.
Try to perceive
what's real.*

CHAPTER TWENTY-SEVEN

MIKKA

LARGER THAN LIFE—LARGER than this small town, at the very least— Jay dominated the first take the next week. He'd promised me he would, swore up and down that he had this challenge in the bag, and even went so far as to tell anyone who would listen about how we were moving in together soon.

Lorraine was thrilled. She literally patted herself on the back and said she knew the iron headboard wasn't banging around up there for no reason.

I could have shrunk away from embarrassment, but Lorraine didn't respect anyone who couldn't dish it right back.

I told her Ray had stopped by the day before and I'd let him know exactly what was in her box shipped from King Chang. She cackled all the way to her bedroom.

We were called to the set at 6:00 AM that morning. I was always astonished when I pulled up and saw what they'd done to make the location match the director's vision.

Greenville Village and its shops had been transformed. Trailers lined the street around the corner, and lights had been placed strategically for camera angles near store fronts. I knew Delilah and Ray had given the crew permission to film inside and in front of their store.

It would be a good tourism boost if the movie did well. Jay knew it, which is why he'd requested that the last scenes be done right here.

He wrapped his arm around my shoulders and whispered that he was ready to finish this thing.

Then he disappeared with hair and makeup and I walked the street. I introduced myself to a few people who were outside, mostly techs working on the mics and lighting.

The director and Lela were still in their trailers. Most times on these sets, they wouldn't come out until it was time to shoot. They avoided the audience forming down the street and talking with anyone they regarded as less significant.

I knew the drill. I wasn't a part of the elite crowd here.

I camped out with Delilah and Ray instead. I wasn't a celebrity, didn't belong on the other side of the barrier, even if Jay wanted me to be there.

I watched from afar for the first few takes and had tears in my eyes when the first one wasn't cut at all. The director let them play it out. Lela and Jay smiled at each other like they knew their onscreen chemistry was explosive.

I wanted to be happy for them; I wanted to support Jay the way I always had. But, as he stared into the beautiful actress's eyes like he had mine, I felt a little bit of our world crumble away. He belonged there, with someone like her. The power she exuded, the attention she held—it was as powerful as the wrecking ball Jay claimed me to be. The first time he kissed her, I didn't know how to handle the stabbing feeling in my heart. It mixed with the feeling of getting lost in them, of my heart melting for the love they portrayed so well.

Delilah squeezed my shoulder, and I sighed. "I'm going to go for a walk. I'll be back later."

I tapped out of the situation for a while, walked the streets of Greenville to take in the colder air. Winter approached with each morning frost but was held back by each warm autumn afternoon. Down the road, the birch trees faded to yellow plums and the grass dimmed from its vibrant green to a golden brown. The colors of nature listened closely to the weather, pulling back their brilliance to make sure the snow stood out when it fell.

I wondered if I would see it, if the first snowflakes would fall while I was here, if the town would give me the opportunity to see another layer of it.

My phone rang when I rounded the corner on Lorraine's block. Mom popped up on the screen.

"Mom, I was going to call you this week."

"Of course you were," she agreed, which wasn't like her. I smiled. Maybe she missed me; maybe she wanted to chat rather than bicker.

My melancholy mood warmed at the idea that I would be seeing her soon.

"I'll be home next week. I'll try to fly in to see you right away. Are Bryan and Anton still there?" My mother had taken Bryan under her wing when his parents had disowned him a long time ago. Now, him and his partner came to visit every now and then.

"No. They left. When Dougie called to say he was coming to visit, I figured he wanted privacy when he asked for your hand in marriage."

"My... wait... what?" I halted in front of Lorraine's, my stomach twisting in knots. "He's there?"

"I'm making him supper. There's only one reason a man comes to visit a woman's parents without her, Mikka. I should have kept it to myself. I was going to because I don't think I'll say yes."

"Mom..." I whispered, trying to gasp for air. I was trying and failing. The fear I'd forgotten descended on me like a hurricane, stronger than any other storm I'd ever had to weather. I could deal with Dougie. I was equipped to. I'd built up my storm doors, cemented myself against the physical and emotional abuse and been able to endure it.

But Dougie, alone with my mother—I hadn't planned for that.

"Mikka, don't sound so dejected. He's not listening. He will listen tonight when I tell him your hand is worth a thousand of his. He thinks he can have you even though he doesn't work. Yue Lao would be so displeased. I mean—"

"Mom!" I yelled, stalking toward the house. "I need you to let Dougie know I'm coming. I need you to be nice to him. I'll be home soon. I'm taking the first flight I can get on."

"Oh, now you want to come home because your boyfriend and mother might quibble?"

I took the stairs two at a time. "He's not himself, Mom." I mustered up the courage; I pushed out the words that stuck in my throat. "He's dangerous."

"Excuse me?" she whispered.

"Just..." I closed my eyes and fisted my hand, trying hard to keep my tears at bay. I wracked my brain for options. I'd never reported him. I'd done everyone an injustice, put lives at risk by keeping it a secret.

Even then I thought of his pain, of what he'd been through. I saw the way he looked at me right before he was about to hit me, like he'd lost the control he'd struggled to keep for so long. Turning him in, putting it on record, calling the cops to let them know our dirty secret felt like betrayal.

"Mikka, are you saying—"

"I'm going to call the non-emergency police line. I'm going to fly home now." I threw everything into my bag. Then I ran to Jay's room and grabbed my book bag too. "Be calm, Mom."

"I'm not going to be—Dougie!"

I heard the phone rustling.

"Get your ass here, Mikka."

My hand shook as his voice rasped into the phone.

"And don't you dare think of calling someone. I deserve a private conversation with you. If I have to hold this knife to your mother until I get one, then so be it."

My phone lit up, signaling that the line went dead. I called back once, twice, and again, but there was no answer. I tried his phone, and it went straight to voicemail.

Adrenaline kicked in. I had to save one of the only people I loved. My mind sharpened, and my instincts, my drive to overcome the impossible, took over.

Jay couldn't help me with this—it would ruin his shoot and possibly his career—so I called Brady. He raced me to the airport without asking questions. I told him I had to leave; it was a matter way out of my control.

I wondered if everyone else on the flight to San Francisco thought the pilot took his time, that we should have arrived in half the time. Minutes passed by so painfully, they tore at my soul, sliver by sliver.

Was my mom safe? Would Dougie have the gall to harm another human? The worry magnified my guilt because I'd ignored the signs.

This was all my fault. I'd ignored the advice I read over and over to report abuse. I even ignored my own advice to friends who'd faced this situation before me. When I saw a woman being hit on TV shows, I'd scream at the screen for her to leave, to call the cops, to do something. And I'd done exactly the opposite.

Abuse was fickle like that. Wasn't that the saddest thing ever? I hadn't really loved myself, not the way I'd loved so many others, not enough to leave. When it was just me, I covered it up. I dealt with the abuse, the pain, the guilt, and the shame. If it had been someone I loved, I'd have fought to the death for them. But I hadn't fought for myself.

We'd all succumbed to the idea of a good man, to the idea that a relationship could work if we just tried hard enough to fix it. But those men, the ones who turned violent and brutal, that continued to hurt the ones they loved, weren't looking for someone to fix them. They were looking for a keeper of their secrets and demons. They were looking for a hollow vessel in which to dump all their fury and to keep it bottled up. Dougie had taken his time bleeding me dry so I was empty enough for him to abuse.

I let him. I bent my soul for him until it broke, and I would have stayed had I not had the support to pull me out.

That support showed me I was more than just a woman trying to be the best, though. I was a woman a whole town loved, a woman who could be good enough just by being herself.

I was the first person off that plane, and even when I saw the texts and missed calls from Jay coming in, I ignored them all to dial an Uber. I needed to get to my mother's. I made a beeline from the terminals to the drive-up garage to catch my ride.

I couldn't worry about Jay or what he would do if he thought I'd just left. It would look that way. There hadn't been time to leave notes or explanations.

The shop's lights were off, but my mother's apartment above it glowed bright against the night sky. I waved off the Uber and grabbed my spare key.

Turning the locks and entering the shop felt like a horror film. I wasn't sure where they were, what I would walk into when I climbed the stairs to her place or if I would be able to withstand the sight.

Still, adrenaline and love for my mother pushed me past the fear. I dropped my bag and suitcase in the doorway. Then I stretched my hand out as my eyes adjusted to the darkness and steered around a table. Stalking toward the glass counter and back door, I breathed in deep, trying to prepare myself. It was the only sound in the shop. San Francisco was eerily quiet tonight, and I heard no movement upstairs. I pictured my mother's knife block. Had he grabbed a knife from there? Surely he wouldn't hurt anyone besides me?

I had to believe I was his only outlet; I wished for it as my only wish ever.

As I was about to open the door to the back room, his voice echoed through the store. "I prefer you come take a seat at the table, Meek. This is where you and your mother used to interview all the perverts about what they really wanted, right?"

"Dougie, can I see my mom first?" I put my hands up like I didn't want any problems, like I was willing to do what he wanted, and I was. I glanced at his hands and saw the knife, the largest one from my mother's block glinting in the moonlight. "I just want to know that she's alright."

"You're concerned about her wellbeing but not mine. That was made clear tonight." He stood in the corner, hiding in the shadows, and waved the knife toward a chair. "Go sit the fuck down. Me and you are going to have a little interview of our own."

I tried the voice of reason. "Come on, Dougie—"

"Get the fuck over there!"

I jumped at his bellow and instantly walked to the white plastic chairs. The day we got them, we sat in them for three hours to make sure they were comfortable and we didn't get backaches. Mom used the time to talk me through a new product and then help me study for a quiz.

I tried not to cry over the memory; I tried to remain calm.

Dougie stalked toward the chair across from me and sat down. It was dwarfed by his large frame. A glare marred his soft face. "When did you decide you could walk away from us? Was it when you thought you could fuck the Hollywood heartthrob? He called and sounded oh-so-sad when I told him we were having dinner here tonight."

My gut clenched. Jay didn't need to know; he didn't need to be a part of this. So much was unraveling and I wasn't sure how to catch the thread. "Dougie, you're being irrational. Think about what you're doing. We can't—"

He slammed his hand down on the glass, and the table rattled beneath it. "Don't patronize me! God. You always were a fucking know-it-all bitch. I'm the one asking the questions. You answer them. Nothing else."

I wrung my hands in front of me, thinking of what I could do. "Ok, ask away," I said, completely monotone. I needed to find my mother, I needed to get her to safety, and then I needed to call the cops. The look in Dougie's eye told me he was so far gone, I wasn't sure he'd ever come back to the man I once thought I loved.

Dougie shifted in his chair, his smile drunk with the power he thought he had. "Did you always have the whore in you? I tried to beat it out, baby. I tried to help you realize you and me are made for each other."

His words had my stomach rolling. Bile rose as he stood and walked toward me. He had changed. Or we'd both changed. I wasn't sure which. Maybe he'd always had this brutality in him and I'd rubbed him the wrong way one too many times. Maybe he'd warped into the monster before me all on his own.

It didn't matter.

For once, I wasn't the only one in danger. I could endure the pain, but when it was someone I loved, that changed everything.

The shaking stopped as he looked down at me, wedging himself between my legs by tapping the knife on the inside of my thigh, signaling for me to spread them. "You know we're made for each other right?"

I stared up at him in the moonlight. He'd let his beard grow, along with his belly, and he pushed his length into my arm like he thought I would get turned on by it.

"Dougie, I can't think with you holding that knife."

He squinted like he wasn't sure he could trust me but he wanted to, wanted us to get back to where we were.

Finally, he turned and set the knife down on the table. I shoved my chair back, remembering how light they were on the floor. I didn't hesitate. I wasn't that girl anymore.

I kicked him as hard as I could between the legs. He folded over, eyes popping out as he screamed, and I scrambled around him, lunging for the knife he'd placed out of reach.

I thought I'd make it. I thought I'd kicked him hard enough.

His meaty hand snarled into my hair and yanked me back. I flew into the air, but this time I fought back. I clawed his face, I dug my thumbs into his eyes, and I screamed like a banshee.

His other hand went around my neck as I hit the ground with a thud that knocked the wind out of me. I tried to gulp in air, but he'd blocked my airway.

"You don't fucking listen." He squeezed harder as he spat out the words. "Why. Don't. You. Ever. Listen?" With each word, he pounded my skull into the ground.

I choked on my words as I scrambled and arched my body to shove him off but, Dougie was so much bigger than me. In a last ditch effort, I groped blindly for the knife. I swear a god or two was on my side because my hand landed right on its base. I grabbed the handle and drove it into his arm with every ounce of energy I had left.

He screeched in pain and flew off me, curling around his arm. Then he lunged for me, getting one good punch in at my mouth. I rolled away, realizing if I didn't get out of here now, I'd be done. He had the weapon in his arm. He had the upper hand again.

He hobbled toward me as I got to my feet to run, and just when I thought it was do or die, a loud crash sounded behind me.

I turned to see him crumble to the floor and my mother standing over him with shattered glass all around.

"Well, my Yue Lao vase was good for something. I knew he didn't want you marrying this abomination of a man."

I choked back a sob. "Mom!"

"Mikka!" She mimicked my tone with a deadpan face and then stretched her arms out for me to run into them. "I called the cops. They should be here..." She trailed off as the red and blue lights pulled up.

"Are you okay?" I whispered as I hugged her.

"He tied me up in the worst knot known to man. You'd think he would have studied a good one before he tried this kidnapping. But I always knew he was a lazy bum."

I laughed and then cried in her arms. When I glanced up at her, tears were streaming down her face too.

My mother held me up as the cops asked questions, and we promised we would be going to the station to file a report. They cuffed Dougie and led him away. He had the audacity to apologize.

My mother didn't give me a chance to respond. "Get help. And don't come around us again. I pay money to the mob and I'll pay them to kill you."

Dougie's eyes widened, along with the cops' that were holding his arm.

"What? This is a porn shop. Not a church. Don't bother us."

"Ma'am..." The cop hesitated as my mother stared him down, and then he shook his head and led Dougie away.

We stared out at the police car in silence. When I glanced at her, she still had tears in her eyes but they weren't overflowing anymore.

My mother was strong. Weakness couldn't find a way in her. And maybe she'd raised me to be the same.

THERAPIST: *Sometimes all you can do is try.*

JAY: *What do you do when trying isn't good enough?*

THERAPIST: *You tell me.*

JAY: *I guess I remember I'm a Stonewood. It means you try until you succeed.*

CHAPTER TWENTY-EIGHT

JAY

MY WRECKING BALL demolished us. She took what we had and smashed it to the ground. I couldn't figure out the reason; none of it added up. Still, I couldn't argue with her. Not after the phone call I'd made to her mother.

When I'd finished the day, I went looking for her. She'd missed half of the takes that I'd nailed and had never come back.

That was the first clue.

I saw the wounded look in her eye when she'd left. She was questioning us again. Delilah shook her head when I asked her where she went. Greenville's grapevine was alive and well, though.

Second clue: someone had seen her get into Brady's car with her suitcase.

I called him, and he said she'd been crying. He only pried as much as she would let him. She'd told him she didn't want to talk about it, that she needed to get home. He didn't ask any other questions.

I knew the scenes would be hard for her to watch. I should have discussed them with her, should have put myself in her shoes. If I had to watch her make out with another man... well, I wouldn't. That mouth of hers was mine, and I didn't share the one thing I'd committed to.

Third and final knife-to-my-heart clue: after numerous calls, I gave in and phoned her mother. The woman sounded delighted when I finally got ahold of her, and Dougie was with her, smarmy as ever. They told me they'd worked it all out, that Mikka belonged there.

With each bit of information, the puzzle pieces fell into place. Mikka had realized she couldn't do it. She'd packed her things and left me behind. She didn't want to start anew with me. The grass wasn't greener with me.

A bump would have made this easier. A hit of any drug I could get my hands on at this point would have made it bearable. My hands shook with the need to use. I tried to talk myself out of it, I paced my room, contemplated calling my therapist, considered bothering my family.

But I'd been doing so well.

The burden piled on to me, crumbling the walls I thought I'd built around my sobriety. And maybe sobriety wasn't necessary if I only indulged in small amounts.

I walked to Lela's and before I knocked, the witch of a woman swung open the door wearing a red silk robe.

"I felt you coming." She smiled and ushered me in with the bottle that dangled from her hand.

"You're a witch." I walked past her, fully aware that she hadn't backed away. It was an invitation but, for her, pretty subtle.

The smell of incense hit me. Reggae played softly, matching the bohemian feel of her forest green curtains and velvet seating. "Jesus, Lela, are you burning that in here all day?"

"Of course. It's good for the soul," she retorted through a laugh. Lela sat down and patted the cushion next to her. "Tell me what's eating you so that we can make sure it doesn't last. We need you alert for the next scene tomorrow."

"Nothing's eating me. I handled each scene today in one take." I sat down next to her and nodded when she lifted the bottle in question.

She poured the red wine into one of the crystal tumblers she had sitting in a golden tray beneath the window. "Your aura shifted."

"My aura?" I raised my eyebrows. The woman and her free spirit always made me chuckle. Now it eased me into being open.

She flitted her hands in front of her and wiggled her turquoise-ringed fingers. "Yes, you know what I mean. The tension ratcheted up, which actually worked well for what we had to film. Is it just our chemistry? I don't know, but I feel your moods. Your tension from before has turned into a fog of darkness. Something is weighing on you so heavily it's dimming my lighting."

Her exaggeration or maybe her description was the only thing that could have made me laugh right then. I shook my head as I did and then grabbed the wine to gulp it down.

"You're crazy."

"I'm the only one that can work well with you in this role. Well…" She looked up to the ceiling, considering it. "Yes, I can safely say I'm the best person to ever play opposite you. This movie will be our Oscar-winning performance, maybe the best onscreen chemistry for years to come."

I nodded. "I don't know if I believe your witchy magic, woman, but I believe that."

She shrugged. "So, what's it going to take to bring your mind back to the set one hundred percent?"

I sighed and fell back into the seat cushions. I rubbed my forehead, trying to find a way to say what I needed to say. Lela was only invested so far as it affected the movie, not as a friend, not as a member of my hometown, and not as someone close to Mikka.

And maybe her lack of care for my relationships made it easier to open up to her.

"What if I relapsed?" I glanced at her. She knew the stakes for this movie and that I could potentially lose my role if I did.

"Will that make you give your best performance at this point?" She narrowed her eyes.

"It might." I dragged a hand over my face. "I lost the one thing I wanted, and I'm pretty damn sure I can't forget that unless I have a pick-me-up for these scenes."

"Okay. Then, I've got just the thing."

She lifted the rest of the crystal glasses from the tray and then slid the bottom of it out. Underneath, I saw small bags of powder, white as fresh fallen snow.

The shaking in my hands started again. My heartbeat raced, speeding up the pumping of blood through my veins.

I'd lost the one woman I'd committed to. The one addiction I wanted to indulge in most. She'd left me for greener pastures.

But my drug, this drug, never left.

It was as committed to me as I was to it.

LESSON OF THE DAY:
Don't assume anything.
Find the truth or
you'll be deceived by the lie.

CHAPTER TWENTY-NINE

MIKKA

I HADN'T SLEPT. AFTER showering away the trauma and sipping my mother's tea in her living room, I told her I was tired. Yet, I lay there wide awake.

When I'd turned my phone on, it lit up with message after message. I read everything. And then reread all the texts he sent.

> **JAY:** Where are you?
> **JAY:** You packed up everything and left. Where the hell did you go, Little Pebble?
> **JAY:** If this is about the movie and Lela, I promise we can talk.
> **JAY:** We need to talk either way.

Then, there were the voicemails.

The first hour of my flight: "Wrecking ball, why did you smash the relationship we were building together? Are you scared? Mad? We'll work through it. Call me when you get this. I need to hear your voice."

The third hour of my flight: "I've called you a million times but it goes straight to this voicemail and I'm not sure what else to say. I talked with Dougie and your mom. Whatever you're doing isn't right. You know how I know? Because we're right. We're the top of the class. The A on your assignment. The best in show. Me and you, little one. Please call me back."

At the hour I'd faced down Dougie: "I'm going to stop calling for today. I'm going to try to get these scenes over with. And then I'm coming for you. You want me to come for you, right, Meek? Damn, woman. I don't know anymore."

The last four words broke the heart that was beating just for him.

I tossed and turned, wanting to keep a level head, wanting to stop myself from rushing back to him. But my body didn't belong to me anymore. It belonged to a man that was worth belonging to.

I jumped from my mother's spare bed and grabbed the suitcase I hadn't even unpacked.

Halfway down the stairs to the front door of the store, I heard soft footsteps behind me. "You're leaving now?" My mother's voice sounded an octave higher than usual.

"Jay doesn't know why I left."

"Jay is what Yue Lao has in store for you. He will be fine if you rest, heal, and take care of your mother for a few days."

"Take care of you? You've been buzzing around, cleaning up the shop all night. You're fine."

"Well, I could have been hurt," she said like a petulant child. "It's not my fault that Dougie was bad at everything. Had he knocked me out, I would have had more reason to complain."

I laughed at her joke, but it made my throat ache where Dougie had crushed my airway. When I turned my head to the side to cough, my mother was there in a flash, lifting my chin to assess the damage. "I should pay Ronnie to take care of Dougie."

Leaning away, I crossed my arms. "Okay. Are you serious about the mob? Is Ronnie a part of this partnership you formed? That's not a clean business, Mom."

I worried she was losing her marbles, that someone was coaxing her into doing business for the mafia.

"Oh, Meek. Don't worry about it. Ronnie knew your father and he helped start this business."

"But, Mom—"

"The less you know, the better. Now, are you going to get your husband or what?" She shooed me toward the doors, completely happy with me leaving now.

"He's not...we...I'm his PA," I stuttered.

"Oh, don't waste your energy on lying, Mikka. You're going to need it to make sure he wants to marry you once the bruises on your neck and face surface. Not to mention that you left him to fend for himself during one of the most important times of his career. You're his PA. You should be there."

I rolled my eyes and hugged her goodbye to hurry and catch the next flight.

I fidgeted in my seat for the next hour, willing the plane to go faster. I finally opened my book bag and placed the planner in my lap.

Jay had hidden it from me all month, and for some reason it felt wrong to open it now. Maybe I wasn't the same person I'd been when I arrived in Greenville. Maybe our lives couldn't be listed out and crossed off each day.

I took a deep breath and opened to the current day. In permanent marker, he crossed out the lesson for the day and wrote:

LESSON OF THE DAY: "I got you, Pebble. No plans."

The next day, it read the same:

LESSON OF THE DAY: "I got you, Pebble. No plans."

I flipped through every page before and every page after. He'd filled them all in. The lesson was always the same and I believed him. As tears filled my eyes, I hoped I would get to him in time. I hoped I would be able to explain why I hadn't told him, that his movie was just as important to me as anything else.

Landing just twenty minutes away from Greenville, I felt like I was almost home.

Crossing into the town, I rolled down the window and leaned my head out so the cool, fresh breeze could hit me.

Almost home. Almost to Jay.

The sun had just started rising in the East over a hill of golden, autumn-painted grass. As we pulled into Lorraine's driveway and the gravel crunched under the tires, I hummed a sound of comfort.

As I scanned the Lodge, I didn't consider whether or not I should knock. I didn't consider what the little town thought of me anymore. I'd faced one demon and it made all the others shrink back. I belonged where I wanted to. I stood tall like my mother.

And this town had accepted me for who I was before all that.

The door opened as it always did. I was sure Lorraine never actually locked them. I called for Lorraine, but there was no answer. Next, I took the stairs a little more quickly than I normally would have to knock on Jay's door.

No answer.

I banged on it before swinging it open and finding his bed made but the dresser wiped clean. The vase, books, and doilies that usually sat atop it lay askew on the ground.

I was like a woman in a horror film; I checked every corner of the house as though he was hiding somewhere, even the closet.

My mind raced with worry, with doubt, with the terrible feeling that Jay had access to everything dangerous with no support last night.

I flew down the steps and burst from the home. I ran down the street, so fast I was sure I could have been a track star, and ended up on the outside barrier of the movie set. I scanned it all, and one trailer's light glowed brighter than the rising sun.

Lela's.

Maybe there was such a thing as an old man on the moon. Maybe Yue Lao really had tied Jay and I together because I felt the pull. I knew Jay was in that bus with her. Each step toward it felt like sloshing through murky waters toward hell. I wanted to believe I would find them both awake, maybe just catching up, sharing stories through the night.

My gut clenched at even that idea, though. For some reason, over these past couple of weeks, I'd solidified in my mind that Jay was mine.

And this time, I was willing to stand my ground because I was good enough. Logical enough. And we were perfect enough to fight for.

I fisted my hand and pounded on the door.

After a minute, Lela cracked it open and squinted one eye at me. "Girl, it is early."

I jerked my head down. "Is Jay with you?"

The silent sun rose, the birds chirped loud, the early workers' cars hummed in the distance. Lela assessed me with her red robe hanging from her shoulder and her dark hair knotted on her forehead. Her presence would enrapture anyone, and this moment was no different. I wasn't sure if she was calculating odds, comparing herself to me, or learning my whole being.

I lifted my chin, though. I wasn't backing down.

Finally, she opened the door wide and sighed. "It's a good thing you're here actually. The stars are shifting in the sky and you both need to connect or you'll lose each other forever."

I was accustomed to my mother talking like that, so I shrugged and stepped up into the bus, not concerned with her omen at all.

Finding Jay laid out on the velvet seat, fast asleep with lines of coke on the table in front of him was the moment all omens flooded me. My gut fell down the nine circles of hell and burned there as I stared.

Jay had relapsed. He'd lost the battle and I knew without a doubt I'd contributed to the chain of events leading up to this.

Tears welled in my eyes at seeing how much we'd destroyed. I wanted answers, I wanted to shake him awake and scream at him. First, though, I needed to lock down the situation.

"Close the door, Lela," I commanded.

She let out a low whistle and did as I said.

"Who knows he stayed here with you last night?" I asked as he stirred on the couch.

She shrugged. "Probably no one." She peered out her window. "Actually, probably everyone. I can feel their whispers. They know."

Unfortunately, I believed her.

Jay sat up from his slumber. His eyes adjusted, so blue and crystal clear I wondered how much cocaine he'd truly sniffed. It didn't matter because he looked at me with so much pain and frustration, I didn't think there was any way we could overcome the next few hours.

"Where the hell have you been? What the fuck have you been doing all night?" he rasped out.

I should have just answered him. I should have taken the high road. I pointed to the table instead. "More important question, what the hell were *you* doing?"

I'd lost him. His eyes turned such an icy blue, I knew right then. We'd lost each other. Our ground rules stated that we weren't broken, but we both had been and we couldn't be honest about it. It'd made for a fragile base, one that was definitely not strong enough to hold a wrecking ball and a larger-than-life movie star.

THERAPIST: *The temptation will come and it will be overwhelming.*

JAY: *My determination will be there too and it will be impenetrable.*

CHAPTER THIRTY

JAY

"**YOU THINK...**" I glanced around, rubbed my eyes and saw what the damage looked like to someone who hadn't been there. A tumbler was on the floor, probably reeking of incense and booze, and powder was laid out on the table.

I tried to tuck my rage into a bottle for later. I tried not to blow up at her, but the distrust I saw all over her face whittled away at my hope. The one person I wanted to believe I wasn't ever going to use again stood there questioning me like I was only ever an addict.

I'd been more.

I was more.

I'd stared at that cocaine most of the night.

I'd held a rolled up piece of paper in my hand ready to sniff it off the table after watching Lela do two lines.

I'd stared at the one drug that had committed to me and always been there for me and turned it down.

No one tells you that breaking off your relationship with a drug is like losing a loved one. That the pain of knowing you won't ever feel that exact same sort of feeling again is a scary fucking thing. Sure, the loved one had screwed with your head, threatened your life, and stolen so many things from you, but they'd still been a part of you.

Saying, no especially when it was only me and the drug, was one of the hardest things I'd ever had to do.

Instead of the woman I loved congratulating me on doing that, she was accusing me of throwing away my sobriety and my career.

I cleared my throat. "I get this looks bad, Meek—"

She cut me off. "It's fine. It doesn't matter. Let's not talk about it."

As she rushed to the sink and grabbed a towel from the counter, I realized what she was doing. "Wait a second." I stood up. "What are you doing?"

Lela piped up from the corner of the bus like a ghost I'd completely forgotten about. "Yeah, what are you doing? Don't you dare wipe my blow. I'm going to hit it soon."

She threw the towel into the sink harder than necessary. "Fine. We need to go, then, Jay. Lela, it's been interesting."

Mikka stormed off the bus, and I stalked after her.

In the middle of the village, I yelled at her. "You have some gall coming here at the ass crack of dawn just to direct judgmental looks my way after you sped back to Dougie yesterday."

As she spun around, her hair whipped through the air. "Go back to him? Are you insane?" she screeched. "I can't believe you think I would go back to him."

Her words didn't even really register. "Oh, so then you know how I feel about you thinking I would go back to using."

"There was cocaine on the fucking table, Jay. You slept in her trailer. Did you fuck her before you took the hit or after?" She threw the first blow swiftly, knocking the wind out of my lungs with the ruthlessness of her words.

I shook my head. Her eyes glistened in the light of the morning sun. "You know what? You're broken."

She took a step back, ready to be done with me.

"I'm broken too, Little Pebble. We never threw stones at each other before, and we're not going to start now. Our ground rules were wrong. We're broken."

She swiped at her eyes. "I can't... I don't know how to not be."

I closed the distance between us and threaded my hand in hers. "I never wanted you to be unbroken, woman. We have to work together to heal."

She snatched her hand away. "Jay, you need to finish your scenes for the day. You need to focus on you."

I nodded and searched her eyes, scanned her up and down and saw the way she was holding herself. "First, I want you to give me a drug test. I want you to call Bob and tell him you found me in the bus with Lela and cocaine. Let's go back to Lorraine's and have me take one."

She shook her head, eyes widening. "No," she whispered and then blurted loudly, "No! You're not doing that. We aren't torpedoing your role in this movie to prove... whatever you're trying to prove."

"The fact that you think I'm torpedoing my career means you don't believe nothing happened on that bus. So I'm going to show you."

She frowned.

"Lela!" I yelled. The wizard of a woman appeared in her doorway immediately. "Did we sleep together or use on your bus?"

She looked baffled by the question, like I hadn't spent the night on her bus. "So, it might be a good time to tell you both that I'm only attracted to women. Also, we don't use anything on my bus, Jay. But if we did, Mikka, Jay would be sober as a judge. Really not a fun guy to pull an all-nighter with, quite honestly."

"See!" I raised my eyebrows at her. "Let's go, little one."

She begrudgingly followed me.

We didn't say a word to each other on the way. I didn't even look back to make sure she was following. She ascended the stairs like she was on death row. I grabbed the supplies and started to unbuckle in front of her. Even then, she rolled her eyes and turned around.

I pissed in the cup and set it down on the table. As I zipped back up my jeans, I walked over to sit on the bed.

She closed the bedroom door and leaned against it. She stared out the window on the opposite side of the room, then murmured, "I don't care one way or the other, Jay."

"You wouldn't care if I fucked her and relapsed?"

She squeezed her eyes shut. "Fucking her is one thing. That's unforgivable. Relapsing is something totally different."

"Meaning what?"

"Meaning we'd get through it."

"Your mom would never want you to be with a man who uses drugs."

"I'm not concerned about what she wants."

"She raised a gold standard of a daughter to be with a gold standard of a man, little one."

"We all have our flaws." She sighed and rubbed her neck.

"Okay." I nodded, urging her on but not asking.

"Are you going to ask where I went?"

"No. I'm going to accept whatever you have to give." I waited because it was her story to tell. I waited because she'd been pushed and controlled before. My anger and impatience to know where she'd been didn't have a place here.

"What if what I have isn't much?" she asked, her voice small.

"It's all I want," I said without even considering it.

"Compared to other women—"

"There's no other woman to compare you to for me. You're it. I'm taking whatever you'll give me."

She took a steadying breath and nodded. "I'm going to tell you what happened last night, and I want you to remember that everything has been taken care of."

Leave it to Mikka to have already solved the problem.

"I left last night because my mother called. Dougie showed up there. He showed up and he wouldn't leave until he saw me..."

I rose to go to her but fell back to the bed when my legs gave out. With a push, I forced myself to her side and cradled her face in my hands. "Why didn't you tell me?"

"Your movie—"

"Means nothing at all, Wrecking Ball!" I said, voice cracking. "What happened? Are you..." I assessed her with a different eye, one that looked for the smallest change in color. The faintest line across her neck and a slit covered in lipstick popped out like black on white paper. "No," I whispered as I brushed the marks. "No, no, no."

"It's okay. He's in custody. He's going to jail." She choked back a sob and put her hand over her mouth. "I fought back. I didn't let him beat me into a corner and into submission again."

The words took the floor out from under me. I almost fell to her feet, I almost let my rage run rampant at the fact that this man had gotten away with hurting her again. "Wrecking ball, you were never one to submit. Remember that."

I pulled her in and lifted her chin. I kissed along the line I saw. I murmured into her neck, "I don't think I'll ever forgive myself for letting the law bring him to justice instead of me."

Her hands fluttered over my arms as she moaned low at my touch. "It's for the best. I didn't want anyone fighting my battle."

"Your battle will always be my battle, Little Pebble. Yue Lao tied us together." I gazed into her eyes. "I believe your mom's story now."

Her eyes filled with tears and she looked to the ceiling, trying her best not to let them fall. "I want to tell you that you're crazy. I also want to believe you."

"Believe me. Or I'll prove it. I'll earn your belief over time."

I stepped back and spun around. I grabbed the cup from the counter and held it up for her to see. "To start, I'm as clean as a whistle."

"Jay... I'm sorry, but—" she started.

"It looked bad. I get it. Lela's never been anything to me, you know that. It's hard to think you'll always be scared that I might relapse, but you're right."

She opened her mouth and then closed it. *That's right, Little Pebble, we are going to be honest. No lies. No false hopes.*

I sighed and rubbed a hand over my face. "I might relapse. I have to accept that about myself too. Last night was hard. It could have been catastrophic, but I proved something to myself and hopefully to you. For now, I'm strong enough. For future reference, call me when you decide to strand the man you love."

The smile that spread across her face was worth the pain of admitting how I felt.

LESSON OF THE DAY:
I got you.

CHAPTER THIRTY-ONE

MIKKA

L**EAVE IT TO** him to make a joke at a time like this.
"I literally jumped on a flight within hours of resolving the situation, Jay," I managed through a laugh.

He shrugged and started stripping as he walked toward the bathroom. "I'm sure your scheduler says we have to be on set in about an hour, and I have to get every take on the first try. So, I'm going to get ready."

"Just like that?" I followed him. We'd opened a Pandora's box worth of problems and he was as relaxed as ever. "Don't you want to discuss all this further?"

He smirked down at me, a twinkle in his eye. "If you strip and get in the shower with me, the answer is yes. Always yes."

"Just so we're clear, we have literally no time and the amount of damage control we're going to have to do when we leave this room will be epic." I was positive that the whole town had heard our fight, that Bob would get wind of Jay's night, and that the film crew was five minutes away from getting started.

He didn't wait. He picked me up with my clothes on and plopped me in the shower with him. "Jay! This is freaking designer."

He unbuttoned my blouse like none of it mattered. "I'll buy you a new one."

As water droplets rolled down my face, I said, "I'm starting with ground rules."

"Good. We need to start over with our ground rules, anyway. You know that, right?"

My eyebrows lifted in confusion as he kneeled before me and slid my pants and panties off. My stomach flexed from the butterflies fluttering through it. Jay kneeling before me, wet in the shower, made me weak at the knees.

"We aren't who we used to be, Wrecking Ball. You told me before you're still you, that you aren't broken. But you are. I am too. Together, though, maybe we can make each other whole again."

I got down on his level and sat right where he could wrap his legs around me. We made out in the shower until the water ran cold.

He was my person, my safe haven, my home.

As we got dressed, I found myself rushing around the room. "You're going to be late for your scene."

"We're on time. I texted Guillermo. He understands."

"Understands what?" I said, confused.

"Understands what a man will do when he loves someone. I guess I found our director's weakness."

My eyes widened. "Are you... did you just say..."

"Meek, Yue Lao tied us together. I'm not wasting any more time letting you think I don't love you. I'm committed to this. One hundred percent. You better be too."

"Jay." I sighed. "This is fast."

"We've known each other for years. It's not fast at all."

I combed my hand through my hair and glanced around the room. When I grabbed my leather bag, I froze. My scheduler was full. I couldn't add anything to it if I wanted to.

He came up behind me and wrapped his arms around my waist. "Read your planner?"

I turned to hug him and nod into his neck.

"Then, you know. I got you."

He kissed me, and I wondered how I'd lived this long so close to a friend without knowing he was really my soulmate.

We jogged back over to the set, and Jay introduced me to Guillermo. He kept saying Guillermo wanted to meet the girl that had brought him to his knees.

When I shook the director's hand, he said, "You don't like my lighting, I hear?"

I glared daggers at Jay and stumbled over my words as I tried to right the wrong. "I love your work. The lighting is perfect. It's absolutely—"

"—atrocious," he finished for me. "We're flying back to San Francisco to film the scene again. Next time, speak up. You'll sit by me now."

He motioned to a crew member, and suddenly a seat stood next to his.

Jay smiled from ear to ear as we talked, then he went off to do makeup.

He filmed every shot in one take.

Guillermo mumbled to himself about the flawless performance but never once complimented the actors, the crew, or anyone.

Just before the final shot, he motioned for them to wait. He turned to me. "Camera angle and lighting good?"

I scratched a temple and realized I'd never been one to accept just good. "The audience needs to see him from her point of view in this shot. The lighting works."

He nodded, listening closely, and then he yelled for the cameramen to do as I said.

They got the shot first take again.

When Guillermo shouted, "that's a wrap," and stalked off, Jay whooped in the background and everyone cheered with him.

Then he yelled for the whole film crew and most of the town to hear, "Our bet's still on, Wrecking Ball. You're moving in with me."

LESSON OF THE DAY:
*You're part of
the family now.
We got you.*

EPILOGUE

MIKKA

"**YOU'RE GETTING NOMINATED.**" The grey-haired man shook Jay's hand enthusiastically after the world premiere of his movie. I'd been his date for the night, and Lela ambled along close to us for post-screening photos.

The words from that man solidified what I already knew. Jay would have his pick of movie roles from now on. He'd made it, and he'd done it during one of the most difficult times in his career.

I squeezed his arm as we walked away. "You're not just getting nominated, you're going to win."

Jay laughed and wrapped me up close to him. "Leave it to you to not settle for just being nominated."

I glanced up at him and took in the man of the night. His black tux was tailored to accentuate his shape, and his hair was parted like he was a 50s icon. His smile was as charming as a 50s movie star's too. "You should be proud, Jay."

"I'm proud I have you on my arm. Everything else is fluff."

I nodded because we'd found a good balance of eliminating a lot of the fluff from our lives in the past few months. Jay reacquainted himself with Hollywood, and we found out what it was like to struggle through constant temptation. He came home a few nights so frustrated, we decided that networking at parties wasn't worth it for us.

I struggled with trusting him too, trusting that we could make it after all I'd been through.

Relationships were work and we'd just started ours. We kept our ground rules: we were broken, but we were honest.

It helped to remind ourselves of that.

His brothers and their wives met us after we mingled with a few other important executives. Bob even came over with tears in his eyes.

Jay announced to them, "We're going to King Chang's. You all are free to join us or you can go have a few drinks, but I promised Mikka's mom we would stop by after all this."

Free to join us? "Jay, I don't think anyone wants to come to—"

"Oh, thank GOD!" shouted Vick, Jett's wife. "I've been dying to get to that porn shop!" She literally jumped as she said the words, and I giggled. I was finding that Vick could be the life of any party and look like a blonde model, all while screaming about porn.

Jett rolled his eyes at his wife. "Pix, if you announce to the world you're going to the porn shop, they'll all end up following us there."

"Oh, the more, the merrier. Imagine the fun we could have..." She wiggled her eyebrows up and down.

Jay laughed hysterically at her joke, but Jett grumbled under his breath, "You only have fun with me, woman."

Brey smoothed a hand over her growing belly and leaned her head on Jay's shoulder. "I'm going with you guys." She looked at me for reassurance. "If that's okay, Mikka?"

"Of course." I could never say no to her now. We'd grown so close over the last few months. She'd become a friend I never knew I needed but had always wanted. I called her for everything, and even though Jay and I were in LA, renting an apartment, I hoped one day we would live closer to them.

We all piled into an SUV and arrived at King Chang's. Vick ran around the store in her silver couture dress, touching every dildo she could find and asking Jett which he'd prefer.

Jett was a hard nut to crack; he barely smiled at all. But he followed her to every corner of that store and responded to every ridiculous question she asked him. When they got to the last row, I saw him push her against the shelving and kiss her like he was starved for her.

Jax and Aubrey took a seat in some of the new furniture my mother had purchased after the incident with Dougie. He rubbed circles on her thigh and whispered to her like they were the only ones there. I swear, in their world, they *were* the only ones there.

Jay had his arm around my waist as he spoke with my mother who was, of course, rearranging a bigger Yue Lao that sat on her glass countertop. "The new and improved Yue Lao looks good there, Ms. Chang."

"Of course it does." She harrumphed. "I wouldn't have gotten it otherwise."

Jay smiled and carried on with her. "Are you ordering Wren's for us tonight?"

"What for?" my mom asked, a look of confusion on her face. "His egg rolls are terrible, and Mikka found her soulmate. It's not him, thank you, Yue Lao."

"Yes, thank you, Yue Lao," Jay murmured into my ear.

"Who is Yue Lao?" Vick asked as she bounced over, pulling Jett by his hand to sit by Brey and Jax.

"Oh, I'm so glad you asked," my mother said. "No one ever asks about Yue Lao anymore."

"Mom, please don't tell the story again," I groaned as I put my face in my hands.

My mother obviously launched into the story about how Yue Lao was the man on the moon who tied soul mates together with a red string. She had a twist now, though. Now, Yue Lao was so annoyed with Dougie that he knocked him out cold the night he'd attacked me.

Everyone listened intently. Jay sat next to me, completely tense the whole time. I knew he hated the story almost as much as me but for very different reasons.

The man still wanted his turn with my ex, and the justice system wasn't going to allow that for a long time.

My mom smiled at her audience. "Yue Lao is making sure Dougie doesn't have a soulmate. He got an extra 10 years behind bars for laundering money. It just came out."

That was new information not even I had heard. "I'm sorry, what? But how? Dougie didn't have any..."

"Oh, Mikka, hush. You know the mob is taking care of us. Right, boys?"

My mother glanced around and made eye contact with every Stonewood brother in the room.

All of them smiled the same smile I'd seen a million times before. It was the one they gave when they were being ruthless, when they didn't really care to smile at all.

"Jay?" I turned to him.

"Don't worry, Wrecking Ball. Lesson of the day: You're part of the family now. We got you."

~The End...or just a new beginning~

OTHER BOOKS BY
SHAIN ROSE

DO YOU LOVE the Stonewood Brothers? Want to read more of them? Here are the other men's books:

INEVITABLE

An angsty, second chance romance that follows Aubrey and Jax through their rollercoaster of a relationship. When Aubrey loses her parents, she loses her heart to Jax Stonewood too. Is it there love that's inevitable or their heartbreak?

Available on Amazon.

REVERIE

A captivating enemies-to-lovers office romance where Vick and Jett are complete opposites that must learn to work together. Can Vick stop living in reverie long enough to be a part of Jett's reality? Can Jett see that life isn't all darkness and be a part of Vick's light?

Available on Amazon.

STAY CONNECTED

RECEIVE UPDATES on all things Shain Rose and get an email once pre-orders are live!

Subscribe to Shain Rose's newsletter here so you can be the first to see teasers, be a part of giveaways, and get updates:

shainrose.com/newsletter

Join Shain Rose's Lovers of Love Facebook Group to keep in touch and get sneak peeks:

facebook.com/groups/shainroseslovers

ACKNOWLEDGEMENTS

TO THE READERS, the bloggers, the authors, and the book world that took a chance on me this year: this is all for you. I couldn't imagine how anyone has any time in 2020 but somehow you have all taken me under your wing and shown me what it means to be part of a family that has the same love for books that I do.

It was a long road to get here. I never used to share my love for romance. I never imagined that there was even a world where I could. I stumbled across it all when I published and now I'll never look back. I can't believe I didn't jump in sooner. I can't believe I've been missing this amazing community for so long. Now I'm just sad I didn't do it sooner.

Thank you for accepting me.

Thank you for telling me I could do this.

Thank you for reading my words like they are worth it.

Thank you for being you.

PS We're all making it through 2020 together. Together, we will thrive <3

ABOUT SHAIN ROSE

SHAIN ROSE is an author of Contemporary Romance and New Adult novels. She writes romance that cuts deep and fights for love one word at a time. Those happily ever afters can sometimes be a bitch to get to.

When she isn't writing, she's spending the days with her husband, daughter, son, and terrible cat. She and her husband drink way too much coffee, eat way too much candy, and laugh way too much. Life is good when the kids are behaving.

On the off chance she's not writing or spending time with family and friends, she's calling them to talk. And if no one answers, then she's reading and watching trashy TV.

FACEBOOK: facebook.com/author.shainrose
INSTAGRAM: author.shainrose
AMAZON: amzn.to/37Nfejt
BOOKBUB: bookbub.com/authors/shain-rose
GOODREADS: goodreads.com/shainrose
WEBSITE: shainrose.com

Made in United States
Orlando, FL
28 January 2023